STRIKER

RACHEL LEIGH

"Revenge is the raging
fire that consumes
the arsonist"—Max Lucando

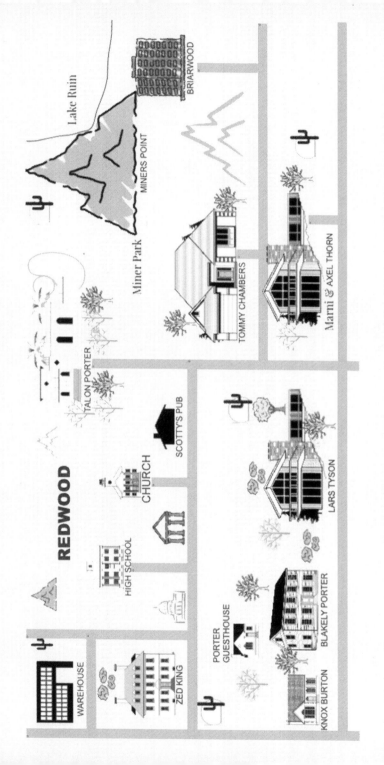

MARNI

RebelSin: Damn, now that's sexy. Let's see another.

NotYourAngel: I'll make you a deal. I'll send you a pic for every question you answer. Grand Finale, you get a private video.

RebelSin: Deal.

NotYourAngel: Why do you hate the world so much?

RebelSin: What's to love?

NotYourAngel: That's not an answer and doesn't warrant a boob shot.

RebelSin: Ass?

NotYourAngel: Nope!

RebelSin: Because the world hates me.

NotYourAngel: (Image sent)

Are you afraid of the dark?

RebelSin: Holy shit! To answer your question, I welcome the dark.

NotYourAngel: (Image sent)

Do you feel like you live in the dark?

RebelSin: You know I'm hard as a fucking rock right now

and I might need to take a break to relieve myself. Unless you plan on coming over and doing it for me.

NotYourAngel: I don't meet up with clients.

RebelSin: Oh. Is that what I am?

NotYourAngel: Have you not paid me massive amounts of money in exchange for my body shots?

RebelSin: Money means nothing to me. To answer your last question, I don't live in the dark. The darkness lives in me.

NotYourAngel: (Image sent)

What is your biggest regret?

RebelSin: Drooling over here. Biggest regret…talking to you.

NotYourAngel: Jerk!

RebelSin: You dig out my demons. I don't like to feel. Unless it's your mouth around my cock.

NotYourAngel: In your dreams.

RebelSin: You are in my dreams. And in my nightmares. You're a fucking storm, angel girl.

NotYourAngel: Oh yeah? Why is that?

RebelSin: Because you're a fucking tease and you know it.

NotYourAngel: I'm not a tease! You asked for this.

RebelSin: I don't like other men seeing your body.

NotYourAngel: That's not your choice. It's mine.

RebelSin: My turn to ask a question.

NotYourAngel: Do I get to see a pic of you?

RebelSin: Not a chance. You'll see my face when I'm ready to show it to you.

NotYourAngel: Ask away.

RebelSin: Have you always been a dirty little tease?

NotYourAngel: Ok. I can see where this is going. You always get so mean when things get serious. I'm logging off.

RebelSin: That's because you're my favorite dirty thought and my favorite little tease. But one day, you'll please instead of tease. Wait and see, angel girl.

MARNI

They didn't see me.

They couldn't have.

It's dark, and the bass is carrying through the floors from the party downstairs so loudly that I can't even hear my own shoes moving. There is no way they can hear my footsteps as I walk steadily down the hall, taking care not to trip over my own feet.

Glancing behind me, I make sure no one is following. Little good it does, considering it's pitch black. The drumming of my heart in my chest is all I can focus on. Can they hear it? I swear it's louder than the music, but then again, it's inside my own chest.

They can't hear it.

A small glimmer of light from the staircase gives way to my shadow as I round the corner. Pressing my back to the wall out of fear, I swallow hard, but slowly, as the lump in my throat threatens to stay lodged in my esophagus. Whoever that idiot was who told me to use the bathroom up here is just that, an idiot.

With my eyes on the staircase across the hall, I give it a few seconds to be sure no one is going to jump out and grab me before I hurry down them. Just as I'm about to make my escape, a door slams shut and voices carry down the hall. Coming closer and closer. I can't hear what they are saying. My focus is solely on not making a single sound. I hold my breath as they draw near and pinch my eyes shut.

"We'll find whoever was out here, and when we do, we'll take care of them." That voice. It's so familiar. It can't be. Talon Porter? Was he one of them? That can only mean one thing, the others are Lars, Zed, and Tommy. I don't even have to see them to know it was them. Where there is one, there are four.

What did they mean, they will take care of them? They know someone was out here but they don't know who it was—not yet, anyway.

Once I hear them go down the stairs, I pull my phone out of my pocket and hit the flashlight. Shining it up and down the hall, my stomach drops.

Cameras.

Of course there are cameras at both ends of the hallway. Talon has enough money to buy the entire state, why wouldn't he invest in a security system?

It's only a matter of time until I'm found out. They will know that I overheard them as soon as they watch the footage. What they plan to do with that knowledge sends chills down my spine. Unless I get to them first. I have the upper hand right now. Their secret belongs to me now, which means they belong to me.

Frozen in place, I give it a minute to be sure they rejoined the party downstairs. As my breathing steadies, I think of my next move.

How can I get to the security footage before they do? Better yet, how do I find it?

Think, Marni.

Creeping around the corner and back out in the narrow, dark hallway, I switch my flashlight on again and shine it directly at the camera. It looks similar to the ones we have. Our system goes straight to a cloud storage that can only be viewed and deleted by those who have the password.

Fuck.

Dropping my phone to the side, I shut off the flashlight.

Why couldn't there just be a room with monitors and one of those ancient cassette tape things like they have in old movies? Why does technology have to be so damned advanced? I'm not exactly complaining; I buy every new iPhone as soon as they are released, but damn, I'd give up all of my possessions just to get out of this mess.

That's it. His phone. I have to get Talon's phone. I'm sure he has the app, and the password is likely saved. I just need to get into it and delete the footage. It can't be that hard. I don't know much about these guys, but I do know what they like— destruction, drinking, and sex.

There is no way in hell these boys will have any part in my life. I'm not exactly a Susie Do-gooder, but I'm sure as hell not on their playing level. They play hard, and they always win. If they think someone knows their secret, they will not stop until that person is silenced. And it's just my luck, that person is me.

Slow and steady steps lead me down the thirty step staircase. My fingers trail lightly on the wooden rail attached to the wall. Talon's house is this huge, luxurious bachelor pad. Zed and Lars live here with him. Apparently, they've all dropped out of high school. I've heard Talon is finishing up online, but I highly doubt that's working out well for him. Tommy still goes to school, and still lives with his parents. At least one of them has life goals.

Glass wrapped walls are on the east side of the house with an automatic door that opens to the fluorescent glow of the underground pool. He bought this house six months ago after returning from a mind-cleansing retreat. We all know it was rehab, but he doesn't make it public knowledge. He and his sister were given millions when their parents disappeared off the face of the earth. Rumor has it, his dad killed someone and his mom was a royal bitch to the kids. No wonder the kid lacks a moral compass.

I don't know Talon well; I'm not sure anyone does. He keeps his circle small, but everyone looks at him like he's some sort of god. He has the world in the palm of his hands with money, power, and zero guidance, since his parents are gone and his sister is only a few years older than us.

The music grows closer, and the bass is so loud I can't even make out the words to the heavy metal song. There are people everywhere, body to body. Some dancing, some trying to hold a conversation over the noise, and most of them holding a drink in their hands. All except for me. A couple of girls walk by and I snatch a cup out of the hands of a petite girl with blonde pigtails. "Thanks." I smirk.

When she stands there looking at me with sheer confusion, I make a move, slamming my foot to the ground and acting like I'm going in for the kill. Shrieking, she backs away with her eyes glued to me. Her friends look like they might piss themselves.

Talon Porter may be a god around here, but I'm not too far beneath him on that totem pole. I have a pull in this town. Namely because of my dad and his influence on the community. Also, my older brother, Axel. He was a legend at Redwood High. Not for sports or honors, but for his "don't fuck with me or my family" mantra. He instilled a level of respect and fear in the residents of this town when it comes to our family.

Talon might have money and connections, but we have them, too. We, Thorns do not cower to threats, and if it comes down to it, we will fight back.

That doesn't matter, though—not yet. I still have time to put a stop to this.

Now that I have a drink in hand and I'm blending in, I spot Talon sitting on a chair with two chicks on his lap, and it makes my stomach turn.

Kill or be killed.

I just need to dump this drink on him and take his phone while I attempt to brush him off with an over dramatic apology. It can't be that hard.

Stumbling over like I'm three sheets to the wind, I use my four years of drama class to my advantage. "Raging party, Talon." Holding my cup up in cheers, he completely ignores me.

Lars comes up behind him, bends over with a look of agitation, and whispers something in his ear that sends a wash of anger over Talon's face. Lars comes back up, looks me dead in the eye, sending shivers down my spine, and then turns away.

The girls on Talon's lap turn inward, one slobbering all over his neck, while the other trails her index finger down his cheek. Both are wearing skintight dresses that leave nothing to the imagination. "Let's take this party upstairs." She leans closer, her face pressed against his as she cups his dick in her hand, giving it a firm squeeze.

My eyes move from her hand, up to his face, and I realize he's watching me. "Can I help you?" His voice is stern, a thin layer of pink shading the whites of his eyes that tells me he's high or has had too much to drink. It's hard to tell with him.

I bring the cup up to my chest and look around to see if there is anyone else nearby that he's addressing right now. "Me?"

Standing up, he lets the girls fall to the ground. They brush themselves off and watch his steps as he stalks toward me. His black combat boots hit the ground like a jack hammer with each step. His fingers rake through his disheveled dark brown hair, stray strands falling back into place as his hand drops to his side.

Talon holds this mystery about him that makes him sexy as hell. He's at least six foot three, and although he might not have the body of an athlete, it's obvious that he works out. His plain white t-shirt fits tightly around his biceps and the ridges of his abs are apparent through the thin fabric.

Being the end of summer, his skin is sun-kissed. And here I thought he was a vampire who only came out at night.

Reaching into his pocket, he pulls out a rectangular metal Zippo with his initials engraved on it. TJP. Talon Joseph Porter. I shouldn't know that, but I do. I know a lot about Talon— now, even more than I care to.

"If it isn't Axel Thorn's little sister," he says as he stops directly in front of me. The smell of weed rolling off of him, invading my space.

I hug the cup tighter to my chest. "Also known as Marni." God, I am so tired of living in Axel's shadow. "My name is Marni."

"I know who you are. But your last name is more important than your first. You share blood with a man I hate; therefore, I wanna know what the hell you're doing in my house."

"Seriously," I laugh, "Talon, we've gone to school together our entire lives. I've been to at least a dozen parties here. What's the problem?" I throw my hands out, sloshing the contents of the cup around. Instinctively, I almost take a sip, before I remember that someone else was drinking this, and I have no idea whose dick she may have sucked tonight.

Cocking an eyebrow, he begins flicking the Zippo. Once a flame stills, he brings it closely to my face. The heat warms the side of my cheek, and I tilt my head away, out of fear of how far he may go with this game. "Did he send you here?"

"Send me here?" I question. I have no idea what he's talking about.

Frozen in place, my mind says dump the cup, but my body doesn't listen.

His eyes linger over the flame as he begins moving his hand back and forth in front of my face. Reaching into the pocket of his black jeans, he pulls out a joint. My eyes skim down his arm, noticing one small black tattoo on his forearm. Bringing the joint up, he sticks it into the flame. "You're in no position to play dumb with me." Using his forefinger and thumb, he draws in a long drag of the joint. His mouth forming the shape of an O as he blows it out into my face.

"What the hell?" I swing my hand back and forth in front of my face, sweeping away the smoke.

The flame diminishes as he leans forward, his lips almost touching my ear and his breath warm on my neck as the smoke still lingers in the small space between us. "Seems you've got something that belongs to me, Axel's little sister."

To my left, I notice Lars and Zed. Tommy stands to my right. All three of them take steps simultaneously as they close in on me.

Talon wraps his hand around my elbow. His calloused fingers feel like sandpaper on my smooth, bare skin. When I attempt to jerk away, he strengthens his grip. Gritting through my clenched teeth, I hiss, "It will do you well to remember that I am, in fact, Axel's little sister."

"From here on out, you have only one title that matters," his mouth ghosts my ear as his fingertips dig deep into my arm, "ours."

2

MARNI

After Talon and his gang tried to claim me while puffing smoke in my face, I slithered from his reach and walked out of the house backwards, slowly, with my eyes on him to be sure he didn't make a move. The house was full, too many witnesses. It's what he planned to do to me in the darkness that had my knees knocking as I ran for my car. Fear doesn't come easily, but they created enough in me with just one word that sent me running for the hills.

Each creak of the floorboards, and every slam of the door by our housekeeper Ruby, sends my heart into my throat. It's only a matter of a time before they seek me out. I have something that I shouldn't. A secret that could destroy their entire lives.

Pacing the bedroom, I graze my teeth over my freshly painted nails. I should just go for it. Lay it all out there, admit that I know, and use it to my advantage. After all, I'm the one who knows what they did. They should fear me, not vice versa.

I drop my ass down onto my bed and grab my cell phone off the bedside table. My thumb hovers over Talon's name as I contemplate whether or not I should call him and tell him we need to talk. Leaning back, I notice something beneath the comforter on my bed. Digging my hand underneath it, I reach until my fingers find something hard and rectangular shaped, with a clasp on the front—maybe a box? I slide my hand out from under the comforter and look down at the wooden box. Feathered corner joints, a handcrafted engraving of a snake-like infinity symbol on the top, and a small clasp on the front give it a vintage and charming appeal. Dad must have picked this up for me on one of his trips. Smiling at the gesture, I click the clasp and push the top open.

As soon as I see what's inside, the box flies out of my hand and across the room. My stomach twists in tight knots as the tongue slides down the wall, leaving a trail of fresh blood. "Oh my God." My hand claps over my mouth. With my heart rate at an all-time high and my breathing staggered, I stand up and walk slowly over to the box. Keeping my hand over my mouth to refrain from smelling the fresh meat. The box sits open on the floor with a blood-soaked, folded up piece of paper sticking out of it. Taking a deep breath, I grab the note and begin opening, taking care not to rip it.

Secrets are for the silent.

Briarwood at 8pm tomorrow or you will be silenced.

Tossing the note down, I take a step back with tears welling in my eyes.

What's that supposed to mean? They plan to cut out my tongue?

Swallowing down the bile rising in my throat, I rush over to the door, tearing it open and slamming it behind me when I step into the hallway. With my back pressed against my bedroom door, I slide down slowly until my legs are bent in front of me. I bury my face in my hands on top of my legs and rack my brain for who I can call for help. I can't call the cops; it's my word against theirs. I can't call Axel because he will make everything worse. Wyatt, my best friend, doesn't have a fighting bone in his body, so he's no help.

I'm alone in this.

It's me against them, and there isn't a damn thing I can do about it.

IT'S HALLOWEEN NIGHT, and I should be hanging out with friends, pulling innocent pranks and having fun. Instead, I'm here, with this eerie weight on my shoulders and a sickness in the pit of my stomach. Shifting my car into park right in front of Briarwood, I look around for the guys' cars, but it appears I'm the only one here. This is just fucking great. Telling me to come here was probably some sort of sick joke.

Noticing the flicker of flashlights on the upper level, I assume they're inside. At least someone is inside. It's quite possibly a psychopath and that almost sounds more inviting.

Startling myself by the shutting of my own car door, by my own hands, the darkness looms. Everything about the last twenty-four hours has me on edge. I slept with one eye open last night, meaning I didn't sleep at all. After convincing myself that I do, in fact, have the upper hand, I planned on walking into this place full of demands, but now that I'm here, I'm suddenly feeling weak and intimidated, and I haven't even laid eyes on them yet.

Go in, tell them that you will keep your mouth shut in return for them going on with their lives. It's not that hard. All they care about is my silence—well, they have it.

An uneasy feeling washes over me as I take steps onto the broken concrete that lead to steps made of more broken concrete. Briarwood sits on one hundred acres of desert land just outside of Redwood. In the early 1900's, the building was used for an asylum, and rumor has it they tortured the patients inside. Screams could be heard even outside of the property. One girl my age escaped and almost made it into town when she was hit by a car and killed right before the county line.

There are stories that the place is haunted by that girl and some of the others. Then again, these are all just stories. I'm more of a 'see it to believe it' kind of girl and I have no interest in finding out the truth tonight. I thought the place was set to be condemned a couple years ago—but here it is—still standing.

Occasionally groups of kids will come here just to try and scare the shit out of themselves. Apparently one girl actually did shit herself when a group of guys were trying to be funny and hid in a closet to scare her. Let's hope that doesn't happen to me.

Walking up to the front of the dilapidated building, my fingers trace over the weathered wooden door, taking note of the carving. It's the same symbol that was on the box they put in my bed. Coincidence? It has to be. It's not like they hand carved this door or that box themselves. Talon might have money, but I don't take these boys to be crafty or symbolic.

Moving to the shaft of the metal handle, I notice it's cold. It's October, but even at night, it's still eighty degrees outside. "Talon?" I say, in a hushed tone. "Tommy? Anyone?" Damn, I really do not want to go into this place.

Just as I turn to walk back to my car, taking only a few steps down to get away while I have a chance, the door creaks open, the wooden structure scraping against the floor. I turn around in an instant and see that it's wide open as I look into the blackness of the house. Not even a flicker of light can be seen inside. Taking slow and steady steps, I holler, a bit louder this time, "Talon? Tommy? Is anyone here?"

I'm such an idiot for being here, and an even bigger idiot for what I'm about to do. Walking back up the steps I just walked down, I take a deep breath.

Something is burning.

It smells like freshly burnt paper, or maybe it's leaves. A fire in these temperatures, along with the drought, cannot be a good thing. Swallowing hard, I step into the entryway. "Talon?" I try once more. "Will someone please fucking answer me." My voice raises a few octaves, agitation and nerves getting the best of me. "Alright you dumbasses, you have one minute to show your faces or I am gone and I'll tell everyone your—"

Strong, calloused fingers wrap tightly around my wrist. Pulling me farther into the house, while the door slams shut behind me. Goosebumps cascade down my arms. "Who's there?" I attempt to jerk away. All I can hear is my heavy breathing and the deep breathes of the person restraining my body.

"Shh," he whispers, his breath warm and heavy on my neck.

Reaching my free hand out, I slap it around in the air, hoping to catch someone or something. I can't see a damn thing. "Talon, is that you?"

"Would you shut the fuck up," he grits through his teeth. Pulling my back to his chest, he slaps a hand over my mouth while his other arm wraps around me.

Impulsively, I bend my head down, biting into the meat of his thumb. The taste of sweat—salt, hitting my tongue.

"You bitch!" he screeches, spinning me around and bringing my hands behind my back.

"Show me your face," I demand.

"Would you shut your damn mouth for two seconds." I can hear his jaw tick as he lifts me up from behind and carries me, step by step, holding me tightly, until I'm faced with a broken window that looks out in the front yard.

Headlights shine in the driveway, right next to my car. "Is that—"

"Sheriff. It sure as hell is," he says. After hearing him speak calmer, I'm assured that it is Talon who is holding me like I'm his own special prisoner.

"Do you think he knows?"

His hand clamps over my mouth as his other arm continues to squeeze my body against his. "I said shut the fuck up."

With my heart hammering in my chest, I remain still. Watching as the sheriff walks around my car with a flashlight, looking inside each window, as if he's expecting to find something—or someone.

Floorboards creak above us, and instinctively, I try to look up, but Talon's hold on me forces too much resistance. It has to be the other guys. They're who I saw in the window. They knew I was here the entire time and watched me in the front yard from the window. Instead of just coming down, they had to instill a little more fear in me first. Bravo to them, they did it. I should have never come here. I should have just gone to the police. What the hell was I thinking?

My heart rate picks up when the sheriff begins shining his flashlight in our direction. Talon takes a couple of steps back as the light beam hits my face. I contemplate trying to free myself, running out to the sheriff and telling him everything, but I can't squirm out of his arms.

His raspy breath hits the fold of my neck. "If you know what's good for you, you'll just stand here and be quiet like a good little girl." His firm grasp tightens around me with my arms still behind my back. Bony fingers hit the skin of my waist while the other is still shielding my mouth from saying a word.

Picking me up again, he continues to walk backwards, until the only thing I can see out the window is a small flicker of light that resembles a firefly. Slowly fading into the distance, it's gone. The sheriff is likely still there, but his presence diminishes from my vision as Talon spins me around to face him. "You are going to walk up these stairs, slowly and quietly. If you say a single word, I'll be forced to use this." He holds up a ring of duct tape.

"This has to be some sort of Halloween joke. Come on, Talon. You aren't seriously—" I stop when he begins pulling the gray tape off of the roll. He tears a long piece off and the sound of the tape ripping makes my body jolt.

"Walk." His voice is demanding and full of warning.

Swallowing down the lump in my throat, I take a deep breath and begin walking up the wooden staircase. It's so dark. I have no idea what exactly I'm walking up to. For all I know, there could be holes in these stairs and one wrong step could send me flying into a cave.

Walking directly behind me, Talon places both hands on either side of my waist, guiding my steps and sending waves of chills through my entire body. If I were to stop abruptly, his face would plant right into my ass. The closer I get to the top, the more I notice that burning smell again. "What's up here?" I mutter under my breath.

He doesn't respond. Instead, he turns my body when we reach the top of the stairs, pointing me to the left, in the direction of a bedroom that shows a glint of light coming from a lantern.

A thick black sheet hangs over the only window in the room, and other than the lantern in the center, it's completely empty. Colorful graffiti is written all over the four walls. So much so, that I can't tell what color of paint is beneath them.

"What is this place, and why am I here?" I ask, looking all around at the artwork. It's apparent that it's the job of many because it's all scattered and each piece is different.

"You talk too much. That's why you're here."

A small breeze hits my bare legs, carrying that smell into the room. Turning around to face the door, I notice a room across from us with the windows wide open, and there they are:

Tommy, Lars, and Zed. All three standing there, with their arms crossed over their chests, glaring at me.

"Come on in, boys." Talon waves his hand through the air. When they join us, Talon tosses something in the air to Lars who catches it with his eyes still pinned on me.

Once he spins it around and begins pressing his fingers into it, the sparkle of purple glitter catches my eye. "Hey, that's my phone." I jump toward him, but Zed's arms wrap around me.

"Calm down, Little Thorn." He sweeps his fingers over my neck, moving any stray strands behind my ear. "I heard you were a feisty little thing. Maybe you can show me just how feisty you can get." His hushed tone alarms every cell in my body.

I look over to Talon, who is watching us intently. Instead of focusing on whatever Lars is doing on my phone, his gaze is secured on Zed's fingers that are creeping underneath my hoodie, grazing against the skin covering my rib cage. Fear washes over me, more intensely than the fear of being in this house with these guys—a fear of what they plan to do with me. They could do whatever they wanted, and no one would ever know. They could rape me, kill me, and bury me on this property, and I'd just be deemed a missing person forever.

Lars tosses the phone back to Talon. "It's done," he says with the phone midair. Talon swings around just in time to catch it.

"What's done?" I raise my voice. "Will someone please tell me what the hell is going on?"

Talon thumbs through my phone. When he hits the button on the side to shut it off, I assume he's going to hand it back to me, but instead, he sticks it in the back pocket of his black pants. "Go check the fire," he says, looking at Tommy, who nods in agreement.

Lars and Zed continue to stand around. "Go with him, dumbasses, and close the door on your way out," he snaps.

It's obvious who the puppet master is in the group.

My entire body jumps when the door slams shut. "Talon, I swear, I'm not planning on telling anyone what I heard. You have my word. Now, can I just go?"

"Marni. Marni. Marni." He circles around me. "You really fucked yourself when you decided to be a nosey little shit." His index finger trails across my cheek, over my nose, and around my head. Jerking my ponytail, he pulls the black scrunchie out, and my hair falls carelessly around my face. My body tenses up, and I close my eyes. "What am I going to do with you?" he tsks.

"I told you—"

"Shut up," he shouts, sending my brows to my forehead and the contents of my stomach into my throat. "You don't get to tell me anything. You're gonna listen to me." He takes my chin between his thumb and index finger, gripping it tightly. "You might think you have something on all of us, but that's not the case. Do you understand me?"

Nodding, I swallow hard.

"Good, because you don't know a damn thing. But, we do. We know about your secret relationship with Josh Moran."

"Josh Moran? As in Josh Moran who's obsessed with me? I barely even know the guy." I really don't know him well. I'm aware that he's had a crush on me for the last couple of years. Even asked me out a few times, but I turned him down—in a not-so-nice way.

A couple of months ago, he began acting very odd. Showing up at my house unannounced. I even caught him in my yard in the middle of the night once. Dad was out of town and I was feeling very uneasy about the whole situation, so I went and stayed in LA for a couple of weeks. Josh is creepy, and he's a jerk who treats women like he is a gift to them, even if we aren't interested in the package.

Tucking my hair behind my ears, his hands drop to mine.

Taking both of my hands in his, he begins tracing his index finger over my palm. Following each line engraved in my hand like it's some sort of puzzle. "Yep, that's him." His nail begins digging into my skin as he drags it on the surface of my vein.

Shrieking at the pain, I jerk away. This time, he lets me. I run my hand over my wrist and notice the red-line he left. Talon reaches in his back pocket and pulls out my phone then slams it into my chest. "What did you guys do to my phone?"

"Go ahead, look at your text messages." He walks over to the window. No longer worried that I might make an escape or scream at the top of my lungs.

Something tells me, he has me right where he wants me.

Something tells me that I'm stuck here, and there is nothing I can do about it.

I unlock my phone and pull up my text messages. "I didn't send these," I say, when I notice that there are messages from Josh. I click on the number and don't recognize it. "Whose number is this?"

"I thought you said that you barely knew him. Funny how your phone says otherwise."

"It's Josh. He's the one who you were talking about in the room when you said you disposed of the body. You killed Josh Moran." My stomach drops. Suddenly feeling lightheaded, I fall to my knees and bury my face in my hands, before looking up at him. "And you're trying to set me up."

3

MARNI

"Walk," Talon orders, as he shuts the door behind us while shining a flashlight toward the stairs.

My eyes are fixated on the blazing fire that can be seen through the open window of the room across from us. What are they burning? Is it Josh? Is this how they plan to get rid of his body? Bile rises in my throat at the thought. Suddenly feeling sick, I stop walking.

"I said walk!" he barks, nudging me from behind.

"I can't. I need to know what is going on. You guys are scaring me, Talon," I admit. As much as I know I need to stay strong and not let them see the fear that is soaked into my pores, at this point, I'll gladly lay it all out there just to get the hell out of here.

Talon gives me another nudge, and I begin walking again.

Baby steps lead me down the staircase while I take care not to touch the rickety, wooden rail on my way down. The last thing I need is my fingerprints all over this place. If they are trying to set me up, as I suspect they are, I need to cover my tracks better.

"Why did you kill him?" I ask in a hushed tone. "I know he was a creeper, but to take his life—why?"

"Josh wasn't just an ass; he was a monster. He deserved what happened to him, even if it was an accident."

"If it was an accident then I'm sure the cops will understand. Can't you just explain whatever happened?"

He snaps at me, "Stop talking."

We reach the bottom, and Talon shines the light down a long and narrow hallway. Old broken floorboards rattle beneath us. The walls are covered in everything except fresh paint. There is more graffiti, dirty handprints, and some weird occult symbols in the middle. A feeling of dread washes over me, chills spread like tiny spiders down my spine, and a cool breeze is felt on the right side of my body as I walk past it. "What is this place?" I mutter under my breath.

Not expecting him to answer, he surprises me when he does. "It's a sanctuary for secrets. Nothing between the walls of this building leaves. Empty souls, dark desires, last wishes. They are stuck in this building for eternity."

"Sounds creepy," I say, folding my arms over my chest and hugging myself tightly.

Reaching a door at the back of the house, Talon shines his light and tilts his head with a scowl, directing me out. With the sleeve of my sweatshirt wrapped around my hand, I push the metal handle to the screen door, opening it up. The smell of the fire strengthens in the dry still night.

All three guys are standing around a large barrel in the middle of the backyard. At least, I think it's a yard. It's more of a wide-open space that looks like it hasn't had landscaping attention in ages. The only thing back here is an old shed off to the side, a rather large pole barn, and the barrel full of blazing flames that stretch at least three feet over the guys' heads.

"Let's get this over with. I'm ready to get drunk and get laid," Lars grumbles with agitation in his voice.

Tommy is tapping into his phone and Zed is looking at me with this blank stare. There is nothingness behind his dark eyes. He always looks so angry and cold. Like he can be standing in a room full of people and he's still alone in his own thoughts. I've never really talked to the guy, but I don't feel like I'm missing out on much. I don't take him as the type to hold conversations easily. There were times in class where I would watch him as he stared straight ahead, his expression never changing. There were also times that I wanted to get inside his head, just to know what he was thinking because he's never given light to any emotion. Though, I imagine it's scary as hell inside his thoughts.

All four of these guys are easy on the eyes. Each one holding his own appeal. They don't have that athletic, jock appeal. They're more grunge and darkness. Mysterious and alluring. There is a blackness about them. A more than confident 'I don't give a fuck' attitude that everyone wishes they could have at one time or another. People follow them, but never walk beside them. They're loners, and for good reason—they have secrets—dark and dangerous secrets.

"Alright." Tommy tosses the phone he was playing around with to Talon. "Let's do this."

With his eyes glued to mine, Talon walks slowly behind me and sticks his hands and the phone out in front of us. "Toss this in the fire." After I take it, he moves a couple steps back.

Looking around from one person to the next, my body shivers. Even in the heat, I feel coldness ride down my back like the ghost of my future is standing directly behind me. "Why?" My voice cracks.

Talon snaps, "Because I told you to. Now do it."

"Whose phone is it?" I look to Zed, who appears to be recording me.

He catches my stare. "You have two choices. You throw the

phone in that fire, or we throw you in that fire. What's it gonna be, Little Thorn?"

Pressing my lips together tightly, I grip the phone and shut my eyes. Without even looking, I toss it in front of me. When I hear Talon breathe a sigh of relief behind me then squeeze my hips, I know that it went in.

Tommy begins clapping. "Atta girl."

Opening my eyes, I pull away from Talon aggressively. "What? You don't like to cuddle?" He smirks.

Rolling my eyes, I turn to walk away as quickly as I can, but someone runs up behind me, grabbing me and lifting me up in the air. "Let go of me." I begin kicking my legs. "I did what you wanted, now I'm going home."

"Oh no you're not."

Talon.

"You think that was the end? That was just the beginning, baby. You do what we tell you to do. You go where we tell you to go." He sets me back down by the fire, where the guys are all watching and finding humor in this insane situation. "Now we're celebrating, and you're celebrating with us."

"Celebrating what exactly? Getting away with my murder?" I eat my words immediately when Talon jerks my body to his. Gripping my face in his hands, he pushes his fingers so far into my cheeks that I could bite down and feel the space they are invading in my mouth.

His teeth clench together so tightly that I think I can hear the crack of a tooth. "Don't you ever fucking say that again, do you hear me? We didn't murder anyone. Josh was a psycho, and it was an accident. We did what we had to do, and now you're gonna do what you have to and keep your mouth shut, do you understand me?" He presses harder.

All I can do is nod. In a swift motion, he pushes my face back. I rub my hands on my cheeks, where I'm sure he left the imprint of his fingers. Feeling like I'm on the verge of a break-down, I choke, "Was that his phone?"

"Yes. And you just threw it in the fire. You just got rid of evidence shortly after you two exchanged text messages." Talon tsks. "Did you really have to threaten him like that?"

"Threaten him? Is that what you made it look like?" I shake my head in disbelief. "What was the point? His phone is gone. I can delete the messages from mine." Turning on my phone, I begin scrolling to the conversation. Without even reading it, I delete the message.

"You can delete whatever the hell you want, but if you think that forensics can't retrieve your phone records, then welcome to the twenty-first century, babe." He slaps his hand to my back.

"Why are you doing this?" I ask, with a hushed voice. Dropping my head down, I shake it slowly. "I told you that I didn't plan on telling anyone anything."

"You're right. You're not." Zed comes to my side, hooking an arm around my shoulder. "C'mon, let's get you a drink." He begins leading me back toward the house. Glancing over my shoulder, I catch Talon watching us with fire behind his stare.

Following Zed's lead, we walk back into the dark building. As soon as we escape the orange glow of the fire, the unnerving feeling returns. Chills wash over every inch of my body. Being in this place—being here with them—feels sinister. My mind is in a constant state of fight or flight.

"Zed, I know we barely know each other." I turn toward him as we step into a small room to the left of the back exit. He flicks on a small flashlight that he must have had in his pocket. "If you could just let me go home. We can all pretend this never happened. Please, I'm begging you."

A smirk grows on his face—a menacing one that's laced with intention. He trails his index finger down the side of my cheek then traces it along the center where my lips meet. I hold my breath, trying not to take in the smell of stale cigarettes on his skin. "Maybe," he watches my lips while he speaks, "but, what are you gonna do for me?" His eyes slide up, meeting mine as his finger presses aggressively between my lips. I clench my teeth shut quickly, not allowing him in any farther, but his other hand grips my jaw, prying my mouth open.

"Stop!" I demand, with my jaw locked from his hold on me. I try to squirm away, but he only presses harder, keeping me in place. With my lips in the shape of an O, he slides his finger in slow and smooth. I squeeze my eyes shut and try not to gag on the metallic taste.

"We can't let those pretty lips go to waste. I bet you know how to work them." My eyes pop open at his words. He continues to slide his finger in and out of my mouth, watching it like some sort of fucking psycho. "Show me how you work them, Little Thorn."

Bringing my knee up, hard and fast, I nail him right in his balls, feeling his hard cock hit the bone of my knee. In a swift motion, his hands drop and cup his crotch. "You fucking whore!"

Attempting to reach for me, I move faster. Running behind him and out of the room into the dark. My body crashes violently into something, or rather someone. "Where do you think you're going?" Talon wraps his hand around my wrist and begins pulling me down the hallway, away from Zed. Thank God. Who knows what that guy would have done to me if Talon hadn't shown up.

Who knows what Talon will do to me now that he has me.

With his fingers like claws around my wrist, he leads me down the dark hall. "What did he do?" Talon asks, point-blank.

"He didn't do anything," I snap, jerking from his reach and walking with hurried steps in front of him. "Like you'd care if he did." I have no idea where I'm going. I can't see a damn thing. But hearing his footsteps thud against the wooden floor behind me reassures me that he'll catch me before he lets me fall to my death.

For whatever reason, I have a purpose with these guys. They know I'm not telling anyone that they killed Josh. They could let me go—but they won't.

Face planting into a wall, I gasp. "Son of a bitch." My hands cup my nose, then dab around to feel for blood.

Laughter rolls behind me as Talon finds humor in my pain. "You ready to stop trying to be so damn tough and let me lead the way?" A beam of light shines in front of me when Talon turns on his flashlight.

"No!" Stretching my hands out in front of me, I walk slowly. Noticing an open door swaying back and forth, curiosity gets the better of me. "Is someone in there?" I whisper.

"Let's find out." He brushes past me and heads for the open door. I don't know why, but I follow him. What better way to scare the hell out of yourself on Halloween night than to walk through a haunted asylum housed with the dead—though, it seems the living ones I'm stuck with are the ones doing the haunting.

Sticking close to Talon's back, ready to reach out if need be, I follow him down a case of raggedy stairs. Reaching my hand out, I take hold of the back of his shirt, balling it in my fist. When we reach the bottom, he flashes the light in the center of the room.

"What the hell?" I draw out. "Is that a swing?" Stepping closer, I get a better look at the fixture hanging from the ceiling. It's some sort of wooden crate without a top attached to a pole with straps inside of it.

"Back in the day, this was used to stimulate vertigo in children. Apparently, it resulted in laughter. And we thought we got to have all the fun toys as kids." Talon chuckles, before popping the small flashlight between his teeth. His hands grab me by the waist, and before I can even react, my ass is sitting inside the crate.

"Get me down, now!" I shriek. "This thing is so dirty. There are probably baby spiders hatching on me as I speak." I kick and squirm, but his hand only pushes me farther in. Before I even realize what the hell he is doing, the straps are over my shoulders. My body jolts at the clicking sound of a lock.

Taking one hand, he sticks it to the side of the box and closes a clamp that I didn't notice before. Then does the same with the other hand. "Talon, I mean it. Get me out of this thing right now." Panic ensues. He's going to leave me here. He's going to fucking walk out and leave me in this thing in the dark. "Please, I'm begging you."

"Kids didn't get to have all the fun, ya know. Adults played, too. Just by cranking that lever over there a few times." My eyes bolt to the lever to the right that is connected. "I could make this thing spin six-hundred times in a minute. You might vomit or shit yourself; you'll probably even pass out. In which case, I could do whatever the hell I wanted to with your lifeless body."

"You wouldn't," my head shakes, my tone shifting, "I know you wouldn't hurt me."

Shining the flashlight up at his face while he speaks, his eyebrows dip. "Your first mistake of the night would be believing that."

"I do believe it. You're not a monster, Talon, I know you're not. You have a heart."

Stepping forward, his hand dips between my thighs, prying them apart. With my wrists anchored in place, I can't even try to fight him off. "Don't reduce me to a man with a beating heart. Just because it's in there, doesn't mean it beats with good intent."

My legs whip out, kicking my feet over and over again. "Get me the fuck out of this thing!"

When he leans closer, a momentary lapse of hope has me drawing in a sigh of relief. Until his warm breath hits my neck and his fingers slither between my legs.

"You're worse than Zed. Here I thought maybe I'd be safe with you. You are just a bunch of sickos," I spit out, my feelings shifting rapidly from frightened to angered. My feet kick again, trying to hit him wherever I can. I scream, "I hate you, all."

When I stop kicking, I notice that Talon is just standing there watching me. His breaths are labored and unfulfilled. I take notice of every inhale and exhale. "You said he didn't do anything in that room." He speaks the words as if each one was a sentence on its own.

Defeat overpowers me. "I just wanna go home, Talon."

His hand retreats from my shorts and grips tightly onto my face. His signature move to get my attention. "What.the.fuck.-did.Zed.do?"

"Nothing. I told you, he didn't do anything. He may have if you hadn't come in the room, but fuck, Talon, maybe I would have been better off. At least he didn't restrain me and assault me."

"I didn't assault you."

"Then what exactly is your endgame here, hmm? Doesn't feel like you are trying to make me laugh in this laughing chair."

"You were curious. Maybe next time you'll think twice before following me into a torture room." He begins shining the flashlight around the room.

My eyes skim the room, following the light. That's exactly what this place is. It's a torture room. One wall holds a row of wooden crates that look like they were used as cages. There are old hospital beds on another side and a bunch of mechanical equipment surrounding a chair. I don't even have to ask; I know exactly what that chair is used for.

"Can you please—" I'm cut off by the sound of the clamps opening. One hand drops free, then the other. Taking a deep and audible breath, I rub my fingers around my wrists. Once he unlocks the straps over my shoulders, I jump down, without even giving it a second thought.

"You're such an asshole." I swat at him with both hands. "I mean it. I fucking hate you, Talon Porter." His fingers grip my wrist, stopping my movements. His body presses against mine as he takes both of my arms into one hand and pushes me against an open space on the wall. With one of his hands free, he slides his open palm down my side, then to my ass, gripping it tightly. His touch sends a rush of adrenaline coursing through me.

"Guess what, baby girl?" he mutters into the thin air between us. "I hate me, too."

"Why are you doing this?" I choke out. "Why won't you just let me leave?"

My head tilts instinctively as his lips shadow my neck. "Shh," he whispers, "No more questions."

Closing my eyes, I fight hard against the feelings that are washing over my body. I fight the imprints of his touch on my skin, every tingle, and every craving for more. Swallowing hard, I try not to feel. Not anger, not fear, not hate, not the longing desire to have his hand between my thighs again. I hate myself even more than I hate him, because the way his body is ghosting me at this moment makes me want to invite him to take all of me. To possess me. To corrupt me—mind, body, and soul.

"Talon, I—" My voice cracks. Hushed, almost unrecognizable, I say, "I think we should go back with the others."

"Since when are you such a scaredy cat? The Marni I remember is tough." His lips continue to trail downward, grazing my collarbone. "She wouldn't shake beneath any man." His eyes find mine. I can barely see the color in them, just the black outline of his orbs.

"I am tough. And I'm not scared of you."

Cold fingers wrap around my waist beneath my sweatshirt. They feel like ice on my bare skin, coursing up my rib cage. "If you're so tough, why are you still standing here? Why not fight me off and leave?"

I draw in a ragged breath. "I can't leave until I know this is over. That I won't find another mysterious box in my bedroom or a cop at my door. I want to know that you guys will leave me alone."

"Is that all? Or are you afraid that I'll strap you to that chair and shock parts of your body that crave electricity?" His chest presses harder into me, sandwiching me between him and the wall.

Even if I tried to get away right now, I'd fail. I should try. But, I don't. I hate that part of me likes the way his touch numbs my skin and his words warm my insides.

His index finger traces my jawline, then glides down my neck to my chest, then slowly down my side. Drawing in a deep breath, I'm unsure how long I was holding it. "I could make you feel so fucking good."

Bringing my lower lip inward, I bite down, holding it between my teeth. My breaths are staggered as I question my own sanity. My mind begging him to keep going as his fingers dip beneath the waistband of my shorts. Tilting my head back, I let him have me at his mercy.

"Do you think I could make you feel good, baby girl?"

Yes.

"No."

He chuckles. "I could make you see fucking stars if you let me."

I'll let you. Show me them. I beg in silence.

"Do you want me to make you feel good, Marni?" His voice is gruff and lust-filled.

Yes.

Only I don't say it. Admitting defeat is not something I'm able to do. If he knew how bad I wanted him to shove his fingers inside of me, he'd hold all the power.

He lifts my leg up, and lets it rest on his strong forearm. His hand pressing against the wall, holding me in place while his other hand slides up the leg of my shorts. I close my eyes tightly, internally begging him to do something. Anything to satisfy this undeniable urge to lose myself in him. I'm not even sure if it's him that I want or just someone to make me feel good. I could just go home and get myself off. My hand moves under the fabric of his shirt.

As I creep higher, unknowingly searching for a grip while I succumb to temptation, his hand slaps it away. "Never do that again," he gripes. His body tenses up for a sliver of a second, but it doesn't stop him.

Two fingers begin trickling the seams of my panties, and then, without warning, they plummet full force inside of me. My body jerks up as I let out a whimper. Each thrust sends me higher and higher as he fucks me with his fingers. "Oh god." I moan, bringing my hands behind his head and gripping his hair in my fists. There is nothing soft and gentle about his movements. It's so rough that it's painful, but I crave more of the pain.

"Oh fuck." I gasp, unable to control my outburst.

"You like that, baby girl?" he says, thrusting so deep that I can feel him in my stomach.

"Uh huh." He sticks in another finger.

"Tell me that I make you feel good."

When I don't respond, he curls his fingers inside of me and digs deeper.

"Tell me!" he urges.

Succumbing to his demands, I choke out, "You make me feel good."

His cock grinds against me as he dry fucks my leg that's still planted firmly on the floor. Completely out of control, I begin panting as he prods at my insides. So fast, so hard, and so unbelievably satisfying. My walls constrict as I feel the evidence of my orgasm pool around the half of his hand that's shoved inside of me.

My leg begins to quiver in his hold, but he doesn't stop. Even when I push my leg down with force to drop his arm, he continues to finger me with the same potency, thrusting his cock harder against me. "Fuck," he growls, "you are soaked."

His rhythmic grunts escalate as he leans his head back, pulling his fingers out as my own liquid dribbles down my bare leg. The pads of his two fingers begin rubbing my clit in a circular motion, sending new waves of electricity coursing through every inch of my body.

Flexing my lower half, I push myself into him further as he rubs faster. I lift my leg up and grind my knee against his solid cock.

"Ready to see those stars, baby?" he mutters through his heady breaths.

Before I can even gather a thought to respond, his fingers begin vibrating against my clit. Bucking my hips out, I lose all control and begin moaning. Fighting back the electricity that is shooting through my body, the voltage so high that I can't handle it. I pull back but want more. Push into him but lose my breath. "Oh god." I moan, before I reach the sky and come floating back down.

Opening my eyes, that I didn't even know were closed, I look down when I hear the sound of Talon's zipper. It's still so dark, but I can make out his hand wrapped around his cock as he pumps it a few times, before shooting his cum all over my leg that is still in his hold.

Once he drops my leg, and my breathing steadies, a rush of guilt hits me. At least I think it's guilt. Whatever it is, it feels dirty. Doing this here—with him. A man who has been taunting me, threatening me, and trying to imprison me.

When he has his zipper back up, he leans forward, and for a moment, I think he might kiss me. "You never speak of this to anyone. Do you understand me? Not a single person."

"Like I'd ever tell anyone about this. I'm not exactly proud of what just happened."

"Good." He gives my cheek a pat like I'm a fucking child. Grabbing some sort of fabric off the floor, he tosses it at me. "Clean up with this."

I step back quickly, not allowing the rag to touch me. "Gross. I'm not touching that thing." There is no saying what that rag was used for.

"Suit yourself." He shrugs a shoulder. "Suit yourself."

"Let's go, we've got things to do."

"You have fun with that." I push past him. "I'm going home."

Before I can even make it to the steps, he's on my tail. Once again, grabbing me by the wrist—his signature possessive, asshole move. "You need to quit telling me what you are going to do and just do what I fucking say."

"Tell me why," I demand. Taking a step closer to him.

"You mean why do you need to listen to me? Because I can make your life hell."

"That's not what I meant. Besides, I told you, I'm not scared of you. Don't mistake me for a weak girl. I can get the upper hand in this if I really wanted to."

"What makes you so sure that I won't hurt you?"

Jerking away, I stretch my hand down between us, getting a firm grip on his balls beneath his now soft cock. "Because you might have had me against this wall, but I've got your balls in my hand. Keep that in mind." I squeeze tighter, making his body jerk up.

Squeezing even harder, he begins to laugh. "You like pain, don't you? Reminds you that you're alive. Shines light on your darkness." Turning my nails inward, I dig into him through the fabric of his jeans.

"Nothing you do will ever hurt me, baby. I've seen it all and felt it all."

I've heard the rumors. I know what he's talking about. The entire town knows that Talon's dad used to beat him like he was a piece of meat on a cutting board. He's never had it easy, and all the money in the world can't cover up his internal scars.

"I don't wanna do this, Talon. I just want to finish out my senior year of high school. Move away and pretend none of this ever happened. So, just tell me that it ends tonight."

In a swift motion, he spins me around and grips both arms over my chest. With my back pressed against him, I can feel his heartbeat mimicking mine.

He can act all calm and collected, but his pulse rate and the fact that he was just humping my leg five minutes ago proves that his body reacts to me.

"I'm afraid I can't do that, because tonight—tonight is just the beginning of the fun we are going to have together." His chin rests on my shoulder. His jaw pressing into my shoulder blade with each word. "You really want to know what comes next?"

I nod.

"There are about five dozen people having the most epic Halloween party at my house right now. We are going to walk upstairs, get in my car and go have ourselves a little fun. Tomorrow, I'm taking you to your house, you're packing all your shit and settling in at your new house."

My eyes pop wide open. "New house? What the hell are you talking about?"

Straightening up behind me, he lets my hands fall free, then begins combing his fingers through my long black hair. "You're moving in with me."

Sucking in a deep breath, I exhale with laughter. "You're out of your damn mind."

"Party is waiting, let's go." He grabs a hold of my hand and begins forcing my steps behind his.

Catching him off guard, I jerk away abruptly. "I'm not going anywhere with you." I can't even see where I'm going, but I manage to find the steps and walk up them briskly. "You really are out of your mind," I mutter under my breath. I can feel his body directly behind me, but I keep on my way. Walking as fast as I can in the direction we came, hoping to find the front door.

I need to get the hell out of this place.

4

TALON

I could walk the maze of this house with a blindfold on and know exactly where I am. Marni, on the other hand, doesn't know the front door from the back.

Picking up my pace, I catch her by the waist, right before she's about to walk into a wall. "You can try and be all independent here, but the truth of the matter is, you need me right now."

"You would think so," she titters, "all you guys think that every woman needs you. Well, newsflash, you are all nothing but scum. The others just don't know it—yet."

Spinning her around abruptly, I pull her close. "Listen closely, you're wasting your breath with these nonchalant threats, and If you think that any of this will work in your favor, you are wrong—dead.fucking.wrong." Our faces are so close that I can smell the fear on her warm breath. Her heart thrashing against the walls of her chest. The sound and her scent turning me on. There is something about making a girl shake with wonder of the unknown—feeling her cling to you out of fear. Even if you are the one she fears the most.

"I'm leaving. You can try to stop me, but one way or another, I'm getting the hell out of here."

Giving her a gentle nudge, I let her think she's going to walk out that front door and leave. I'll let her hold onto that hope for now.

Pulling out the pack of smokes from my back pocket and my Zippo from the front, I stick a cigarette in my mouth and give the lighter a flick. She glances back for a moment, and I watch her eyes through the flames as I take in a drag.

"You're not stopping me?" she asks, surprised.

Keeping the flame alive, I hold it out in front of me and give her a nod toward the door in front of us. Her brows squint together in confusion. I just stand there and watch as she walks out the door, not even bothering to shut it behind her.

Five.

Four.

Three.

Two.

"You motherfuckers!"

A grin draws on my face. Giddiness washes over me. The way that one might feel when they do something good. The way happiness rolls through your body, hitting every nerve.

Marni Thorn has no idea what we have planned for her. The Rebels have a new pledge. She just doesn't know it yet.

"Where the hell is my car?"

I draw in a long drag of my cigarette with a smirk, exhaling a laughter-filled cloud. "It's not out there? Hmm, that's weird."

Her long legs stalk toward me with ambition, her open-palmed hand swings and meets the side of my cheek. "You stupid motherfucker! Where the hell is my damn car?"

More laughter rolls. The sting of her imprint on my cheek is noticeable, but not in a painful way. Instead of pissing me off, it does the exact opposite. I'm beginning to find her little outbursts sexy as hell. My dick hardens instantly as I grab her by the waist and pull her close. "You're gonna pay for that one, baby girl."

Hands continue to flap around, hitting my chest. "I fucking hate you! Now, let me go!"

"Where ya gonna go? You plan to run ten miles into town?"

"Tommy! Lars!" She begins shouting at the top of her lungs as she continues to flop like a dead fish in my arms.

"It's pointless, no one can hear you." I lean forward, grazing my teeth over the lobe of her ear. "They left. It's just you and me."

My words shut down her movements, her body frozen in my arms. The beat of her heart pounding against my chest. "Wh-where did everyone go?" Her voice cracks.

Trailing my lips up the crease of her neck, I stop when our noses touch. "I told you. There is a party and we are going. Now, if you'll quit acting like a disobedient child and do what I say, we can go have a little fun while the night's still young."

She breathes out a sigh, reacting as if just breathing is painful for her at this point. "Why are you doing this?"

"I know that none of this makes sense right now, but some-day, it will. What you need to do is quit asking questions, do as you're told, and keep your mouth shut."

"You made a ridiculous comment about me moving in with you. Why?"

"Oh, it's not ridiculous. You will be moving in."

"And if I refuse?"

"Is that a question? Because that's not an option. You *are* moving in with me."

"I'm not scared of you, Talon. You think that you can plant fear inside of me and keep me on a leash so I won't go blab your secret. You can't. I won't tell anyone, but not because of this." She looks down at the small space between us. "It's because I don't give a shit. Josh Moran was an obsessive freak. Maybe he deserved what he got. Personally, it's not my business, and I could give two fucks about him. And I give zero fucks about you and your chain gang friends. So, let me the fuck go." Catching me off guard, two hands meet my chest, and she shoves me backward.

In one swift motion, she's back where she belongs with her breasts pressed firmly against my chest. Her feistiness almost more than my hungry cock can handle. It's taking everything in me not to lay her down and fuck her in the company of every spirit in this place. Cupping her ass in both hands, I lift her up. Her legs straddle around me. The blue in her eyes shines through the darkness, landing on mine. This time, she doesn't swing or kick. Her arms fold around my neck. "Guess what, baby girl, I'm not scared of you either."

Her fingers rake through my hair before she fists a handful of it and jerks my head back. "Then why don't you let me the fuck go?" She grits through her clenched teeth.

"Contrary to what you might think, this isn't about what we did. This is about why we did it. So drop your goddamn attitude and walk with me to my car, so we can go home."

"If I go, I want answers. All of them."

"In time. You will know all that you need to know. Do we have a deal?"

"No. We don't have a deal. But I will go with you. Because I'm not calling for a ride and answering a dozen questions about why I'm in this place alone."

"Works for me." I drop her down, and her legs catch her fall. When she begins heading for the front door, I grab her hand and pull her in the right direction. "My car's back here."

"And my car?" she questions. "I swear if there is a single scratch on it, you're paying to have the entire thing repainted.

"Don't you worry. No one scratched your precious BMW.

Tommy went and picked it up from the impound, and you can have it back tomorrow."

Her hand jerks away abruptly. "Impound!"

"Why else did you think the sheriff was here? He got a call about a trespasser from the owner of this place. I told him to tow it."

"Was this all part of your elaborate scheme to silence me?"

Grabbing her hand once more, I pull her forward, and we continue walking. "Let's just say that with the text messages, the video and the fact that your car was impounded on private property, we have no doubt that all suspicion could be directed at you with just the drop of your name."

"Where is he? I mean, his body. Where did you...dispose of it?"

"Don't worry about that. We've handled everything. No one will ever suspect that you killed Josh, if you just do as you're told."

For the first time tonight, she goes quiet. Giving me a chance to recollect my thoughts about the events of tonight. I've learned that this girl can turn me from soft to hard just by running her mouth. I've also learned that she has no idea about her part in Josh's death. Let's just hope we can keep it that way.

"Wait a minute? You own this place? Why in the world would you ever buy this pile of garbage?" she spits out, as if she's had an epiphany.

"The place was set to be condemned. I couldn't let that happen. It's one of my favorite places in this town. It's full of mystery, darkness, and secrets. While some may believe this house harbors death, it brings me to life. It's a reminder that things could always be worse."

Instead of speaking, she just nods and continues to walk. No fighting, no resistance.

Hopefully she finally realizes that she isn't going anywhere.

Not unless I'm there with her.

∞

THIS LITTLE FIRECRACKER riding copilot has no idea how much her life is about to change. Most men would feel guilty for what we're doing, but me and the boys aren't most men. We've all grown up in a darkness that has fucked up any feelings of empathy, regret, or compassion. A couple of us worse off than the others.

I look over and catch another glimpse of her innocence. Her head pressed back against the headrest as she stares out into the ugly world.

I'd suspected that she would drill me with a dozen questions, toss out some insults, maybe even try to flee from the moving vehicle, but to my surprise, she's been quiet on the ride home. I'm not one for small talk, and I really have nothing to say to this girl, so I let the sounds of Breaking Benjamin blast too loud for either of us to get a word out.

When we reach the house, I turn down the private drive through the open gate. Cars wrap the turnaround, and a few people loiter around outside with drinks in their hands. Pulling up to the front of the house, I tap her leg to get her attention then turn down the music. She looks at me with tired eyes. "Remember everything I said. Not a word—about Josh or about tonight. Go up to the bathroom and clean up, then join me downstairs with a smile on your face." I curl my lip. "It's time to party, baby."

She closes her eyes and lets out an exhausted sigh. "Whatever. Just get me out of this damn car." She reaches for the handle as I click the unlock button. We both get out simultaneously, and I leave the car running.

Tossing the keys to Stan, the valet, I pick up my pace to catch up with her. "What's the hurry? We have forever." I hook an arm around her shoulder, but she brushes it off right away.

"I can't get your jizz off my leg fast enough. That's what the hurry is."

"You are such a snarky little thing. You better knock that shit off or I'll be shoving my other hand up your pussy later."

Her eyes roll. "Fuck you, you sicko."

Pulling her back over with my arm on her shoulder, I press my lips to her cheek. "Promise?"

"Never!"

When we walk inside, I drop my arm immediately. I don't need anyone in this house getting the wrong idea.

"Porter!" Jameson slaps my back, "about time you show up to your own party." His eyes skim up and down Marni, who is still at my side.

I lean and whisper in her ear, "Go upstairs and clean up. I'll be up in a minute." Once she's gone, I turn back to Jameson. "I've been around. You seen Zed?"

His eyes skim the party. "Yeah, that fucker is around here somewhere. Probably dunking heads in the toilet."

Sounds like something Zed would do. Only most people do it as a prank, he'd do it to attempt a drowning. "Alright, I'll catch ya later."

Layla and Cara did a stellar job of decorating this place. I'm pretty impressed. I slapped a few hundreds in their hands this morning and told them to throw together an epic Halloween party, and they delivered. Half of the guests are wearing costumes, half aren't. I look around the front room for Zed, but spot Marni taking part in what looks like a very serious conversation with a couple of her girlfriends. I'm not surprised, of course she has friends here. We all live in the same small town. However, I'm not comfortable with her interacting with people, without me, this early in the game. It's too risky.

"Let's go." I grab her hand and begin pulling her away from the three chicks she was talking to. I don't even look back at their reaction, nor care what any of them thinks. "I told you to go upstairs. Why are you still down here?"

"Stop it. You're embarrassing me." She tries to slither from my reach, to no avail.

"You embarrass me when you don't do what I tell you to do. Quit fighting me or I will drag your little ass up these steps. How much would that embarrass you?"

Once we reach the top, I drop her hand. "You know where the bathroom is, right?" I nod my head toward the end of the hall. "After all, that's what got you into this mess."

I watch her as she starts walking, but she stops and turns around. "Wait, how did you know that I was using the bathroom that night?"

Biting the corner of my lip, I look up at the camera directly above me, then back at her.

It satisfies her curiosity, so she continues on her way.

With my back pressed against the bathroom door, I wait. And wait. And wait. "What the hell are you doing in there?"

The sink faucet has been running for ten minutes. Granted, I haven't busted a nut in a few weeks, but it couldn't have been that much of a mess to clean up.

"I need a different pair of shorts," she hollers from the other side of the door.

"What's wrong with the ones you have on?"

The door slowly opens, causing me to straighten up. Her head pokes out of the crack. "Mine are all wet."

"So dry them and hurry your ass up."

"I can't, Talon. I really soaked them. I can't wear these downstairs."

"Come on." I grab her hand and walk her down to the other end of the hallway to the door to the next level. Cupping my hand around the keypad, I punch in the code then open the door.

"I've never been up here before," she says, as we reach the top.

"No one has."

This level is my space. No one comes up here. Aside from one time that Blakely came up to check on me because she thought I was on the verge of suicide—which I wasn't—no one else has seen my lair. The boys, the ladies, the guests, they can have the rest. This is mine.

"Wow. This is nice," she says, looking around. "I didn't even know this part of the house existed."

"Good. Because this is the first and last time you'll see it." I walk over to my dresser, open the drawer, and pull out a pair of boxer shorts, then toss them at her. "Put these on."

She holds them up. "Umm, I'm not wearing your underwear."

"They're clean. Quit bitching and put them on. You're welcome."

"You expect me to thank you." She laughs sarcastically. "There is no way that I am putting these on and going back downstairs to a house full of people." The boxers fly back at me.

"Guess you'll be partying in your panties. That, or your cum-soaked shorts. Your choice."

Steady steps lead her over to me as she grunts and groans in agitation with each movement. "Seriously, I'm so tired. Can I just go to bed?"

I drag my teeth over my bottom lip as she stands there with one hand on her hip in just a pair of underwear and the hoodie she's been wearing all night. "Fine. You're sleeping in my room tonight." There are too many people here, and I don't want anyone fucking with her. I don't need to dispose of another body any time soon. "Don't even think about trying to leave. The door will be locked, and the alarm will be set. I've kept people out of this part of the house for a year, I can keep you in it." I bend down and grab the boxers then push them at her chest. "T-shirts are in the bottom drawer. I'll have the house-keeper wash your dirty clothes, just put them in the basket."

I give her one last glance before I leave. Shutting the door behind me, I walk down the stairs and step back into the main hallway, before setting the alarm.

"Where is she?" Zed comes stalking toward me. His boots heavy on the hardwood floor.

"She's here. Don't worry about it." I push past him and start walking back toward the staircase when I see Tommy and Lars.

"Killer party, man." Tommy holds his beer. He's already three sheets to the wind, not surprising.

Zed joins us at the top of the stairs. "Why is she up there?" he asks. All too concerned about the way I'm handling the situation.

"She's safe up there. She can't leave and no one can touch her."

"Including you." Zed pokes a finger in my chest. "Or was that your plan all along? You think you're gonna get her all to yourself?"

My hands meet his chest, shoving him forcefully back-wards. "Fuck you."

'Woah, woah. Knock it off you two." Lars steps in. "It's only night one. You can't start this shit already. We have a deal. No one touches her." He looks between the two of us. "Got it?"

"No one is fucking touching her, including me. A deal is a deal." I hold my fist out to Zed, who bumps it back.

"Deal," he agrees.

I'll make damn sure no one lays a finger on sleeping beauty. If they do, I'll kill 'em with my bare hands.

"Do you think she suspects anything?" Tommy asks, as he sways back and forth with a now empty beer bottle.

"She doesn't know a damn thing. And she never will."

5

MARNI

R eality hits me like a glass of cold water to the face when
I wake up. The silk black sheet that tangles around my
body is not my own. Pushing myself up as my back slides
against the wooden headboard, heavy breaths from someone
beside the bed warn me that I'm not alone.

Without looking over at him, I acknowledge his presence.
"How long have you been here?" I ask, watching as he stands
up in my peripheral and steps beside the bed.

"Long enough to know that you sound like an eighty-year
old man with sleep apnea when you're sleeping." He fists the
black sheet and jerks it off of me in one swift motion. "Get
your ass up. We have shit to do."

Hugging my legs to my chest, I catch a glimpse of him.
Fully dressed in a pair of black jeans, black boots that lace up
to his ankles, and a solid gray tee that hugs his muscular form.
His hair is swept over to one side of his head and a brown
cigarette filter peaks out from above his ear. I divert my attention quickly and resume staring at the closed door in front of
me. "It's the day after Halloween. Everyone skips school the
day after Halloween."

His hand wraps around my wrist as he pulls me off the bed. My feet hit the floor next to his while I fight to avoid eye contact. "I never said we're going to school. I said we have shit to do. *We* includes you."

Dragging me like a ragdoll, he takes me over to his dresser where my shorts and underwear sit neatly pressed and folded. He finally releases his hold on me when he tosses them at me. "Put these on." I catch the shorts as they hit my chest and wait for him to turn around—to leave and give me some damn privacy. "I said put them on." He taps his bare wrist. "We ain't got all day."

I start walking to the adjoining bathroom, but he stops me. "Uh uh. Right here."

"You're delusional. I'm not taking my clothes off in front of you."

Crossing his arms over his chest, his eyes slide down to my bare legs. "Fine, you can wear my boxers to your house. Hope Daddy doesn't mind."

Hope washes over me, and I'm sure the smile on my face gives me away. "I'm going home?"

"Just to pack your shit and get some pants. We're taking a little hike today. Might wanna dress the part."

Any hope is quickly diminished. "A hike? Why?"

His shoulders steel, and agitation gets the best of him. "No more questions. Change. Now."

He stands there with his eyes glued to me, and I have no choice but to slide down his gray and white checkered boxer shorts. Thankfully, my hoodie hangs down low enough to hide the parts that I don't want him to see. I watch him as I kick them to the side. His gaze following every move I make. Like some sort of sick pervert who gets off on watching me strip out of his clothes.

Unfolding the shorts, I give them a shake. "Where's my underwear?" I look up and see him twirling my pink thong on his finger with a shit-eating grin on his face. My stomach churns when he shoots them toward me like a rubber band. "Seriously? Was that necessary?"

Tugging the corner of his lip between his teeth, he smirks. "Might wanna pick those up."

Closing my eyes, my cheeks fill with air. Puffing it all out at once, I pull the hem of my hoodie down over my ass and turn around, then bend to pick them up. Glancing at him behind me as my head hangs low, his arms are still crossed over his chest. He bends at the waist; his head hangs forward and his eyes meet mine. But not before skimming every part of my body beneath the hoodie. He curls his lips upward. "Nice. But I've seen better."

Such a fucking asshole. Quickly snatching up my underwear, I tuck my shorts under my armpit and slide them on before even turning around. "I don't even have a toothbrush." I wiggle into my tight jean shorts and zip them up.

"Use your finger. Or you can use mine."

"Gross, I'm not using your toothbrush."

"I know you're not. I meant that you can use my finger. I'll even let you suck the toothpaste off."

Pulling my hair out of a ponytail, I comb my fingers through my hair and snarl at him, "Are you always this much of an asshole?"

"Not always. Sometimes I'm a dick, too."

Shaking my head, I sigh. "Let's get this over with." Pushing past him, I head for the door, but he beats me to it. Grabbing the handle and pulling it open as he watches me out of the corner of his eyes.

"No funny business, got it. We go get your stuff. You tell your dad exactly what I tell you to say."

We step out of the room and start walking down the stairs. Then out another door, where Talon begins punching in a code to set the alarm.

"What about school?"

"You'll still go to school. But don't think that you won't be watched, because you will." He hooks an arm around my neck, pulling me close, like we're old friends. The scent of pot and cigarette smoke no longer lingers on his clothes. He actually smells good. Really damn good. Like cedarwood and citrus— pineapple maybe. I catch myself sniffing him, and when he looks down at me with a cockeyed stare, I look down the long stretch of the hallway and see his henchmen waiting at the end.

"Oh yeah, do you have an army of men lined up to keep track of me now?"

"As a matter of fact, I do."

"Who? Them?" I laugh, but I really don't find it funny because, the truth is, these guys probably will be watching my every move. I just hope no one else plans on me stripping down in front of them. The one and only reason that I didn't slap Talon and lock myself in the bathroom is because he already learned, and probably memorized, every fold and curve with his fingers anyway. I've never been self-conscious about my body. In fact, I've done things that most would call deplorable —though I find it satisfying in a weird way. But still, it's different when it's not by choice.

"Amongst others," he finally says when we reach the guys. "You can't be trusted." He gives me a push into the arms of Lars. "Until you can, you'll be handled in the way we see fit."

Gulping air, I peer up at Lars who has his lips pressed into a firm line. He looks down at me, and my stomach twists in knots when I feel his dick harden against my thigh. His dark brown hair, about the same color as Talon's, hangs down on his forehead. He throws his head back to brush it out of his eyes while still holding me tightly in his arms. "You hungry, pretty girl? I've got something for you."

"Eww, get away from me." I push off of him and sneer with disgust.

Talon begins walking down the stairs, and Lars gives me a gentle nudge to follow. All the while Zed is staring at me like I'm some sort of meal that he plans to cut into and devour. I wanna say something. Ask him why the hell he's looking at me like that, but if I know Zed like I think I do, he won't even answer me, and if he does, it will be all lies. I'm starting to think that all these guys know how to do is withhold information, lie, and prey on women like their dicks are a gift to us all.

"Come on, shithead. We have to get this over with," Talon barks at Tommy, who is still standing at the top of the staircase, too busy tapping on his phone to even notice that we were walking downstairs. He quickly sticks his phone in the pocket of his black cargo pants and jogs down. Jumping over the last three steps.

Tommy has more of a babyface than the other three. With ash blonde hair that is shorter on the sides. His eyes mimic the blue sky, dappled with specks of green, and I can see how it would be easy to get lost in them. He offers more of a surfer vibe. Minus the array of black ink sleeving his arm, the small tattoo on his neck and the silver chain linked from his back pocket to his front.

I lean closer and notice that the tattoo on his neck is the same symbol as the box and the door, then it hits me that it's the same one on Talon's forearm too. I never even noticed it that first night here when I overhead the guys talking. I guess it didn't dawn on me until now. I give Zed and Lars a onceover, curious if they have the tattoo as well.

Lars lifts up his shirt, turning his side to me. As if he knew exactly what I was thinking. Staring back at me is a distorted face—half-skeleton, half-girl covering his entire side. On her neck is the snake infinity. "We all have them." Even more than the tattoos, I notice how well-defined his body is. A six-pack, maybe even eight. A v-line that leaves nothing to the imagination. I already know what it leads to, I felt it digging into me only moments ago. Needless to say, it doesn't disappoint.

Shaking my head, I try to dismiss the image that is now engraved in my mind. Yes, these guys are all sexy as hell, but they are obviously psychopaths.

"Let's go." Talon walks back in the room. I didn't even know he had left. "Get the car and meet us at the spot in one hour." He points to Zed. "Do not fuck this up."

Zed smirks, tossing his hands out in front of him as he walks backward. "Wouldn't dream of it."

Talon's eyes burn into him, and it makes me wonder if there is some sort of animosity between them. "I know how you are. Reckless and careless. One wrong move and we all go down. Got it."

Zed salutes him then proceeds to flip him off. Talon shoots daggers at him one more time, before grabbing me by the hand and pulling me toward the kitchen.

"And don't you forget our deal," Zed hollers when we round the corner.

Entering the mud room, Talon pulls open the door that leads to the four-stall garage. Three black vehicles are inside. A car, a pickup truck, and an SUV. Opening the passenger side of the SUV, he nods for me to get in. That reminds me, I still don't know where the hell my car is. Talon stands outside the driver's side door for a minute, tapping on his cell before he gets in. His eyes catch mine for a moment and there is a calmness I haven't seen before. It feels so weird to be alone with him like this. Granted, we were alone on the ride last night, and again this morning. But this feels different.

All those feelings wash away as soon as he speaks. "When we get to your house, I'll walk you in. You tell your dad that you're staying with a friend for a while. The fucker probably won't even give a shit, he's never home anyway." He turns the key and the engine purrs.

"How do you even know that?" I question. Talon barely even knows me.

"Are you forgetting that we live in the same small town. And that I fucking hate your brother. I know a lot more than you think."

His words send chills down my spine. I wonder how much these guys really do know about me. I'm sure they've done their research. The idea that they have been digging into my past so that they can control my future is painfully surreal.

"Where's my car?" I ask, as the garage door slowly opens in front of us. My question is immediately answered when I see it parked on the side of the driveway. As we pass by it, I inspect the white paint quickly for any dings or dents, but it looks just like it did when I left it yesterday evening.

The garage door closes behind us as we make our way down the long-paved driveway, hidden by trees on either side of it. Talon's house isn't visible from the road, and it's apparent that a guy like him would prefer privacy. After all, he seems to have a lot to hide. Once we turn onto the main road, I shield my eyes from the sun as Talon flips down the visor in front of me and slides on his black Ray Ban sunglasses.

Engulfed in silence, I internally beg him to turn the radio on to drown out the sounds of my galloping heart. Taking deep breaths, I try to calm myself, but it's impossible. I have no idea how I will ever convince my father to let me go stay with anyone for a couple weeks. He all but had a stroke when I went and stayed in LA with Axel at the end of the summer. He's always kept me on a much shorter leash than my brother. He tightened that leash when my mom passed away last year. There are times that I feel like he is choking the life out of me by trying so hard to keep me safe.

We pull into my driveway, and Talon kills the engine. When

he reaches for the handle, anxiety kicks into high gear. "You're coming in?"

"Of course, I'm coming in. You think I'm gonna risk you walking in there and running your mouth?"

"My dad will never let me pack my things and leave with you. It won't work. You can come, but I'm telling you, you're gonna ruin your own plan." I open the door and hop out, shutting it behind me.

Dry heat fills my lungs as I take a deep breath, suddenly parched. As soon as we walk in the house, I go straight to the kitchen and grab a bottled water. Talon stands by idly, watching me as I slam it.

Ruby, our housekeeper, walks into the kitchen. "Good morning, Ms. Thorn."

I set the empty bottle on the counter. "Ruby, have you seen my father?"

She begins rubbing the rosary that hangs in front of her heart, mumbling something in Spanish as she looks Talon up and down in distaste.

"Ruby." I snap my fingers until she shifts her attention to me. "My father?"

Rosary still in hand, she scoffs while eyeballing Talon. "Mr. Thorn is in his study."

When she continues to glance back and forth from me to Talon, out of sheer concern for my safety, I excuse her. "You may leave."

Ruby is extremely religious, and I get the feeling she thinks that Talon is part of some sort of cult and he's here to take me prisoner. Actually, that's exactly what is happening. Let's hope her little prayer just now has spared my soul from the reapers.

"I'll be right back," I tell Talon, but he grabs my arm before I can even attempt to step past him.

With his face mere inches from mine, he narrows his eyes

and shakes his head. His way of telling me that I will not be going anywhere alone. I huff, "Seriously?"

"You have no idea how serious I am."

Jerking my arm away, I lead the way. "Fine. But remember what I said. He's not going to be happy."

"I'll take my chances." He smirks then slaps a hand to my ass.

I spin around quickly, giving him a shove. He's lucky that I don't slap him across the face. "Do not do that again." I grit through my teeth. But he doesn't even shudder, he just smiles. A sinister smile that trails goosebumps down my entire body.

His breath prickles my neck as he walks behind me. "My apologies. I was just remembering how much you liked it when I touched you last night." Bringing my elbow back forcefully, I nail him right in the gut. When he lets out a grunt, I know I made my point.

Walking up the steep and winding stairs, he's hot on my trail. Getting a perfect view of my ass. I'd love nothing more than to kick my foot back and send him flying down. I'm sure Ruby wouldn't mind the mess of his blood; she'd probably sing one of her church hymnals with a smile on her face as she mops it up.

When we reach the top, I give him one more chance to change his mind. "Are you prepared for the possibility that in three point five seconds, my dad will have a gun to your head demanding your intentions?"

Reaching into his pocket, he whips out a sling blade. My eyes widen as I take a step back. "I'm always prepared." With a flip, the blade goes back in and he sticks it in his pocket.

Ok then. Let's hope that it doesn't come to that because Ruby would not be as inclined to clean up that sort of mess. Knocking on the door, Dad speaks before I announce myself, "Come in, Marni."

Dad watches every move made in this house. He's already

expecting Talon and me. He has a monitor in his office with coverage of every camera in the house. The prison-like feel of my home has made sure that my high school days are anything but thrilling. My bedroom is the only place I get any privacy, and it's not until I'm on the outside of this prison that I am able to fully unwind.

Dad is sitting all high and mighty—the king of his castle. A stern look holds tightly to his face as he glares at Talon. "Hi, Dad." I walk over to his side and greet him with a kiss on his cheek.

"Where were you last night?" he asks. His words are directed toward me, but he is still staring at Talon.

"I stayed at Shay's. I told you this before I left." I didn't really, but Dad doesn't pay attention to half of what I say, so he'll just play it off like he forgot.

Finally, he turns in his chair and looks in my direction. I pop a cheek on the edge of his desk and glance from him to Talon. "This is my friend, Talon. Blakley Porter's brother."

"I know who he is." Dad picks up a cigar on his desk and sticks it between his teeth. Something he does often when he means business. The angrier he gets, the harder he bites down on it. I'm not sure I've ever even seen him smoke one.

Talon stands tall with his hands in his pockets and a blank stare as he glares right back at my dad. Being in this room with the two of them is actually enlightening. They are more similar than I thought. Both have this need for power and dominance. Only, Talon wants power over me. Dad's goals are much bigger. He prefers to rule an entire nation in the black market, while also controlling me so that I don't draw any negative attention to the Thorn name. Not that Axel hasn't done that already.

"Dad, I'm here because I was wondering if I can stay with Shay for a couple of weeks. You're leaving for Dallas in a couple of days anyway, and you know how much I hate staying here alone."

Dad's chair slides back so fast that you'd think his legs were on fire. He stands up and forcefully smacks both palms to his desk. "And what the hell do you have to do with this?" he snaps, looking Talon dead in the eye.

Still not budging from his position, Talon's lips curl upward. Pulling his hand out of his pocket, he pops a toothpick between his teeth while Dad bites down so hard on his cigar that I'm surprised it's still intact. I want to reach over and smack the shit-eating grin off Talon's face before he gets us both in trouble, but that would only draw more attention to the situation. I shouldn't even care. If Talon wants to screw this up, so be it. It would actually work in my favor because the idea of staying in that house with those guys for God knows how long is worse than living in this one with eyes on me twenty-four-seven.

"I'm just here for moral support, Sir." Talon smirks, pinching the toothpick between his thumb and forefinger while he chews on it.

"Moral support my ass." Dad turns to me. "What the hell are you doing hanging out with this beatnik?"

Laughter erupts in the form of sarcasm as Talon steps forward. "Beatnik? Pretty hypocritical coming from someone in your position. Tell me, Mr. Thorn, what exactly is it that you do for a living?"

My heart feels like a jack hammer in my chest. The continuous pounding is so loud I can feel the vibration in my ears. "Stop it, both of you." I stretch my arms out between the two of them, even though the desk is separating them from any direct contact. However, in a matter of seconds, one of them could be on the other side and it wouldn't be a good ending for any of us. "Dad, I'm going to stay at Shay's for a couple of weeks. I'm packing a bag and I'll text you every day to check in." I step behind the desk while him and Talon continue with their staredown. I give him another chaste kiss on the cheek then walk over and grab Talon by the arm to pull him away.

"You lay a finger on my daughter and you won't live to brag about it, young man." Talon takes the toothpick out of his mouth and gives it a toss. I watch as it lands on Dad's desk, and I know that we need to haul ass out of here right fucking now. "Do you hear me?" he shouts, once again, smacking his hands down so loud on his desk that the echo carries out into the hall.

As soon as we are far enough away from Dad's office, I shove both hands hard into Talon's chest. "What the hell was that?"

"Just making sure he knows that I'm not intimidated by him." His thumb flicks across my chin. "I cower to nobody, baby."

I'm not sure if I'm appalled or turned on. I've never seen anyone stand up to my dad like that. Most of the people in this town fear him. Not Talon. Something tells me that Talon has no fear.

Without fear, we have no limits.

For my sake, I hope that's not true.

6

TALON

"Where exactly are we going?" Marni asks from the passenger seat. Her back is pressed firmly against the leather with her hands folded tightly in her lap. She looks tense.

I glance over at her, and as anxious as I am to tell her what we're doing, I'll let the curiosity fester inside of her a bit longer. "You'll see."

Driving down Old Highway Eighty-Eight, the sun has disappeared behind the clouds. An unusual darkness lingers outside as we drive in complete silence. Ironic, considering what we are about to do. In less than an hour, there is no going back, and she will officially be at our beck and call. She will kneel when we say kneel and speak when we say speak.

Straightening her back, she leans forward to get a better look at our surroundings. "Why are we leaving Redwood? I assumed we were going to Briarwood."

"Wrong." I click my tongue against my cheek as we drive past the road that leads to Briarwood. "We're going to Miners Point."

Her body jerks up in a swift-like motion. Fear written all over her face. "Miners Point? As in one of the tallest and most dangerous points on this side of the state?"

"You got it." I smirk. I know that I'm a sick bastard for relishing in the pain and fear that I instill in others—namely her. She just makes it so easy. Marni isn't weak by any means. I don't know her all that well, but I do know that she has a name for herself in the halls of Redwood as a badass bitch. Something about watching her squirm is satisfying.

"If you think that I'm climbing up to the point, you're as delusional as I thought you were."

"There will be no climbing." I throw my arm out in front of her and push her back against the seat. "Sit back, relax, and enjoy the scenery."

Shoving my arm away, she rolls her eyes so hard that I worry they will get stuck up in their sockets. "Ok, if we're not climbing the point, then why the hell are we going there?"

"Has anyone ever told you that you ask too many questions?"

"I think I'm warranted a few here and there, considering I just packed up my clothes to move into a house where I'm forced to sleep with one eye open because you are all fucking lunatics. Not to mention that you are driving me out to Miners Point with zero insight into why. So, yes, I do ask a lot of questions."

"You talk a lot, too."

The sound that escapes her sounds like a mixture of a woman giving birth and a dog growling. "Ugh, I hate you." She crosses her arms over her chest and resumes looking out the window.

"I like the way your hate feels. You said the same thing last night and it poured into my hand as my fingers were fucking your pussy. Tasted pretty good, too." I pop two fingers in my mouth, then pull them out. "You're welcome to hate me tonight if you'd like."

She snarls, "You're so disgusting."

We pull down the dirt road and the dust kicks up, which tells me that the guys are already here. Quickly changing from a smooth ride to a bumpy terrain has Marni grabbing the 'oh shit' handles and looking like she's ready to attack me with her bare hands. "Would you slow the hell down?" she snaps.

"I thought you liked it bumpy, my bad."

"Oh my God, would you quit it with the sexual innuendos? They're getting old."

I tsk. "My, my, you have a dirty mind. I was referring to the ride. What did you have in mind?"

She doesn't even humor me with a snappy response.

Razor sharp edges that reach the tip of the point cover our entire viewing area. Tommy's car looks like a Hot Wheels toy parked in front of it. The closer we get, the more life-sized it becomes, until we're parked right next to it. Tommy is sitting in the driver's seat with the door open. His head shoots up from his phone when we get out. Zed is laying back on the hood of the car puffing on a joint and blowing smoke circles into the still air. He doesn't even acknowledge our presence. And Lars is taking a piss right in front of us and makes no attempt to hide his pencil dick.

"Bout fucking time." Lars huffs as he gives himself a shake and zips up his pants.

I glance around for the car. "Where is it?"

"Don't worry. Everything's in place," Lars says, as he walks over and throws an arm over Marni's shoulder. "Should have put on some hiking boots. Those white tennies won't be so pretty when we're done here."

Marni tosses his arm off her and takes a step back, planting her hands on her hips and looking around. "What's in place?"

RACHEL LEIGH

Zed jumps off the hood, still pinching the joint in his hands. "Oh, didn't our boy, Talon, tell you? We're planning to gang bang you then hike up that point and toss your beaten body over the ledge."

Tommy finally pockets the phone his face is always shoved in. "Don't listen to him. He's a bit fucked in the head." He snatches the joint out of Zed's hands and draws in a long drag.

Zed undresses Marni with his eyes, and I clench my fists at my side. "I mean, we could change the plans. Sounds like a good time to me." He says with a wink.

Marni turns around to face me. "Please, just take me home. I don't like this," she whispers. As if she's seeking comfort in me. Like I'm the one who would save her from this madness. Little does she know, I'm far from a savior. I'm a whole goddamn nightmare.

I spin her around to face the guys. "Walk," I demand. "Zed, lead the way. You're the one who parked the car out here."

The terrain is difficult to drive through, but, somehow, Zed managed to get the car back there last night and walked back when it was in place.

Tommy passes me the joint, and I take a couple drags while Marni is fanning the smoke away from her face. "Oh come on, don't act all innocent. I know you indulge." I offer it to her, but she side-eyes me with a glare that has the veins in my dick pulsating. For some reason, angry Marni turns me on. Which could be very bad for me, considering she's gonna be angry for the foreseeable future.

"Did indulge. Now that I'm living with you whack jobs, I need a clear head. One eye open at night and a deadbolt on the bedroom door. Make that happen, please." She smirks, and it's loaded with sass and sarcasm.

Tommy laughs. "I like her." His shoulder nudges mine. "Looks like you're gonna have your hands full with this one."

"Don't forget, we're in this together. She's not just my problem." Sure, I'll cut off the fingers of any hand that tries to touch her, but as far as her attitude, we get to share in that misfortune.

"I'm not anyone's problem!" she shouts, "and if you all think that I'm a problem, you can gladly take me back home and forget you even know me." She grabs the joint so fast from my fingers that I'm pretty sure she just burnt the tip of her thumb. Drawing in a puff, she holds it for a minute then coughs out a cloud of smoke.

Tommy pats her on the back. "Easy there, girl, we need you alive."

"Could someone give me my fucking joint back," Zed grumbles in front of us but doesn't bother turning around.

Marni skips up next to him and sticks it in front of his face. He takes it away and glares daggers in her direction. Zed is a bit of a robot. Heartless, cold, and made of steel. He's unbreakable, because you can't break what isn't even whole. We're all used to it, but Marni, she has no idea what he is capable of. The thoughts that go on in that head of his are satanic and eerie. All the more reason why I need to keep an extra eye on him. Marni is with us for a reason, and I'll be damned if he pushes her over the edge before she serves her purpose.

Twenty-minutes later, we've finally made it to the backside of Miners Point that looks out over Lake Ruin. The old beat-up tan Chevy sits right at the edge of the cliff. We keep walking, but Marni backsteps once she realizes how far down the drop is. "Holy shit." She stretches her neck to try and look without getting too close. When she stumbles a bit, I instinctively grab her by the waist.

"Watch yourself," I say. She looks at me and giggles. Noticing that her eyes are small and squinted leads me to believe she doesn't indulge as often as I thought she did. "You ok?"

"I'm fine, but what's with the old car?" She takes a step forward, and her eyes widen. "Wait, that's Josh's car." Clapping an open hand over her mouth, she gasps, "Oh my gosh. Is he in there?"

Zed casually lets the joint drop to the ground and digs the toe of his boot into it. "Maybe he is. Maybe he isn't." His monotone voice comes out gruff.

Marni's eyes shoot to mine. Wide and searching for reassurance. Once again—something she seeks from me that I can't give her. "Move." I give her a nudge toward the car.

Her entire body steels as I push her forward, reminding me of the big tractor tires that Coach would make us push up and down the field during practices my junior year. "I don't think," she stumbles over her words, "I don't think I can go near that car."

"I said, move." I walk into her back, forcing her body to move forward. Leaning in, I whisper, "He's not in there."

Her body relaxes a tad, but she's still resisting. "He's not?"

"No, of course not. You think we'd let his body sit in a car in this heat and rot? We aren't that inhumane." I pause for a beat, letting her absorb that information. "He's buried. Beneath the concrete in the basement of Briarwood. Remember that wall I pressed you up against?" When she doesn't respond with words, but I feel her body tense up again, I continue, "Let's just say that Joshy boy was watching the whole thing. I heard he likes to watch you. Did you know that?"

Her entire body spins around to face me while the guys gather behind the car. With flared nostrils, she clears her throat. "What's that supposed to mean?"

She knows exactly what I'm talking about. I tsk. "You didn't think we were the only ones with a secret, did you?"

"How do you know?" When I stand there idly with my hands in my pockets and a smirk on my face, she plunges her hands into my chest. "Damnit, Talon, how do you know?"

Leaning forward, my mouth ghosts her ear. I take in her hitched breaths and relish in the sound of her trumpeting heart. "Because I like to watch you, too."

U nease ripples through my body. Talon's hot breath sticks
to my skin like a thirsty leech. Running my fingers over
the dew on my neck where his words hit, I realize that I'm
sweating. Frozen in place but burning up.

"How does that make you feel?" he hums, "Knowing that
I've not only touched you in the dark, but also seen your naked
body in the light?"

Playing dumb, I shrug my shoulders. "I don't know what
you're talking about?"

Sure, I did some things that I'm not proud of. But he
shouldn't know that. No one should. Especially not Josh. Especially not Talon Fucking Porter.

"Are we doing this or what?" Zed growls from the backside
of the car. The guys are all standing idly, waiting for whatever
it is we are supposed to be doing.

"We'll talk about this later." Talon places his hand on my
back and begins walking toward the guys.

"Yes, we will talk about it later, because I also want to know
what you meant when you said that Josh is buried in that
basement."

"I meant he's buried in the basement. What more is there to talk about?"

The thought sends a quiver of nausea through me. There was a body decomposing just beneath the floors where my arousal was dripping as Talon gave me one of the best orgasms of my life.

"Little Thorn." Zed waves me over, and if he calls me that one more time, I swear I'm gonna scream. Hating myself more and more with each step, I move to his side like an obedient puppy. I shouldn't be putting up with this shit. This is not me. I'm not one to be pushed around. "Stand here. And once Lars jumps out of the car, you push." He looks me dead in the eye as he stretches a pair of black leather gloves on his hands. I struggle to catch the thoughts in my head. *I have to push.* "Do you hear me? You push," he repeats again.

"What? No?" I shake my head, "I'm not being an accomplice to this. I already burned his phone." Zed clenches his fists at his side and the possibility that he could lay those fists on me at any given moment has my stomach turning. My eyes hold tightly to them at his side. "Please, just let me sit this one out."

His eyes narrow and in one fell swoop, his hands are gripping the side of my face. "You will do what I tell you to do or my joke earlier about tossing you over this ledge will become a reality." He pushes my head away as he drops his hands. "Got it?"

Zed scares me. He really fucking scares me. There is nothing I wouldn't put past him at this point and he is one of the reasons that I'm still standing here. If it were just Talon, Tommy, and Lars, I'd probably knot all three of their dicks together and run like hell. I'd fight back. But I take Zed's threats seriously. His heart isn't just black; it's non-existent.

Swallowing hard, I nod. "I hear you, but why am I pushing? Why can't they help you?" I look at Talon and Tommy. I am not putting my fingerprints on this car. Nope. Not happening.

"Because you're part of this now and because I told you to," he looks to Talon, "She really is a pain in the ass."

Talon nods in agreement as he stands there puffing on a cigarette.

"And do you plan on recording this little stunt, too?" I ask, for obvious reasons.

"We've insured your silence after everything else. This one's just for us. Just a little something extra to stomp on your soul when you need a reminder of your part in this."

My part in this. It seems that whether I like or not, I am part of this, and we are all in this together. "I want gloves, too, then. I'm not touching this car."

Zed's eyes shoot to Talon who nods. He then directs his attention to Tommy who's shaking a can of spray paint. "Tommy, gimme your gloves."

"Take his gloves," he points to Talon, "he's not doing anything."

Zed's body straightens, his shoulders drawn and his back stiff. He shouts, "Someone give her some fucking gloves!"

Sticking the cigarette between his teeth, Talon bites down on the butt and reaches into his pockets. He pulls out a pair of the same gloves that Zed is wearing, then tosses them right in front of him, which is at least three feet away from me. I watch as they hit the ground. "Really? This shit again?" I huff as I walk over and pick them up. "You're lucky I have clothes on this time."

Zed's eyes drill into Talon. "What's that supposed to mean?"

"Not a damn thing. Do this shit." Talon is quickly at my side; he grabs the gloves from my hands and begins putting them on me like I'm a child. One finger at a time while he stares me down with unsaid words. He doesn't want Zed to know that he made me change in front of him. But why? Zed hates my guts. He'd probably encourage Talon to shred my comfort zone to pieces. "Tommy, get your ass over here and help them."

"They've got it covered," Tommy says, as he continues to shake a can of paint and begins spraying leaves—weirdo.

"Now!" Talon demands.

Once the gloves are on, I walk over to Zed's side. Lars has one foot in the car and one on the ground, as he stands there waiting to take his foot off the brake. Dozens of questions are shooting through my mind, but I don't bother asking them— not yet.

Closing my eyes, I press my hands to the back of the trunk. "Ok, let's just get this over with," I say, as my eyes open. Lars shifts the car into neutral and then jogs behind the car where Zed, Tommy, and I are and we all press against the back. My hands, entrapped in black leather, push as my feet dig into the dirt beneath me. To my surprise, the car rolls effortlessly. I can feel the weight of the car drop forward as the front tires go over. I follow the car as it moves right to the edge. Step by step, until it drops.

Strong arms wrap around me and pull me back. Only it's not Talon, it's Zed this time. Standing there, held securely, we all watch as the car disappears. Three seconds later, there's a swoosh, and I swear I feel it ripple through my body like an earthquake.

Zed squeezes me tightly. "Yeah, baby." He laughs. Something I wasn't sure he was capable of. I can feel my hair part as he draws in a deep breath. One hand smooths over my breast and his thumb begins making circles around my nipple. Apprehension sweeps through me, but before I can react, he releases his hold on me. Scanning my shoes, I realize why Zed said I should have worn different ones. My white Air Force Ones are covered in sandy black dirt.

When I look over at Talon, he doesn't hold the same enthusiasm. Instead, his jaw is locked and his eyes are zeroed in on me like I did something wrong. I'd swear my heart has stopped beating just to prepare itself for my death, because if his looks could kill, I'd already be dead. My shoulders shoot up and I raise a brow. "Did I do something wrong?" I pull the gloves off and tuck them into my back pockets.

In two seconds flat, he's at my side, grabbing me by the wrist and pulling me away. I look back at the guys who are just standing there, watching him take me back down the trail we came up. I attempt to jerk my arm away once they fade into the distance. "What the hell?"

"Yeah. What the hell is right!" He snaps at me like I did something wrong. "You just let him touch you like that." It comes out as more of a statement than a question.

"I have no idea what you're talking about." I give my arm a swift jerk once more, and this time, it frees. Zed was excited. For the first time ever, I did something good in his eyes, and for some unknown reason, even if it was criminal, I felt proud to be acknowledged by him. "Why are you so mad right now?"

The next thing I know, Talon's hands wrap around my waist as he pushes me up against a boulder. My head hits the rock and my legs instinctively wrap around him. My mind enters a state of fog from the blow to the back of my head. I'm sure it was unintentional, but Talon is forceful, nonetheless. With my entire body stiff, one of the ridges digs deep into my back as he holds me in place. Something awakens inside of me and I'm not sure if it's a desire to grind myself into him as he's pressed between my legs or the urge to spit in his face.

"Quit playing dumb with me. And when someone touches

you and you don't want them to, you make them stop. You got it? You fight back. If Zed lays a finger on you, you tell me or you handle it. Do you understand me?" All I can do is nod. Releasing his grip, he lets go, but raises his voice. "You're lying to me."

My own hands grip the side of my head, feeling the throbbing as I blink my eyes a few times. I choke out, "I'm not lying. I got it. Ok?" Sliding down the rock, it scrapes against my skin through the fabric of my t-shirt. I keep going until my ass hits the ground. It's apparent now that my hormones are confused because all I want to do at this moment is slam his head into the rock.

"You're still lying to me," he raises his voice, "because if you heard a goddamn word I said then you would have just fought me off. Get your ass up and toughen up, or you'll never survive this."

Just as I get to my feet, the guys round the corner. "What the hell is going on over here?" Zed quips.

Talon brushes off my shoulder with a smirk. "Just making sure our girl here is on the same page as us."

Balling my fists at my side, it's taking everything inside of me not to punch this fucker square in the face. I've fought men over less. "Same page?" I laugh. "We're not even in the same fucking book." I walk past him, my shoulder nudging hard against his as I head back down the trail to the parked vehicles.

My heart rises into my throat when I think about this mess I've gotten myself into. Now that I've helped them dispose of Josh's car, I'm more than an accomplice. I'm guilty, too.

If they fall, I'm falling with them.

∞

THE RIDE back to the house was quiet. In fact, the entire day was quiet. As soon as we got back, I brought my things inside to the spare bedroom and took a quick shower in the adjoining bathroom. I didn't bother to unpack because I don't plan on staying long. Unzipping the small pocket of my black backpack, I stick the gloves inside. It's time to start thinking ahead. If they turn on me and try to take me down, I'm taking those fuckers with me. These gloves might have my prints on them, but they also have Talon's. The video of me throwing the phone in the trash might have my face on it, but it also came from Zed's phone. Two down, two to go.

Shay's name flashes on the screen of my phone. For a moment, I decide to ignore it. She'll likely have a dozen questions that I can't answer. Remembering that I need her to go along with the plan I told Dad, though, I answer her call.

"Hey, Shay."

"Hey, Shay? That's all you have to say? How about, I'm sorry I've ignored all of your texts and blew you off on Halloween?"

Dropping back on the bed, I stare at the ceiling and sigh. "I'm sorry I've ignored all of your texts and blew you off on Halloween."

"That's better. Now tell me what the hell is going on and why you haven't been at your house?"

My entire body shoots up. "Wait. You went to my house?"
Shit.

"Yeah, and Ruby said that you left with the devil and haven't been home since. Spill. Now."

There is so much truth to that statement that I don't even know where to begin. "She's right."

"And does this mysterious horned man have anything to do with why you left Talon Porter's party Saturday night without saying goodbye?"

After my altercation with the guys that night, I booked it to my car and didn't even tell Shay or Wyatt that I was leaving. In my defense, I had no intention of sticking around. At first, I was just planning to drop them off because they were catching a ride home with some guys. Then, she practically dragged me inside.

"You could say that." I pause before continuing, "Listen, it's a long story but the bottom line is, I need you to say that I'm staying with you for a bit if my dad or Axel ask."

"Ok…" she drags out the word, "Where are you *actually* staying?"

"Would you believe me if I told you that I'm staying with Talon Porter?"

"What?!" she huffs. "Tell me you're joking. Why would you ever stay in that house?"

"Like I said, it's a long story. But they're not so bad." I lie.

The sarcasm in her voice is apparent. "No, no, they're not bad at all. They're just four of the sexiest and most mysterious men in the school who are also dangerous and probably deadly. Do you remember what they did to Willa Mack?"

I do remember that. Very clearly. Willa is the pastor's step-daughter and the quietest girl in the senior class. She's cute and all, but she has zero personality. At least she doesn't show it if she does have one. At the end of the summer, Lars asked her on a date to Tommy's birthday party and to say she was elated is an understatement. Needless to say, Lars had his way with her. Though, he claims she consented, and she's never claimed otherwise. The real kicker, he recorded the entire thing and blasted everyone's emails the following day with the video footage of her losing her v-card to him.

"That was shitty. I'm not claiming that they are saints. I'm just saying that they aren't as bad as everyone thinks." Another lie.

A knock at the door startles me. "Hey, I've gotta go. I'll call you later, I promise." Ending the call, I set my phone down and straighten myself up on the bed with my feet pressed to the floor.

I don't respond because whoever it is will likely just come in whether they are invited or not. They said it themselves; I belong to them now.

The door opens, and Talon steps inside, shutting it behind him. "Are you hungry?"

I shake my head no, but it's a lie. I'm starving. I'm just not sure that I'm hungry enough to risk eating whatever he plans to serve me. Soup with a side of a date rape drug—no thanks.

"You haven't eaten all day. The chef is gone for the night, but I ordered pizza. Come eat." His hair shimmers on the ends, and it's obvious he just stepped out of the shower.

Curling my legs up and tucking them to my chest, I rest my chin on my knee. "I said I'm not hungry."

"And once again, you're lying." His footsteps come closer, and my body tenses up, hugging my legs tighter. Kneeling in front of me, his index finger slides between my knee and my chin and he pushes up so that my eyes are level with his. "You need to eat."

Closing my eyes, I fight the tears that I feel coming. I'm emotionally and physically drained and it's only day one. I open them, hoping that he will be gone, but he's still there. Still touching my face.

A single tear slides down and his finger trails along my cheek, sweeping it up. "Don't cry."

Twisting my body away from him, I turn to face the wall. "What do you care if I cry? That's what you want, isn't it? To break me?"

"Not at all. My plan isn't to break you, but to build you up. You're one of us now, Marni. We're all in this together."

For a single moment, looking back at him, I believe his words. But that moment passes quickly when I remember everything him and his merry band of psychos have done in the past twenty-four hours: framed me for murder, forced me to push Josh's car off a cliff, threatened me, assaulted me. "Now who's lying?"

The back of his hand finds my cheek and the way he moves it so gently, so effortlessly, has my body relaxing. Warmth radiates from his touch and I despise that he has this effect on me. "No lies," he whispers quietly. His eyes skate down to my lips. I lick them instinctively then fold them between my teeth. "Tell me, Marni—what would you do if I kissed you? Would you fight me or would you let me?"

Internally, my lips are begging to feel his press against them; they're screaming for his touch. Shifting my whole body back around, I let my legs fall on either side of him, caging him in. I hate him so much, but my body loves him. It craves him, and right now, it's taking control. Falling back onto my elbows, I give him a nudge with my feet until his hands are pressed on the bed at my sides.

When I scoot up, he crawls toward me. The magnetic pull between us is too strong when his lips crash into mine. I'm not sure if it's the emotional trauma I feel or just the need to be noticed in a way that doesn't involve crude remarks and aggression, but whatever it is, I take it all. His tongue seduces my mouth, slithering in as I taste the vile words he's said to me. All the lies. The secrets. The hate. All the bottled-up tension pours into my mouth and I reciprocate by giving him every bit of my disgust. Bringing one hand to the back of his head, I fist his hair and force his mouth harder into mine as his cock grinds against my thigh.

When his fingers snake down my side, leaving a trail of goosebumps, reality hits me smack dab in the face. "Talon, we can't," I mutter into his mouth.

"Sure we can." He begins pushing my shorts down, then sits up to pull them off. Both legs slide free and when he begins tracing his finger along the line of my underwear, my hand slaps over his. "Don't fight it. I know you want this."

God, I want him so badly, but at what cost? So tomorrow he can push me around some more. Make me destroy more evidence, while incriminating myself further. "No," I shake my head, "Not until you start treating me with respect. I'm not your little toy."

His lips curl at the seams before he presses them hard against mine with a closed mouth. So hard that I can feel his teeth grind against mine through the skin of our lips. Pushing himself up, his black orbs stare back at mine while he takes my hand into his and presses it down between us. Sliding underneath my panties, he curls my fingers inward. "You like to touch yourself, don't you?" His face nuzzles into the nape of my neck and his hot breath sends chills down my spine. With his fingers shadowing mine, he presses them against my entrance. "Answer me."

My entire body floods with humiliation and I know that no matter how I answer this question, he is only going to try and humiliate me further. He's admitted that he's watched me. "It's not like that." I force the words out.

"Then tell me how it is." His hard cock grinds against my leg as he pushes my index and middle fingers inside of me. "Talon, please."

"Please, what? Please stop?"

Yes. No. I don't know.

Will he ridicule me for not stopping him? Choke me for not sticking up for myself? I'm not sure I even want him to stop. My body and mind are at war, and when his fingers press against my knuckles, forcing my fingers to slide in and out, my body wins.

"You like it, don't you? You like the attention? That's why you do it, because you like knowing that all those eyes are on you. Watching while you get yourself off."

My heart pounds on the inside of my chest. I want to fucking scream, but I'm silenced by the way he's making me feel. The way I'm making myself feel.

Straightening his back, he gets up on his knees. When he lets my hand go, I pull it back and drop it to my side. "What are you doing?" I ask, when he begins sliding my panties off.

"Don't worry. I won't touch you if you don't want me to." He tosses them to the side and then proceeds to lift my shirt over my head. I took my bra off as soon as I came in the room to lie down, and now I'm laying here, in this bed, stark naked with his eyes dancing over every inch of my body. "Show me how you like it." He takes a step back and slides his pants down along with his boxers. His rock-hard cock sticks straight out and I can't help but wonder if all of these guys are well-endowed. "I'll do it, too." He begins stroking his hand back and forth.

Trembling, I slide my hand back down but quickly retreat. "No, I can't."

"Don't be shy, baby. There's nothing wrong with making yourself feel good."

No, there's not. But not like this.

Walking back over to the bed, he grabs my hand and pushes my fingers back toward my entrance. My hormones take control when he begins stroking his cock again as he stands over me. Tingles course through me and every pulse point throbs as temptation stares back at me.

Dropping my head back, I close my eyes. Wanting this. Needing this. I slowly trail the back side of my fingers down my breast then over my stomach. Turning my hand around, I begin touching my clit with little pressure.

"That's right. Show me how you like it."

Opening my eyes, I lean forward. Allowing my legs to drop to the side as I watch Talon pump himself. I begin rubbing faster in a circular motion.

An electrical current darts through me as my clit pulsates at my touch. I slide two fingers inside myself, feeling my arousal pool inside of me. All the while Talon watches me intently as he continues to slide his hand up and down his cock. Precum beads at the tip of his head and the urge to jump off this bed and take him into my mouth is strong.

But, I just watch him instead. I watch as he watches me.

Leaning further up on my elbows, I let my legs fall completely to the side. Pushing my fingers in farther and faster as Talon moves his hand in the same rhythm. "So fucking beautiful," he rasps with hooded eyes. "Faster, baby."

Curved fingers hit the walls inside of me and I feel my nails scrape against it, jolting my body. But I don't stop. I press deeper and farther and watch as Talon's mouth forms an O and his chest vibrates with the pounding of his heart. "Fuck yes." He moans.

Right as his cum shoots all over my body, I pull my fingers out and rub my clit forcefully as my body fills up with an over-powering sensation that is so potent I feel like my entire body is going to combust. The high is like nothing I've ever felt before in my life. Exhilarating, immobilizing, and so damn satisfying. I can feel my arousal pool underneath me as I come down slowly. My body twitches in response to every nerve ending being zapped with such a high voltage.

I look at Talon and I feel my face flush with embarrass-ment, but when I picture his face as he was coming, that embarrassment quickly fades. He wanted this. He asked for it, and he loved every minute of it.

Dropping my head back down, I feel two hands on the inside of my thighs. Pressing my legs up, I'm completely exposed to him. The warmth of his tongue sweeps up from my ass to my clit. Licking in hard and thirsty strokes.

Sucking my clit between his teeth, my entire body twitches at the sensitivity. I put a hand on his head to brace him. When he comes up, his eyes stare back at me. Bunching the flat sheet in his hand, he begins wiping us both off. "I'll grab you a new one," he says, as he tosses it on the floor. With a satisfied smile on his face, he slides up and presses his mouth to mine, giving me a taste of myself.

"That was the sexiest thing I've ever seen in my life."

Pressing my lips together, I turn my head and close my eyes.

"I'm serious. Watching it in person tops the videos any day."

I still can't believe he watched those. I'm not sure how I am ever going to come to terms with that fact. Or the fact that I just gave him the real show, up close and personal. "I don't do that anymore. It was just a one-time thing."

"More lies. You're just full of them."

"Ok, twice." I lie again.

He shakes his head no.

My heart sinks deep into my stomach. "My God, Talon, how long have you been watching me?"

"Longer than you think, Angel Girl."

Scooting myself up to a sitting position, he rolls to the side of me with his hand holding his head up and his elbow sinking into the mattress. "What did you just say?"

"You're not an angel though, are you?"

"No fucking way." I push myself up further. "You're not him."

"Not who? RebelSin?" He winks and the action sends a shiver down my spine.

He's not lying. It is him. RebelSin sent me four thousand dollars over the course of the last few months. He was one of my VIPs on the site. Making personal requests for late night chat sessions about more than just sexual pleasures. He doesn't just know who I am or what I do; I showed him the depth of my heart.

As hard as I tried to get him to open up, he never shared an ounce of emotion with me.

Except for one night.

I don't live in the darkness; the darkness lives in me.

I'll never forget those words.

TALON

Six different pizza choices later, Marni finally ate. I have no clue what the girl likes, so I got a little bit of everything. She ended up grabbing a piece of the veggie and going back to her room, without even a thank you. Not that I'm surprised.

Zed comes charging into the kitchen. "What the fuck?" he huffs, his hands shove hard against my chest, sending me back a few steps. With my back against the refrigerator, anger ripples through me.

"What the fuck is right." I shove him back. "What the hell is your problem?"

Nose to nose, I can see the unpleasantry in his eyes. That blank black stare that he gets when his inner demons are unleashed. The look that tells us all to just walk away and let him be. "You said you'd look after her. We had a deal."

"And I have been." I reach behind him and flip the top open on a box of pizza. Unsure of what kind it is, I grab a slice.

"Don't play dumb with me, Porter. You think you can just take her for yourself?"

Smirking, I tip the pizza up and bite off the triangle end.

Mmm, pepperoni. Lucky grab. "Didn't take her. Don't want her." I take another bite.

"You're crossing the line that we all made crystal clear. Don't step over it because, once you do, there is no going back."

Holding up a finger, I continue to chew. Pissing him off even further. His jaw ticks with fury and in a swift motion, his hand slaps across mine, sending the pizza flying across the kitchen. "Listen close," he grips the collar of my t-shirt and gives me no choice but to listen and also smell the stench of whiskey on his breath, "Don't push me, Porter. I don't give a shit if we've been friends since grade school." His teeth clamp down and he speaks slowly, "I will fuck your life up."

Swallowing down the rest of the pizza, I shove him back. "Keep in mind, we made a deal that she's off-limits. That means you, too, asshole. And what the hell is with you? Since when do you have an interest in Marni Thorn?"

Zed takes a step back, turns around and I don't even see it coming when his fist meets my left cheek. My head whips to the side and something inside of me snaps. Barreling at him, I wrap my arms around his waist and drive him back into the island counter, hearing his back hit the black granite. Coming up, I cock my fist and release, but his head moves just in time. "I'll fucking destroy you!" I shout.

Ignoring the numbness of my cheek, I keep swinging, hitting him a few times. Taking a few blows myself.

"Seriously, you two!" Tommy comes hurrying into the kitchen. His arms sweep between us as he attempts to pry us apart. "Lars, get your ass in here," he shouts.

But before Lars even has time to come, we separate. Both huffing and out of breath. Pointing a finger at me, Zed shouts, "She's not your fucking toy!"

"She's not yours either," I retort.

"Are you two idiots seriously fighting over that girl. It's been one day. One fucking day," Tommy snarls, shaking his head in disappointment as he holds out his arms, filling the space between Zed and I.

I should have known it wouldn't be smooth sailing like we anticipated. I also never expected her having this sort of effect on me. This overpowering desire to keep her away from Zed. I'm not sure why, but the idea of him touching her fills my entire body with a burning rage. It's unnerving—taunting.

"You see what he's doing," Zed snaps, "he's treating her like his own little puppy."

"Isn't she? Wasn't that the plan?" Tommy says, as he opens and closes the boxes of pizza. "What's all this food for?"

Clenching my swollen cheek in my hand, I look at Zed who's doing the same. "I ordered it. She needed to eat."

Tommy pulls out a slice. "She? As in multiple women? Because you bought enough to feed the entire varsity cheer squad *and* their families."

"I didn't know what she liked. What's the big fucking deal?"

Zed doesn't take his eyes off me as I talk. He's waiting for me to say the wrong thing. The guy is so on edge all the time and needs to just calm his ass down. It's apparent he has some sort of fascination with Marni, and if she's on his radar, it can only mean one thing—trouble.

I pull out my phone and slap it to Tommy's chest. "Round one is done. It's time to move on to the next phase."

"Already?" Tommy questions. Zed grabs the phone from his hands and begins clicking through it.

The volume is turned all the way up, and Marni's voice can be heard through the speaker of the video. "Turn that shit down!" I attempt to snatch the phone away, but he pulls back with his finger held down on the volume button. Her sounds quickly fade away until the volume is off.

It irks me that these guys are watching her as she orgasms

intensely—one that was meant just for me. Glad I remembered to crop the footage before showing them; they'd have a field day if they saw all of it—especially the end.

Zed tosses the phone back to me while his eyes sweep the room as Lars walks in—ten minutes too late.

Zed walks out, without even acknowledging him, but then stops and turns to face me. "Just because you're on the verge of fucking up your own agenda, doesn't mean we will let you fuck up ours."

I can't, and I won't fuck this up. This is my one shot.

Looking down at the tattoo on my arm, the pact we made replays in my head. *Start to finish, we stick together. Four games of revenge, one shot each.*

We all have our demons. We all have our vices. But we are all in this together, no matter what fresh stain of hate is dredged up during the in between.

Lying in bed that night, thoughts of her swirl in my mind. Wrapping around every crack and crevice, refusing to leave. I've never had a problem sleeping; in fact, sleep has always come easy to me. It's my escape from this hellish place. I search for my dreams in hopes of finding some sort of connection to the world. Mornings come too soon, and I'm forced to leave behind the illusion of a life with color. Closing my eyes tightly, I imagine myself running toward Dad's open arms. He picks me up, spins me around, then calls me, Sport. Still not asleep, I open one eye, then try again.

He's there.

I'm running.

Only his arms aren't open. He's angry. A bottle hangs from his left hand.

No. Don't go there. Open your eyes. It's not real.

The bottle flies across the room. The sound of the glass shattering has my body jerking and my seven-year-old heart thumping against the walls of my chest. Mom stands by watching apathetically with a hand over her mouth, though she doesn't stop him. His arm lifts and comes crashing down on me. A karate chop straight to the top of my head. I don't even cringe. My body has learned not to react because he feeds off of it.

Wake up, Talon.

Fingers close around my wrist, and he begins dragging me up the stairs. My limp body hits each step with a thud. No, Dad. Please. I internally beg for him to stop. But he doesn't. Fully clothed, he grabs me by the leg and arm and swings me into the bathtub of scalding hot water.

Open your eyes.

My body burns as I lie there floating in the water. Motionless. Emotionless. Forcing my ears to drift just below the ripple of the water to drown out the sound of his sadistic laughter.

My body shoots up. Wiping at the dampness of my hairline, I look at my hand expecting blood. It's just sweat. It was just a dream. Slowing my breaths, I lie back down with my head on the black satin pillow. My hand grazes the skin of my side beneath my t-shirt. Hitting every bumpy ridge of the scars that decorate it.

Closing my eyes again, I try to sleep, but she slithers back into my thoughts. Like a saint there to rescue me from the darkest of nightmares—the darkness of my past.

In slow motion, the gust of wind catches her hair as she stands in a dark room. A smile tugs at the corners of her lips, drawing them up as her eyes stay fixated on whatever is in front of her. My body shoots up again when Josh's face replaces her. Bloodied and dirt covered.

I gasp for breath then tear the blanket off of me. Grabbing my phone off the nightstand, my feet hit the floor and I head straight for the door in just my boxers and t-shirt. I have to get the hell out of this room.

As soon as I open the door to the hallway at the bottom of the stairs, I hear her. Whimpers, followed by a deep sob.

Fucking A. Ignore her, Talon.

With each step, her cries ring closer.

When I'm directly in front of the door to her room, I stop. Pressing my hand against it and giving it a push to see if it's open, but it's latched shut. Suddenly, the cries stop. Right when my ear touches the door, it pulls open. Marni stands there in just an oversized t-shirt, but it's not the shirt she's wearing that grabs my attention. It's the swollen skin beneath her eyelids. Her blush tipped nose and the dampness on her cheeks. "How long have you been out here?" she sniffles.

I press my palms against the inside of the door frame. "I just got here. Why aren't you sleeping? You have school tomorrow."

She sweeps her hand across her cheek aggressively and grimaces. "Yeah, like I can get any sleep after everything that's happened." Turning around, she walks back into the bedroom, leaving the door open.

I stand there for a moment, telling myself that I need to leave. Get some fresh air and then go back to bed. Leave her alone. But the magnetic pull between her and I has me following her in.

My phone begins buzzing in my hand, but I ignore it and end the call. Her eyes dance from my phone to my face. "Shouldn't you get that? It's pretty late. Must be important." She sits down on the bed with her hands in her lap and her bare feet on the floor.

"Nah. If it's important, they'll leave a message." I step closer, but stop in my tracks right next to her bed when she jerks her head up and snarls, "What are you doing?"

I point at the door. "You left it open. Assumed you wanted—"

"You assumed wrong." Her face drops into her hands. "This is all your fault. I should have never...*we* should have never..." Her voice trails off.

She doesn't have to say it. I know what she's talking about. She's having regrets about tonight. For good reason. It was nothing short of fantastic, but the end result isn't going to make this any easier on her. I'd like to tell her it's going to get better, but that would be another lie. I run my fingers through my hair. "Hang in there. That's all you can do." Turning around, I head back for the door and keep walking, even when she says my name.

Should have never gone in there. I can't let this girl weaken me. I can't care. I don't fucking care. It's just that when girls cry, it makes me think of Blakely. My sister shed so many unnecessary tears because of the fucked-up life we were given. I could never even console her because Dad told me that it made me look weak and weakened her in the process. *Our pain makes us stronger. We cry, then we get up and fight back.* That's what Mom would say. What the hell did she know? She never fought back. She took every beating that was handed to her and watched while we got ours.

Thinking about it fuels the fire inside of me. He will get what's coming to him and I will savor every moment of shredding him with my own bare hands.

When I get down to the kitchen, I tap my screen and my fingers shadow over the missed call.

What the hell does he want?

MARNI

Walking out of the bedroom, I leave the door open and step quietly down the hall. I hear someone talking—arguing actually. Yet, there is no one arguing back. It's a one-sided conversation, and I'd know that voice anywhere. Taking a couple steps down the staircase, I'm shielded by walls on both sides. Sitting down, right before the wall turns to banister, I hold my breath while trying to listen. His words are muffled from the distance between us, but it is definitely Talon, and he's definitely engaged in an intense conversation.

"I told you fifty fucking times that she's safe. No one is going to lay a finger on her."

Her? As in me?

"We are all well aware of the deal. Have been since day one."

There's a pause.

"You're in no position to try and call the shots here. Seems you're the one forgetting the arrangement. Now quit calling my fucking phone before you raise suspicion."

There's another pause, followed by the sound of a thud.

When he stops talking, I assume it's his phone meeting the countertop.

Getting to my feet, I go back up the stairs and tiptoe down the hall. Shutting my door quietly behind me.

What the hell was that all about?

∞

NEWS SPREAD like wildfire of Josh's disappearance. Every time his name was mentioned, it felt like a dozen whistles were sounding off in my ears, vibrating through my entire body. My knees buckled a couple times, but all things considered, I've held it together pretty well.

There are so many rumors circulating that I can't keep up: he's addicted to heroin and is staying with his dealer. He fled after his parents caught him raping his sister. Someone murdered him and dropped him in the ocean.

My mind has been replaying Talon's one-sided conversation from last night and I've been racking my brain like hell trying to figure out who Talon was talking to. It could have been one of the guys, I suppose. But was he talking about me? And what deal was he referring to?

"I know you said that you'll fill me in later, but please tell me why he is still following us," Shay says, as she glances over her shoulder for the fifteenth time as we walk from third period to lunch.

Wyatt slides up to us and throws an arm over my shoulder. "She's alive!" he singsongs.

The halls are packed with the senior student body as we all head to the cafeteria. Passerbys look at me and then their eyes shoot to Tommy, who is walking no more than six feet behind us. "Just ignore him," I tell her, keeping my focus on the cafeteria doors in front of us.

"How are we supposed to do that?" Wyatt whisper-talks.

"He's been watching you like a hawk since you stepped out of *his* car this morning. Which, by the way, is really fucking weird because I've never even seen you talk to the guy."

Drawing in a deep breath, I silently beg for them to stop talking. "How was the haunted trail the other night?" I ask Wyatt in an attempt to change the subject.

He drops his arm from my shoulder and begins talking with his hands. "Scary as shit. I may have accidentally grabbed Shane's cock when I all but jumped into his arms."

I laugh. "Accidentally my ass. You probably planned that shit." Wyatt and Shane have a secret crush on each other. Well, they think it's a secret, but everyone knows. Personally, I think they need to just scream it from the rooftop because they're cute as hell together.

When we reach the cafeteria, I stop and turn around to face Tommy with a hand on my hip. My eyes plead with him, and he knows exactly what I'm asking. When he shakes his head no, I stomp my foot like a child. "Really?"

"Really." He nods in the direction of the line. "Your friends can come, but you *will* sit at my table."

Shay and Wyatt exchange glances with each other and then look to me for answers that I can't give them. Not yet.

"Come on," I say to them, "we're eating with Tommy today."

"You two go ahead. I'll pass," Wyatt says. I'm not surprised. He hasn't had the best experiences with these guys. Bullying is too kind of a word to use. They've made the lives of half of the student body hell just because they existed in their world. Yet, everyone still goes to their parties because there is free booze and zero parental supervision.

Shay leans in and whispers in my ear with her eyes on Tommy, "Would you mind if I sit this one out, too?"

Dropping my shoulders, I scowl. "Seriously you guys! You're

both ditching me and leaving me to sit with the likes of that?" I point to the table where Tommy's buddies are sitting. I don't even know all of their names, but I do know that the guy with the leather jacket and purple mohawk was caught selling pills out of his locker junior year. I don't even know why Tommy associates with those guys. Sure, he doesn't exactly belong with the jocks, but I get the feeling Tommy has more layers than the people he calls his so-called friends. He's artistic and, every once in a while, shows a glimmer of kindness. Now that I think about it, he might be my only hope for survival in all of this.

With a shrug, they head to the line while I'm left there with Tommy. "Better get in line before all the good food is taken." He grins, giving a nudge toward the line that is now stretched to the door.

"This is so stupid. Do you guys really think that I'm going to say anything? You think I want my friends to know what I've done. That I pushed Josh's—" Tommy's hand claps over my mouth.

"That…" he snaps. "That is exactly why I'm not letting you out of my sight." He removes his hand and looks around, making sure no one heard us. Everyone is carrying on with their conversations about football, dances, and the luxurious life of a high school student. While I'm here. With him. Drowning in thoughts of dead bodies, asylums, and cliffs. "You can't say his name. Ever. Got it?"

Tommy steps in front of me in the line, and I'm drawn to his back pocket that bulges out. It looks like a rolled-up newspaper stuffed in there with his black t-shirt curtaining it. I lift up his shirt from the back, curiosity getting the better of me. "Why the hell are you carrying around a can of spray paint?" I chuckle then let his shirt fall back in place.

His head turns while his body still faces the line. "Because you never know when an opportunity will arise."

Sighing, I shake my head in disgust. "Please don't tell me you huff that shit."

"Not gonna lie and say I never have, but that's not why I have it. I like art." We take a few steps forward, filling the empty space as the line gets smaller.

"You mean you like graffiti?"

He turns around to face me, a look of wonder in his eyes. "How hungry are you?"

"Not at all." It's true. I don't think I could even force myself to eat right now. Nausea is swimming around in my stomach, and if I let myself, I could probably throw up.

Grabbing me by the hand, he pulls me out of line and walks us briskly toward the doors. "What are we doing?" I look back and see Shay and Wyatt watching us with confusion. Ignoring them, I turn back around and follow Tommy's lead.

"I think we both deserve to let loose and have a little fun. What'dya say? You down for that?"

As I continue to walk beside him, my mind's made up for me. Something about Tommy gives me this feeling of contentment. Like I can trust him. I really shouldn't, but even the excitement in his eyes right now is something that is foreign to the others. Tommy is different. "Alright, I'm always game for a little fun. As long as it doesn't involve dead—"

His finger presses to my lips. "Shh. Don't say it." He smiles, then winks, which sends a rush of adrenaline through me.

Pressing my lips together, I refrain from smiling back. "Cows. Geez, what did you think I was gonna say?"

Looking back and forth down the hallway a couple times with a serious expression on his face, he pushes open the gymnasium doors and nods for me to go in. It's dark inside, aside from a sliver of light coming from the men's locker room. "What's the plan exactly?" I ask, when the door closes behind us.

Pulling out the spray can from his back pocket, Tommy

begins shaking it. The sound of the metal ball inside hitting the aluminum trumps the sound of my reverberating heart. I love the thrill of a rush—being sneaky, taking risks. I always have. These sort of pranks and games, I'm okay with. It's ones that involve murder that I'm not a fan of.

Tommy begins walking behind the bleachers, and I follow him. "What's your favorite quote?" he asks, as we both duck our heads and step underneath the backside of the bleachers.

"That's an odd question."

"Come on, everyone has a favorite. Let's hear it." He begins spraying something onto the brick wall in front of us. Black splatters hit the white slab of brick, and I can't make out what it is just yet. His arms sweep the air as he extends his reach, making the circle of whatever it is bigger.

"She wasn't given wings to keep her feet on the ground."

Tommy stops spraying for a moment. With the can straight out in front of him, he turns to look at me. His eyes are soft and inviting, and I see something in them. I see purpose and depth. Light in the darkness. I see a guy who has dreams and plans for the future but no idea how to reach them. When he turns back to the wall and leans closer, bringing the can right in front of it, he releases small spritzes that form the face of a snake. I watch him work intently, creating his own beautiful art. He takes a step back and I slide over to his side to get a better view of it.

"What's the meaning behind this?" I ask him, as we both face the snake infinity symbol. Same as the tattoos, same as the door handle at Briarwood, and the same as the trinket box left on my bed.

"It's the beginning and it's the end," he pauses, glancing over at me to see if I'm following, "the Ouroboros reminds us that every life starts and stops somewhere. The only control we have is the in between. We can live to die, or we can live to survive. We choose survival."

I nod, thinking that I understand. Though, I'm not really sure I do. "Why do you all have the tattoo? Is it some sort of occult symbol?"

"No." He shakes his head. "Not at all. It's a pact. No man left behind. No man falters alone. We face the in between together and we ride 'til we die."

Taking a few steps to the right side of the sprayed symbol, he begins shaking the can again. "We might seem like we're just a bunch of fuck ups to the world, but really, we have purpose. Everyone does. Me, Talon, Zed, and Lars have our own scars. Scars that brought us together, and scars that keep us bound." Pressing his finger to the nozzle, he begins spraying. This time, his arm spreads and sweeps. He bends and slouches, and I'm mesmerized by his intensity.

When he finishes, I'm in awe. My breath is taken away, and my eyes are cemented to the angelic painting in front of him. "You've got your wings. Use 'em," he says as his arms drop to his side.

Two black, unclipped wings. Fringed with tousled edges. If I could touch them, I imagine they'd be weightless—delicate— soft in the center with pointed ends. "I can't believe you just did that with a can of paint."

The bell sounds, and his eyes widen. "We gotta get out of here," he says a moment too late. The gym door opens, and voices carry over to us as we stand beneath the bleachers. Taking my hand in his, I notice that his fingertip is stained black and his nose is freckled from the out spray of mist. "This way," he says, as we duck all the way down and walk beneath the low seats of the bleachers, trying to hide our steps and faces.

Basketballs dribble against the floor continuously as sneakers squeak across. Five seconds later, the whoosh sound of the ball going in the net has everyone shouting.

"Fuck," Tommy bellows, as his head scrapes against the

metal of the bleacher. He rubs his hand over it, and I'm not sure why, but I laugh, and his laughter follows.

"What have you gotten us into, Tommy Chambers?" I whisper-talk. We may be late for fourth period, might possibly get caught vandalizing the gym wall, and possibly create rumors about ourselves, but this is the first time I've felt alive all week—possibly longer. Definitely longer. Ever since Mom passed away, the days have sort of just blended together in one big fog. Then Axel left. Dad's always gone. I often question what this life is even for and then I have a moment like this and I'm reminded. Sometimes life is simply about living. It's not wrapped in fancy paper in a pretty box. It's a mess of emotions that change from one moment to the next. It's the highs and the lows—and like Tommy said—everything in between.

We finally make it to the end of the bleachers, and Tommy looks from me to the door in front of us. "Slow and quiet," he whispers, before we both emerge from under the stands. I don't even look over at the class, out of fear that someone is looking back at us. Tommy slowly opens the door, and I book it. Hurried steps lead us down the hall and we both burst out in laughter.

Stopping at my locker, I pull it open. I have it rigged up so I don't even have to turn it to my combination. "You better get going. You're already late," I tell Tommy as he lingers next to me.

"I'm always late. I'll walk you to class and maybe I'll make an appearance in mine."

There is something about his expression and tone. It's comforting and kind, and I get the feeling that him walking me to class has nothing to do with the rules the guys set forth, but more so because he wants to.

As we're walking at a leisurely pace down the quiet halls, I start to feel a sliver of respect and dare I say trust in the guy walking next to me. "Hey Tommy?" I pause when he looks at me. "Everything is going to be alright, isn't it?'

"With J? Yeah, it'll all be fine. Don't worry."

"No," I grip my books tightly to my chest, "with the guys? With me?"

When he doesn't speak, but looks over at me with a face full of remorse, I get my answer. Nodding my head, I accept my fate.

When we reach my class, I stop before opening the door. "It was fun. Thanks."

Tommy begins walking away but turns and looks back over his shoulder. "I'll never hurt you. That I can promise."

His words give me a warm and comforting feeling that has the corners of my lips tugging up.

I think I may have just made a friend—and I could really use one right about now.

10

TALON

"Would you quit pacing and sit your ass down," I grumble from the couch as Zed takes long strides in front of the door. He's been there since school got out ten minutes ago, while chewing nervously on the skin of his thumb. "Tommy texted and said everything's been fine. No suspicion, no questions."

We've all been a ball of nerves ever since Josh was deemed a missing person. It won't be long until his car is found, and they assume that he's lost in the bottomless lake.

His movements stop. "She's a loose cannon. I don't trust her."

"We've got enough insurance. Don't start plotting again. There is no way that girl is gonna say anything."

"It's not enough."

Dropping the PS4 controller on the couch, I jump up. "It *is* enough. If you push her any further, it'll be too much. Just let this play out."

My phone begins vibrating in my pocket, so I pull it out. My gaze darts to Zed. "Fuck. He's calling again. I thought we settled this shit last night."

"Don't answer it. They're here." He pulls the door open and walks outside.

Dropping the phone down on the couch, I get up and meet them at the door.

Thirty seconds later, they all come inside. Marni actually looks happy for a split second until her eyes meet mine. "How was school?" I ask, as I walk over to her and position my hand between her back and the straps of her backpack. Sliding it down her arm, I take it and drop it on the couch.

When her only response is her nose in the air and a scowl, I look to Tommy for an answer.

"It was fine. No problems. She was a very well-behaved student," Tommy says, as he and Marni catch a look from each other and both smile.

Marni grabs her bag off the couch. "I'm going to my room."

"What was that all about?" I ask Tommy, who is still sporting a shit-eating grin.

"What?" He plays dumb. "It was nothing. Just a good day. Is that a problem?"

Zed untucks a cigarette from behind his ear. "Shit, maybe we should have had Tommy get the goods from her. She seems to like him more than your ass." He walks out the front door, leaving it open as he takes a seat on the porch steps and lights his smoke.

Just because they had a good day at school doesn't mean she's suddenly falling for Tommy. A burn smolders inside my stomach. If he seriously thinks he's gonna form some unbreakable bond with Marni just so he can try and weasel his way between her legs, he's dreaming. I'll break every fucking bone his body before I let him, or any of these assholes, lay a finger on her.

Tommy holds out his hand for a fist bump. "I'm out. I'll pick her up tomorrow."

Refraining from bumping it back, I push it away. "Don't bother. I'll bring her to school."

Cocking a brow, Tommy scowls. "What's with you lately?"

"Nothing. There's just no reason for you to drive all the way here when I can just bring her myself."

"He wants her all to himself. That's what's with him." Zed huffs from the steps.

Sweeping the air with my hand, I brush them off and stalk toward the stairs. I want this plan to work. That's all I care about. That's why she's here. I need her leash short so I can keep an eye on her. Any move that draws attention to us could destroy everything. It also doesn't help that I don't trust Zed. Tommy's harmless, but I could see her falling for his wit and charm and I can't let that happen. I've staked a claim for her—they just don't know it.

Knocking my knuckle on the bedroom door a couple times, I wait for Marni to open it. When she doesn't, I knock again. "Open the door," I grumble.

Pressing my ear to it, I wait for a sound of movement, but there's nothing but silence. I wriggle the handle, but it's locked. "Marni!" I shout. "Open this goddamn door." I knock more aggressively this time, but still nothing. The only sound is the wallop of multiple feet coming up the steps down the hall.

"What's the problem?" Zed hurries to my side. Nudging me out of the way, he begins tinkering with the handle to no avail.

I pound my fist on the door continuously. "She's not answering."

"Jesus, you guys. She's probably sleeping." Lars comes toward us. I didn't even know he was here yet.

"What are you doing here?" I ask, as Zed disappears down the stairs.

"My bitch of a step-sister is losing her damn mind and

decided to throw a fucking vase at my head, so I figured I should probably skedaddle before I kill her, or vice versa."

I chuckle. "Good call." Reaching into my pocket, I remember that I left my phone downstairs.

"Hey, go get my phone off the couch. I've got her location turned on. Even if she's not in there, she won't get far."

A minute later, Zed comes back with a screwdriver in his hand. "Move," he orders us both.

Two minutes later, Lars is back. "Couldn't find it."

"I assume the cameras are up if you got that video?" Lars asks, as he pulls out his phone and I know exactly what he's doing. He's going to the app to check the footage.

"They're in there, but I shut them off."

"Why the hell would you do that?" Zed grumbles. A screw drops to the floor beside him, followed by another.

"Because," I raise my voice, "I'm not letting you bastards sneak a peek whenever you feel like it."

Lars is still fucking with his phone when I catch his glower. "So you just figured you'd be the only one who sneaks a peek." He holds his hand out to show me that the password failed, but I don't need to see it. I know, because I'm the one who changed it.

Zed springs to his feet and the door handle drops to the ground. Grabbing Lars' phone out of his hand, rage consumes him. With one glance at the screen, his arm extends up and Lars' phone slams to the ground. "What the actual fuck, Talon!"

"Dude, that's my phone." Lars bends down and picks it up, brushing off the screen, even though no damage was done.

"What kind of game are you playing here?" Zed steps closer, but I give him a push, sending him two steps back where he belongs. "Give me the fucking password, now!"

"Are you forgetting that this is my fucking house!" I shove him again and again, until we are halfway down the hall.

"This is my game!" My teeth grind as my fists clench.

His gaze drops to the balled knuckles at my sides. "You wanna fucking punch me?" He steps up. "Do it. I dare ya."

"You try and screw this up just because you've sprouted an obsession, I'll do more than punch you."

"Me." He laughs. "You're the one about to drive your own plan into the ground with Josh. You plan to hand her over to another man. Get a grip, jackass. She's temporary, and once you're finished with her, she'll never even look at you again. In which case, I'll step in. Dry her tears, give her a shoulder to lean on." He pats his shoulder with a smirk, then leans closer and whispers, "I'll fuck you right out of her system."

Heat spreads through my entire body as I cock my arm back. Just as I'm about to release it, Lars flies to my side, grabbing hold of my arm and pulling me back a couple feet. "Would you two shut the hell up. She could be in there listening to this shit."

All eyes shoot to the door. An open circle replaces where the handle once was. Pushing past the guys, I walk over and slouch down to look inside. If she was in there, she would have heard us. She would know that her handle was just taken off. I peek in the hole and see her perfectly made bed. "She's not in there." I stand back up. Pushing aside all the anger toward Zed, I realize we have to work together on this one. I point to Lars. "Get the number of those two nitwits she hangs out with —Shay and Wyatt—call them." I look at Zed. "You're obviously obsessed with the girl, pull anything from memory and check it out. I'll go to her dad's house."

Lars and Zed stand idly watching me, so I snap my fingers. "Now, damnit!" Then we all break apart and, without any further discussion, we go our own ways. Walking down the steps, I pat myself down, thinking that maybe I grabbed my phone and didn't realize it. Sure as shit, nothing.

I tear off every cushion and even tip the couch back and

still can't find it. It's like it just fucking disappeared. My mind replays the last time I had it. *He* was calling. I ignored it and set it down. Marni came home. I took her bag off her shoulder and tossed it on the couch.

Next to my phone.

That bitch!

My little rebel will pay for this stunt she's just pulled.

11

MARNI

"Thanks for meeting me." I lean into Wyatt and rest my head on his shoulder. "I just had to get away from there for a little bit." Nuzzling my head closer, I find comfort in my friend. Wyatt is the kind of guy who would drop anything for someone he cares about. He'd pick you up at three o'clock in the morning on the side of the road when your car broke down after a heated argument with your ex-boyfriend. He'd take you to the doctor for a pregnancy test when you thought that just maybe you were pregnant. And he'd also hold your hand when you get the results. Negative. We celebrated that night. He's also the best person to sit in the bleachers with during football practices just to watch the guys in their tight pants. Though, he only has eyes for one guy—Shane West.

"I'd like to say that I understand, but I have no idea why you're even staying in that house."

"I wish I could tell you, but it's better this way right now. I do need your help, though." I lift my head and turn my entire body toward him, tucking one leg underneath the other. The weathered wood of the old bench pokes into my skin. The bench sits between a couple large trees down one of Miners

State Park's trails. It felt like a good place to go and not be found.

"Aw hell, Marni. Don't tangle me up in this shit. You know those guys already hate me."

"They don't hate you. They just don't know you and they look at you as an easy target because you're too nice. Besides, they won't even know that you're helping me." I place a hand on his arm. "I really need you, Wyatt. I don't have anyone and there is no way I can ask Shay for help. She's a parrot." I love the girl, but if you want to keep a secret safe, don't share it with Shay. She will repeat everything you say and the next thing you know, you're hearing your own story in different words from someone else.

His expression becomes earnest. "You're serious?"

"Dead." I nod, while chewing on my bottom lip.

"Alright. What do you need me to do? Kick some ass? Kiss some ass? You name it and I'm on it." He chuckles, searching for humor in this whole situation.

There's a beat of silence between us before the wind picks up and rustles the dry leaves at our feet. Unzipping my backpack, I pull out Talon's phone and hand it to Wyatt. "I need you to tap into this phone and get a list of every single call, text, and voicemail. Anything you can get for me, I want."

"Woah," he throws his hands up, "I'm not touching that."

"Calm down," I snicker. "It's Talon's phone. He was having a very in-depth conversation on it last night and I'm pretty sure it was about me."

Wyatt gets to his feet and begins pacing in front of the bench. Pulling up the hood of his sweatshirt, he stuffs his hands inside the front pocket. "I can't do this." His head shakes continuously. "Do you know what they'll do to me if they catch me with his phone?"

Unfortunately, I do. I'm more aware than anyone of what they could do. I'm also aware that they'd probably get away with it. I stand up and brace my hands on either side of his shoulders. "They will never find out. I wouldn't ask you to do this if I thought you would get hurt." It's only a semi-lie.

I'm confident they won't find out, but I'm not one-hundred-percent sure that they won't come after me. Wyatt isn't the most tech savvy guy around, but his dad owns Magna Tech, and they are a world-renowned tech company that specializes in cellular devices. They've helped crack cell phones for the local police, FBI, and even the CIA. It's one little device and takes only minutes to download all data onto any SD card.

Chewing on the inside of his cheek, I can see that he's nervous as hell. "Let's say that I do this. What exactly do you plan to do with whatever information you're given?"

"That depends." I'm not even sure. I just need something to go on that could explain what Talon has been up to. I'm starting to think that there is much more to Josh's death than what the guys are letting on. They still haven't even told me how he died. Just that it was an accident and he deserved it. I need more. If I'm involved, and possibly implicated, I have to know exactly what happened that night. "I do need you to promise me one more thing."

"Nope," he shakes his head, "I'm out." He actually begins to walk away. I drop the phone back in my bag then zip it up, catching up to him quickly.

Wyatt is the guy who doesn't do haunted houses, doesn't even watch scary movies. He almost pissed his pants when a monster jumped out of a treasure box on *Scooby Doo*. "Please, Wyatt. I'm begging you." I fold my hands in prayer. "The only promise I need is that you give the card straight back to me, without looking at it first. I don't want you getting pulled into whatever mess they have going on."

The same mess that I'm currently entangled in. I would never want Wyatt to know about what they did to Josh. Not because I'm worried he'd snitch, but because I know he wouldn't, and he'd live with that knowledge and guilt forever.

Drawing out a sigh, I can tell he's thinking about it. When he drops his shoulders, a smile inches up on my face. "Ok. Under one condition," he says.

"You name it. I can handle a condition."

He perks up. "You're coming with me."

Hooking my arm around his, I agree with a nod. "You don't even have to ask twice. You know how much of a rush I get by being sneaky." I waggle my brows and laugh.

"Yes. Yes, I do. And that is exactly why you need me," he pauses and looks at me with a grin, "to keep your ass out of trouble all the damn time."

It's true. Wyatt has saved me from a mountain of regrets. He's a good friend. Which is exactly why I feel like the worst friend in the world right now for getting him involved.

I just need to protect this phone and make sure Talon doesn't find it, then hope like hell that I can get out of that house as easy as I did today. No one was even paying attention when I snuck out the back door. Now that my phone is back on and dozens of messages are coming up on my screen, it's obvious they are well aware of my absence. It makes me smile knowing that they are all panicking and trying to figure out my whereabouts. Almost makes me feel a little special to be this important to them, even if it is because they fear I'll share their secret.

Pulling down the driveway to my house, my stomach twists into knots when I see Talon's truck parked out front.

Fuck. I should have known he'd come here looking for me. At least Dad is in Dallas and I don't have to worry that they may have tried to kill one another. Creeping down the driveway at five miles an hour, I use the time to unzip the bag and grab the phone. Keeping my eyes on Talon to keep suspicion off me, I lean forward and toss it underneath the driver's seat.

When I finally come to a stop, he's already at my door attempting to pull it open. I try to hit the unlock buttons, but he's still pulling. "Open the fucking door." He growls from the other side of the glass.

"Let go of the damn handle and I will," I shout back. He finally lets go and I toy with him a little bit by hovering my finger over the button.

"Get. Out. Of. The. Car," he says each word like it's its own sentence.

Finally, I humor him and unlock it. Before I can even attempt to open the door, he beats me to it and grabs me by the arm. "Can I unbuckle the seatbelt first?" I snarl, as he continues to pull on me like I'm a damn baby doll.

"You think this is some sort of joke?" He slams the door shut then backs me up against it with his fingers still coiled around my bicep. "Gimme my fucking phone, Marni." His brows lower as he bares his teeth. Having him so close to me and hearing the way my name rolls off his tongue is actually calming my anxieties. It's replacing them with an overpowering desire to bite into his lower lip and suck his tongue into my mouth. "Did you hear me?" he barks.

Not even realizing that I was watching his lips, my eyes shoot up to his. "Your phone?" I question, playing dumb. "Why the hell would I have your phone?" I attempt to squirm out from beneath him; I am a terrible liar, and he'll see the truth all over my face. I bite down on my lip to refrain from smiling when he doesn't even give me an inch. Dad always told me he could tell I was lying because I'd smile.

"I don't like being lied to and that's exactly what you're doing right now. Don't make me give you a cavity search in your driveway. I'm sure Daddy wouldn't like seeing that on his cam footage."

"Seriously, Talon, I have no idea what you're talking about. Did you lose your—"

The smack of his hand against the car jolts my body into a tense position. My back steels against the door, and my eyes grow wider. "Don't fuck with me!" He lashes out.

I slap his arm away and duck underneath it when I see an opening. Picking up my pace, I head straight for the house. I have to get him away from this car.

Naturally, he follows me. He doesn't try to catch up, though. Just slow strides behind me like Michael Myers does before he takes you out.

I attempt to close the door, but he speeds up at the last minute and sticks his arm in. But that doesn't stop me from trying. "Goddamn you!" He pounds his whole body into it full force, and I stumble backward as the door comes open. Giving it a swift shove, he slams it shut. "You're gonna pay for that. For all of this."

Ignoring his threats, I keep walking and end up in the kitchen. Not exactly my plan, but we are away from the car and away from his phone, so I relax a bit.

With my palms pressed against the cold countertop, I swallow hard and remain silent.

Spinning me around, so my back is pressed against the counter, he clicks his tongue against the roof of his mouth, a sinister grin replacing his indignant look. "Gimme my phone or I'll find it myself."

When I don't respond, he inches his face closer to mine. "Spread your legs."

"What?" I huff. "No way!" His hand sweeps from my thigh upward as he pries my legs open. "Is it here?" He cups my crotch.

"Do you really think if I had your phone," my voice raises a few octaves, "I'd hide it in my fucking vagina?"

"You're a kinky girl. Wouldn't put it past you. Maybe you like the vibration when I get a text message."

"Now that's just gross. And for the record, it would never fit." He begins rubbing aggressively against the fabric of my jeans and I want to tell him to stop, but once again, my body is at war with my mind. Hormonal fucking bitch that she is.

My head tilts to the side impulsively when his mouth trails the lobe of my ear. "Where is it, Marni?"

Closing my eyes, I mutter, "Still don't know what you're talking about." Using my lies as his motivation, he begins rubbing harder. Sending a current of shudders between my legs, spreading to my belly then straight to my heart as it begins palpitating at an unhealthy rate.

"Cameras." I manage to choke out. "They're on."

"I don't give a flying fuck." He grabs me by the waist and hoists me up onto the counter. His fingers snake up my shirt and tickle the skin of my sides just beneath my bra.

Goosebumps spill down my body when his mouth pulverizes mine. Rolling my hips, I straighten my back and coil my fingers in his hair. He lets out a breathy moan that arouses me further. When his tongue darts in my mouth, taking mine hostage, I allow it. Inviting the taste of mint gum that still lingers on it.

Pushing everything out of my head—the cameras, the phone, the fact that this is wrong—I force his body into me, craving the friction between my legs.

Our mouths disconnect as fast as they linked. I wipe the back of my hand across my mouth. "What's wrong?" I ask. Out of breath for no reason whatsoever. I feel like I just ran a mile and it was only a twenty-second kiss from a guy who hates me—who I hate.

"Stand up." He grabs my waist and helps me down. "I still need my phone." His eyes hold that look of lust and desire. Wide, dark, and fully dilated. Unbuttoning my jeans and taking down my zipper, he gets on his knees then tugs them, along with my panties, all the way down in one swift pull.

I'm standing pantless, in my kitchen, where my dad could be watching, where Ruby could walk in at any moment, and all I want is for him to shove his tongue inside of me while he's knelt at my feet on the mosaic tile.

The sliding of a drawer has me looking down. "What are you doing?" Completely ignoring me, he takes something out. "What is that? An ice cream scooper?"

When he begins brushing it against my inner thigh, moving it up leisurely, I tense up. Chills shoot up from the touch of the cold aluminum. "Talon?" I say his name as a question.

"Where's my phone?" he asks again.

"It sure as hell isn't in the ice cream container, if that's where you plan to look. I told you—"

I gasp. Body shooting up, eyes open wide, and my heart fleeting when he sticks the tip of the handle inside of me.

"Where is it?"

There is no way I can tell him where it is. There is also no way that I am allowing him to stick…

My thoughts trail off when he begins pushing it in slowly. Spreading me open, as I close in around it. I don't stop him. I don't even think I'm breathing when I feel it against my clit. He begins sliding it in and out, and my mouth gapes open. Looking down at him, his eyes are fixated on the object in his hand. As if he feels me watching him, his gaze shifts to my watchful stare.

He smirks, pleased with himself. "I knew you were a kinky little shit."

"Fuck you." My breaths hitch when he picks up his pace. Foolishly, I spread my legs apart farther, relishing in the unthinkable pleasure that a kitchen utensil is bringing me right now.

Fighting to fill my lungs, I draw in a deep breath and the

exhale comes out as a raspy moan. Talon grabs my foot and lifts it up so that it rests on his shoulder. "Oh my God." I whimper when it begins sliding in and out so fast that it feels like my vagina is having a seizure. "Fuck!"

I throw my head back. Taking what is being given to me. I don't even give a damn what is delivering this insane amount of pleasure. Humiliation be damned. My hand slides down my chest, cupping my breast in my hand and giving it a firm squeeze. Talon stretches up his free hand and takes mine off of my breast then drags it underneath my shirt. When he removes his hand, I continue to massage my breast beneath my bra. Tugging at my nipple and letting out sounds I didn't even know I could make while he power drives the ice cream scooper in and out of me. My breaths shudder uncontrollably when I begin to pulsate around the aluminum handle.

"You like that, don't you?" He looks up at me again, and I get the feeling that he's enjoying this just as much as I am.

I don't answer. Instead, I get a good grip on his hair and slam his face into my core. His teeth clank against the aluminum, but I don't let him pull back. I wrap his hair around my fingers and tug until he begins sweeping his tongue up and down over my clit. Just when I'm at the highest high of my entire life, he jerks the scooper out.

I lift his head up so that he's facing me. A devious grin is on his face as his tongue darts at his lips, taking my arousal into his mouth. "Why are you stopping? Please, Talon—"

"Phone. Now." He shoves one finger inside of me, but I need more.

"Finish me off now or I'll find someone else to do it." I tap my finger to my chin. "Zed, maybe."

The reaction I get from him is everything I didn't expect when he bolts to his feet. The aluminum hits the tile with a thud when he grabs me by the waist and spins me around. I hear the sound of his zipper then feel his pants slide down the back of my legs.

Taking my hair into a balled-up bunch in his hand, he forces my head down. "What the hell did you just say to me?"

Knowing that it will piss him off and, in return, give me exactly what I want, I push him further. "Or maybe Tommy."

His hard cock plunges into me so forcefully that the bone of my hip can be heard grinding against the countertop. Taking both legs straight out, Talon stands in the center and begins thrusting his cock inside of me. I grip the other side of the center island to brace myself from sliding back and forth.

"You want Zed and Tommy's cock inside of you?" he grumbles as he drives himself so deep inside of me that I can feel him in my belly. "Answer me, you little whore."

Normally that would piss me off, but not this time. This time I play along. "Maybe I'll let them when I'm through with you."

One leg drops down, and his fingers wrap repeatedly around my hair until he gets a tight enough grip. When he jerks my head up, he presses so far inside of me that, for a moment, I feel an inkling of pain. Beautiful, intense pain. "I'd kill every single one of you."

Dropping my head back down, his hand finds my shoulder, and he uses it as footing. His pace begins to slow, but the depth of his reach doesn't cease. I can feel his head swell inside of me as his cock gains a pulse. Taking me along for the ride, I lose complete control as I cry out in pleasure. One final thrust and then he pulls out and I can feel the warm liquid shoot all over my ass. Running down my leg, to my feet, and then dropping to the floor.

"Clean your ass up. No pun intended." He jerks up his pants. "We have a phone to fetch and then you need to tell me exactly where you were the last two hours." Without even giving me a second look, he turns away.

I'm still bent over the kitchen island when he walks out. I have no idea where he's going, and I don't even care.

My words had an effect on him that I didn't predict. He doesn't wanna share me with the guys. I just got exactly what I wanted. I now have ammo.

TALON

I t's obvious this family has a thing for the color white. White walls, white furniture, fake white flowers in vases. Picking up a picture frame, white of course, I see a child with a smile on her face. One that probably carried so many dreams in that little mind of hers. Her hair is just as black and sleek and her eyes are the only color in the image. Then there's her brother, who was just beginning his years of being a douchebag at the age of eleven or twelve.

Something about Axel unnerves me. It's not because he got the girl I pined for, for a few months. No, it goes much deeper than that. Back to when I was a sophomore playing football on the varsity team. It was parents' night and, naturally, mine were a no show. He bought his mom flowers and she returned the gesture with a kiss to his cheek. There's nothing like the relationship between mother and son, or so they say. I stood on that field alone with my head held high. Not allowing anyone to see that my insides were in the process of being gutted.

When we walked off the field and the happy family parted, the asshole turned his head with a crooked grin, leaned close and whispered, "Pretty pathetic when your own family can't even stand to be near you."

I overdosed that night. Had to leave Blakely behind to endure the wrath of our monstrous father. Then I spent three months in rehab and the rest of the year living with an aunt and uncle who I'm pretty sure grew to hate me just as much as the rest of the world. I'm unlovable—what can I say.

A loud banging on the door has me dropping the picture. I rush over to it, as the thudding increases in intensity. Peeking out the peephole, I turn the handle and open it for the familiar angered face. "Where is she?" He plants two hands on my chest and pushes me out of his way.

"I never invited you in. Shouldn't you be catching fire or something?" He completely ignores my bad joke and begins heading down the hall. When I go to shut the door, resistance has it coming back toward me. Tommy looks concerned; Lars looks bored. Waving my hand through the air, I let them in.

"You were supposed to call us when you found her," Tommy says. Being the most respectful of this disrespectful crew, he kicks his shoes off.

"Oh yeah, let me just pull my invisible fucking phone out of my pocket." I growl.

"You still haven't found that thing?" Lars asks.

"No!"

My eyes sweep down the hall as I bend and twist to try and see where Zed went. Two seconds later, Marni comes down the hall with her phone gripped tightly in her hand. Her eyes land on mine, and we exchange what I hope to be a silent agreement that what we just did stays between us. The last thing I need is these guys harping on me because I'm breaking our number one rule—don't touch the girl. I doubt these two would give a flying fuck, but Zed's head might literally explode.

"Hey, guys," Marni says, with an immediate sarcasm in her

tone. "While I'm so happy that you all wanted to come and hang out in my home, I prefer that you don't." Her arms cross over her chest and her cleavage peaks out the top of her white V-neck.

I look to the guys and, sure as shit, they're gawking. Smacking my hand to the bottom of Lar's jaw, his eyes shoot up. "What the hell!" He slaps at my arm that's already back at my side.

"They're not on display for you," I grumble. I'm starting to think this girl eats up all this attention. Of course she does. Why else would she be on the WatchMeNow app? Sure as hell isn't for the money. I walk around her to go find Zed, but stop and whisper in her ear, "Go put on a sweatshirt and while you're up there, delete the last two hours on your security system."

Marni's fingers grab a hold of my arm, stopping my movements. "Where do you think you're going?"

"To see what the hell Zed is doing roaming around your house." I shake her hand off, but her expression leaves my feet planted.

Blinking a few times, her jaw clenches. "Zed's here?" With a loud groan, her feet begin moving. "Zed!" she shouts, "you better not be in my fucking room."

I follow after her. "Highly doubt he's in your room. I'd guess some place like your dad's office." I step in front of her and walk up the stairs, skipping every other step. I pull the location of his office from memory of the last time I was in there and as guessed, the door is wide open. "What the hell are you doing?" I snarl at him, as he sits comfortably in Anderson Thorn's chair.

"I don't understand what the buzz about this guy is. He doesn't even have a gun in his drawer. What kind of big top cartel leader doesn't have a fucking gun?" He speaks calmly, as he rocks back and forth with his arms resting on the arms of the chair.

Marni comes storming in the room. "Are you trying to get us all killed?" She points at the door. "Get out of here."

"Calm down, Little Thorn. It's highly unlikely that your dad would murder his only daughter."

Heavy steps bring her to his side where she begins pulling on his arm to try and get him up. All the while, I find it comical. She is a feisty thing when she wants to be. "Get up! If my dad notices the cameras are off this long, he will send security in here. If he finds out that you all are lurking around like a bunch of nosey little shits, we'll all be in trouble." When Zed doesn't budge, she directs her attention to me. "And you. Don't think I didn't see that you were in my house long before I even got here."

"You have my fucking phone. I'll search every inch of this place if I have to."

Her hands flap in the air like a flock of angry birds. "I'd just gotten here. How would I have hidden your phone in this house?" She looks so fucking sexy when she's angry.

Zed rolls the chair back and stands up. "I hate to break up this cute little fight, but I've got important shit to do." I watch as he pushes down a folded paper in his front pocket, but I don't think Marni noticed. When he catches my glance, he gives me a subtle nod.

I have no clue what it is or what he might want from Anderson Thorn, aside from some blackmail material or a possible link to his own father, and I really don't care.

"Come on," I throw an arm around Marni's shoulder, "we gotta get home. Our student has to do homework before bedtime."

"Ugh, get away from me. And quit treating me like a child. I'm the exact same age as you are. Just because you're a high school dropout, doesn't give you authority, and it certainly doesn't make you wiser. In fact, you're the exact opposite."

I'll let her have those words for now. She can view me as just a high school drop out if she wants. The truth is, I've just about completed my senior year early. After rehab, I did round the clock virtual schooling to catch up. Somehow, I ended up ahead. I guess when you're knee deep in the muck of depression, and you don't wanna go anywhere or see anyone, you strive for more.

The problem now? I have nothing left to strive for, except for my revenge.

As soon as we step out in the hallway and Marni closes the door behind us, a more chipper side of Zed emerges. "Who's up for a party? It's Thursday. I'm thirsty." His tone is cheerful and everything that Zed is not. Whatever paper he just pocketed must have been something useful to him.

Marni gets all too excited. "A party sounds fun."

Lucky for me, I get to be the bearer of bad news. "Can't. She has school tomorrow."

"Fucking A. Really?" Zed sighs.

"Yes, really. She needs sleep and there is no way in hell that she can sleep with a party going on downstairs."

"I'm eighteen years old. If I wanna stay up late and go to school tired and hungover then I will."

My jaw ticks as I think. This could work in my favor. Give her a few drinks. Soften her up. Get my damn phone back. There is so much shit in there that could destroy me if it fell in the wrong hands. And that's not even what has me worried. It's the video. All she has to do is open that up and bam, I'll lose all leverage, and she'd hate me more than she already does.

Tommy and Lars are raiding the cupboards when we walk downstairs. "Where are the bowls at?" Lars pulls open the freezer and grabs a tub of chocolate ice cream.

Marni stretches on her tiptoes and reaches into the

cupboard behind him. Her shirt rides up and the ruby red string of her thong sticks out from the back. This girl is going to fucking kill me. An overdose couldn't do the job, but she will fucking kill me if she doesn't stop showing her body like this.

Marni's eyes shoot out at me when Lars grabs the ice cream scooper on the counter. "No!" she grabs it from his hand, "you don't wanna use that."

"Oh come on." I smirk, as I take it from her hands and dig it into the ice cream. "The boy wants a taste of this sweet stuff." I drop a scoop into Lars' bowl then hand it to him. "Enjoy."

Shaking her head at me with disapproval, I literally fight myself not to mirror the smile that creeps on her face. When her eyes soften and I look at them deeper, it's impossible not to feel something. This moment is ours. These secrets are ours. And her smile is mine.

∞

WHEN THE GUYS LEAVE, Marni insists on cleaning up any remnants of our being here. She seems to think that her dad would lose his shit. What she doesn't know is that none of us fear the old man.

Marni is tossing all the dirty dishes in the sink from the guys' ice cream social when she holds up the scooper. "Maybe I should just throw this thing away." She fights back a smile.

"Oh no you don't." I grab it and drop it into the sink. "We might need it again."

"Not a chance."

"Don't act like you didn't enjoy it. And definitely don't be embarrassed. It was hot as fuck." I push my hair back over my dampened hairline. I'm still sweating from the explosion.

"I'm not embarrassed. I'm just not proud that it was with you."

"Oooh, burn." I make a sizzle sound with my tongue. "Why's that? Because I'm so repulsive?" I know that girls like Marni don't typically fall for guys like me. She's the former head cheerleader. The girl that all the other girls hate and the one all the guys want to fuck. She's also extremely fucking sad and a bit rough around the edges. She's too damn good for me. I might have money and power but I'm the reason that dads with daughters have loaded guns at their doors.

"Repulsive? No. You're not repulsive at all, Talon. You're just..." she searches for the word and I find myself hanging on it, "...daunting."

"Daunting?" I laugh. "As in, scary?"

Grabbing a rag she begins wiping up the slop of melted ice cream on the counter. "Why is that so funny? Should I remind you of everything you've done and said to me?"

"And should I remind you, that I knew you before all of this started?"

"Maybe this was all part of some elaborate scheme. Maybe Josh wasn't the obsessed psycho." She presses her hand on the counter and turns toward me. "Maybe you're the one I should have feared all along."

If only that weren't true, this would be a hell of a lot easier. Unfortunately, it is. I take a step toward her and watch as her breaths skip when I tangle my fingers in the back of her hair. "You're smart to fear me, but you'd be a fool to deny me." I pull her mouth to mine and allow our lips to melt together without movement. Stagnant like a still pond. Captivating, yet unmotivated. There is no manipulation behind this kiss. It's just for the plain and simple fact that I wanted to do it—if only just to feel her. Or to let her feel me and see that while I might be a monster, I also tremble when we touch.

13

MARNI

"Listen," I whisper, "there is no way that I can hold on to this phone any longer. We need to do this tonight." I look up and down Talon's driveway, behind me and in front of me, making sure that no one is around.

"I can't do it," Wyatt says. I hate this all so much. Dragging him into this mess. Asking him to do this. But, I don't have a choice.

"Wyatt, Please. I'm begging you." I turn on my sweet voice. The one that always gets me what I want. The one I used on Dad when I told him that I wanted to stay in L.A. It's not the same one I used when I told him I was staying with Shay. That one was demanding and, somehow, it still worked.

"How do you plan on getting away from them this time? They're not stupid, they'll never let you leave."

"I have a plan," I whisper into the phone. "Please, Wyatt," I repeat, "I'm begging you."

Another beat of silence.

"Fine."

Adrenaline rushes through me. "Really? Oh my gosh,

thank you, Wyatt." I jump up, and I know he can hear my smile through the phone. "I knew I could count on you. Ok. The party is at seven. I'll need until at least nine o'clock to get Talon off my back. Pick me up at the end of the driveway at nine-fifteen. If I'm running late, don't call. I'll be there."

"If I die because of this, my blood is on your hands."

The line goes dead. I know he's not pleased with the situation and what I'm asking him to do. But, it'll be fine. We'll get the info, and I'll put the phone back like nothing ever happened. Talon may know I have it, but I'll never admit it.

Talon's truck comes down the driveway, and I can immediately tell that he's pissed. I may have driven a little too fast and took a different route to get here before him. When his eyes widen, and he tilts his head backward, my jaw drops open and any sense of elation or calm that I did have is quickly diminished when I see the red and blue lights on the top of the car directly behind him. My first instinct is to run, but that's obviously not an option.

When Talon's truck stops right next to my car, he climbs out and slams the door shut, which is followed by the shutting of the officer's car door. "Is there a problem?" Talon asks when he comes into view.

There's a beep, then a voice on the other end of the receiver the officer is wearing. "I'm here now," he says, while holding down a button. When he releases it, he looks to Talon. "Talon Porter?"

I try to remain calm, even though my heart is galloping inside of me and I'm pretty sure all the color has drained from my face.

"That's me," Talon says, calm and collectively. How does he remain so composed? If that officer does so much as look at me with suspicion, I'll probably pass out.

"I'm Officer Klein, and I just have a few questions." He moves his attention to me. "And you are?"

Oh shit.

"Marni," I manage to choke out with wobbling legs and dazed confusion. "Marni Thorn."

"Ah, Anderson's little girl. How have you been, hon?" he asks with a smile.

My nerves calm a tad. "I've been good. Thank you." I have no idea who this man is, but I'm not surprised he knows my dad.

"I'm sure you've both heard that a student from Redwood High has gone missing. Josh Moran, does the name sound familiar?" he asks, as his eyes dart back and forth from me to Talon.

I just nod. It's all I can do. I can't speak out of fear of saying too much or not enough.

"Yeah, I heard about that. Did ya find him yet?" Talon asks, as he stuffs his hands into the pockets of his jeans.

"Not yet, but we're working hard to track down his whereabouts." He pulls out a small notepad and pen, giving the pen a click, he presses it to the paper. "This is your home, correct?" He poses the question to Talon.

"Yes, Sir," Talon responds, respectfully.

"And Zed King lives here with you?"

Taken aback, Talon's tone shifts. "Zed stays here. Why do you ask?"

The officer begins writing something down and then lifts his head. "We spoke with his father, Martin King, and he mentioned that Zed hasn't been home in months and that we might find him here."

Confused, I speak up. "What does Zed have to do with Josh's disappearance?" Talon shoots me a look that pretty much says *shut up*.

Completely ignoring me, he continues to talk to Talon, "Can you tell me where Zed was on Halloween night?"

"Easy. He was with us. We had a party right here at my house."

He looks at me with his pen still pressed to the paper. "You can attest to this, Ms. Thorn?" When I nod, he continues writing.

"Can you tell us why you need to know where Zed was?" I ask, warranting another glare from Talon.

Officer Klein closes his notebook and sticks it into the pocket on the front of his uniform. "Josh's sister mentioned that she may have seen someone matching Zed's description driving his car that night. She gave a couple names of possible guys. Zed was one of them. Thanks for clearing it up." He gives a nod and walks to his car.

We both watch as he gets in his car and does a U-turn. I stand frozen until his brake lights let up, and he disappears out of the driveway.

Releasing the breath that I was holding, I bend over with my palms pressed to my knees. "Holy shit."

When Talon wraps his arms around me and stands me up, I collapse into his arms. He holds me for what feels like minutes, though it's only seconds. Pulling back, he tucks a stray strand of my hair behind my ear. "You did good."

I close my eyes and bite my lip, hoping and praying that this was our only visit from Officer Klein.

"Hey." He cups my face in his hands. His touch feels warm, comforting, and like something I might actually want. "It's gonna be ok." He blinks slowly, trying like hell to give me the comfort that I need. It looks painful for him. Like he's fighting some inner demon who wants him to push me away; yet, he doesn't. He stands here exposing a vulnerable side that I don't think the world has ever seen. A side that I didn't even know existed.

His eyes widen. Surprising himself at his momentary lapse

of treachery. He tries so hard to be stone cold, but little by little, I'm chipping away his layers of ice. Unfortunately, no matter what side of him I see, there is no happy ending. Talon doesn't give a damn about me. All he cares about is making sure my lips stay sealed.

14

TALON

Without a word, I walk away.

Something inside me does this weird like flicker, which I blame on not eating today. As if there is a string attached from her to me, I turn my head around, feeling the pull of her eyes on me. She stands there looking all innocent, and I want to scream at the top of my lungs that she's not. So loud that maybe I'll actually believe it. She's an attention-crazed, spoiled rich brat. She's got Daddy's money, her mom's hot as hell looks, and her brother's holier than thou attitude. She's no angel. She uses her body to tease the fuck out of men, just to get high on their want for her. But the truth is, they don't want her—they want her body.

She's the only one to blame for the mess she's in. If she would have kept her legs shut and her life private, I would have never even targeted her, and I would have never tasted her. I'd give anything to rid myself of this uncontrollable desire to explore every inch of her body and uncover every single scar inside.

She's a weapon! Get her out of your fucking head!

I slam the door shut so hard that the ten-foot painting of

Gothic City rattles on the wall and threatens to fall down. I push it upwards and set it back in place, before the door swings back open. Without even taking my eyes off the painting, I know it's her. I can smell her. It's like my scent has found home on her body, and I've marked her as mine. Yet, somehow, she also lingers in my clothes and my hair and my cologne. Masking every inch of me, no matter how hard I try to wash her off. I can't rid myself of her, even if I wanted to. Even if there was another way.

But there's not. It has to be this way.

She has to be sacrificed so that I can have somewhat of a normal life. Whatever normal is.

"You ok?" she asks. Like we didn't just get questioned by the police. As if she didn't just invade a part of me that has been closed off to humanity. Part of me that I didn't even know existed, and I'm still not convinced it does.

Why can't I look at her the same way I did before this?

Yell at her. Call her a bitch. Do something to show that I still have the upper hand.

"Just hungry. You want something?"

Yeah, sure. Feed her. That's really putting her in her place.

"Nah, I think I'm gonna lie down for a bit before the party starts." She walks away, and with every step, I fight not to shadow her. To go up there and get in her head and rattle shit around just to get a rise out of her—though, it would likely be a fall, my fall.

"Dude. What the fuck?" Lars bellows, as he and Tommy come trudging down the hall from the kitchen. "What the hell were the cops doing here?"

I pull open the door and don't see their vehicles out front. "Where'd you two come from?"

"We parked at Zed's and walked." He swats Tommy's shoulder. "This asshole was too scared to drive up after we saw the flashing lights."

Waving my hand through the air, I brush it off as no big deal. "They were just wondering where Zed was on Halloween. It's all good. They have other people to question. We're little fish on their radar."

"You're downplaying this too much. I know you've got your own shit going on, but don't get too comfortable. We still need to be on our toes," Lars says.

"It's fine. Quit stressing so much, you're just gonna get Zed all worked up again."

"Yeah, well, Zed has come unleashed. He's pissed off that you're sheltering this girl like a lost puppy," Lars says, as Tommy flops down on the couch.

"Good. He's been getting on my last nerve lately." I look at Tommy, who's just standing there listening. "What's with him?" I ask Lars. Tommy has been particularly quiet since this whole plan took afloat and it's unnerving.

Lars rolls his eyes. "Don't worry about him. He actually thinks she is a lost puppy."

Tommy finally speaks up. "I just don't think she deserves this shit. You're tempting a lion, and she's the bait."

"Don't go getting soft on me, Chambers. We talked about this, and if you think for a second that you'll be her knight in shining armor, you're dead wrong."

Taking a seat on the couch, Tommy pulls a black sharpie out of his pocket. "You're the fucking devil. You and Zed both." He seethes as he begins marking up his white canvas shoe that's crossed over his leg.

"Damnit, you two. Is that all any of you guys do anymore is fucking fight?" Lars shouts.

I change the subject quickly. "Back to Zed. He's a problem. I feel like he's losing control. I'm pretty sure he's got a thing for this girl."

"Yeah. We're pretty fucking aware of that. But it sounds like you do, too," Tommy chimes in.

I flip him off, neither confirming nor denying his claim.

Lars taps his phone on. "Gimme the security password. You don't have your phone. Someone needs to keep tabs on the house and on her."

He's right. We have too much going on to let our guards down at this point. No one can be trusted, not even the three guys I call friends. The same guys who I made a pact with to face the in between together. Real times bring out true colors.

"Redwoodrebels. All lowercase. Do not share it with Zed. Not until we know what he's up to. Something tells me, it's not good."

Lars tosses his hands out. "He's our boy. He wouldn't betray us for her."

My brows shoot up. "You'd be surprised." If I almost thought she was worth it, Zed definitely thinks she is. Zed misconstrues love and hate. He loves the chase. He hates that he can't catch her. In his eyes, his actions are plausible.

∞

WE'RE all playing Call of Duty in the rec room when Lars gets a call from his step-sister about some family emergency. He leaves and tells us he'll be back for the party. There's an abundant amount of tension sitting between Tommy and I, and I wanna reassure him that we're cool, but the good thing about these guys is, we don't need words to show our loyalty. And the truth is, if I had to trust one of these guys with Marni, it would be Tommy. He has that empathy that most people do. He was raised by good people, and for the most part, he makes good choices, aside from running around with us since he was six years old, vandalizing private and public property with paint, and stealing glances at his dad's wife.

Grabbing the metal tin on the end table, I pull out a joint and spark it up. After a long drag, I pass it to Tommy in an attempt to break the ice. "You going to school tomorrow?" Smoke rolls out of my mouth and I cough on the last exhale.

He smirks. "Guess we'll see what the night brings." Taking a drag, he passes it back to me then begins cursing at the game.

Tommy is passive aggressive when it comes to our vile ways because he knows what a mess we all are. I'm pretty sure he pities our past and that's why he's always stuck by us and defended our actions.

We continue to puff and pass and I use this opportunity to do a little digging. "Now that it's just us, you ready to tell me why you're so damn protective of her?"

"I'm not protective of her. I just think you and Zed both have some seriously fucked up motives. I told you both that in front of her house and when you and Zed made the deal."

"Yet, you agreed to it?"

"What choice did I have? We stick together, right? You'll do the same for me when the time comes." He looks over at me, and I nod in agreement.

I'd absolutely do the same damn thing for him.

Tommy drops the controller on the seat then sticks the roach end of the joint in the tin, before smothering it with the lid. "And why are you so protective over her? You sprouting the feels for this girl?"

Laughter in the form of air blowing out of my nose has me shaking my head. "Not a chance in hell. You've seen her. She's a handful. Besides, relationships aren't my forte."

"Probably for the best. No girl would ever put up with your ass. Besides, she's only temporary. When this is all said and done, she'll never forgive any of us."

When it's all said and done, she just might burn the fucking house down with all of us inside.

15

The party is in full swing, and it's not even seven o'clock yet. I questioned whether or not we should even proceed, but Talon insisted that we carry on like normal. Anything else would raise suspicion. Partying is a normal thing in this house, so partying we are.

Zed hasn't been seen or heard from since we left my house, and even though I don't give a shit about that jerk, I'm getting worried. Not for him, but for the rest of us. If Zed is on the cop's radar that means they could start nosing around more often.

Talon's hand reaches around me with a red plastic cup. I take it from him and spin around to speak, but I'm rendered breathless when he stares back at me. His hair is flipped to one side and he's wearing a white t-shirt that hugs tightly to his chest and a black leather jacket over it. The scent of the leather alone is intoxicating. Then there's his eyes. I haven't even had a sip of my drink and I feel off-balance.

"You plan on standing by this door all night?" He tips back his cup and takes a drink.

I give the glass a sniff, and while it smells overpowering, it also smells really damn good. "Do I dare drink this?" I tease.

"I didn't drug it if that's what you're insinuating. I prefer my woman to be active in bed rather than limp."

Against my better judgement, I take a sip. What are the chances that he would try and knock me out on the same night that I'm doing it to him? With my free hand, I pat the pocket of my jeans nonchalantly, just to make sure the pea-sized pills are still intact.

"Just waiting for Shay. So go on, hang out with your friends and I'll hang out with mine."

Tilting his head to the side, he tsks. "Nice try. But you'll be by my side all night. You're also sleeping in my room again. I don't like you alone when people are getting drunk like this. I need to keep an eye on you."

"Seriously?" I huff. "Even after the run in with a cop out front, you still think I plan on snitching?"

"I'm not sure that you haven't already. You might not plan on telling the law, but I wouldn't put it past you to talk to your friends. Speaking of, I know you went to Miners Park earlier today."

My stomach drops. "How do you know that?"

"I know more than you think." He winks. "Come on, I need another drink."

Stopping him with a hand on his shoulder, I quickly slam the contents of my cup. "Let me get it. I could use some more."

He raises a brow. "Since when do you do nice things for me?"

"I don't. Unless there's something in it for me." Complete and utter truth right there. I walk away and give him a glance over my shoulder then blow him a kiss. "Goodnight, Asshole," I mutter under my breath.

When I return to Talon with his drink, I give it a whirl to

make sure the sleeping pills are fully dissolved. Mom used to take like three of these at a time and she was out cold within ten minutes, so I know two won't kill him. He'll just get a good night's sleep, which he could probably use.

Handing him his drink, I hold mine up. "Cheers." He bumps it back, and I watch him over the rim of my cup as he takes a drink. Trying not to be too obvious, I let my eyes dance around the party.

"What the hell is this?" He smacks his lips together.

My expression goes bleak. "Whatever they had mixed in that jungle juice bowl." Plus a few extra shots of vodka, but I don't tell him that.

"Tastes like straight alcohol." Yet, he still tips it back and takes another swig.

"Probably was, knowing your friends."

The front door comes open, and Shay walks in, and it's obvious she's already been drinking before she got here. She's with a couple of the girls from the cheer squad and I can't help but feel a tinge of envy. I should be enjoying my senior year. I didn't even make it to the end of the season family cheer banquet a couple days ago. Though, I wouldn't have gone anyway, because I lack the family part.

∞

A FEW DRINKS LATER, I'm feeling pretty buzzed and far too brave for what I'm getting ready to do.

I turn around and see Talon's eyes half-closed with his chin to his chest. Tucking my arms under his, I guide him away before anyone notices his semi-comatose state.

"What you...." he stutters, "What did you do to me?" His head continues to bobble around, and his full weight begins to feel heavy in my arms.

"Guess you just can't drink like you used to." We make it

halfway up the stairs before he begins to put more weight on me, and I fear that one wrong move will send us both crashing down.

We finally reach the top of the stairs, and just as we round the corner, I hear Zed. "What's going on up there?"

Oh shit.

Pushing Talon up against the wall, I hold him in place with one hand. Thankfully, he's still got some strength in his legs. I peek around the corner and look down at Zed. He's standing at the bottom of the steps in a solid black t-shirt and black jeans. His dark hair is flipped to the side and his eyes zero in on me. "Talon had a little too much to drink. I'm just helping him to bed." I steal a glance at Talon whose eyes are completely closed.

When I look back down the stairs, Zed is gone.

That's too fucking weird. Zed is constantly suspicious of everything that I do, yet now, he's not even questioning me. Brushing it off, I lead Talon down the rest of the hallway.

It suddenly hits me that I don't know the password to get upstairs.

My room is only three feet away, so I push open the door, and just as we step inside, Talon collapses to the floor. There is no way that I can get him on that bed and there's really no point. He's already asleep; what does he care if he's comfortable or not?

I go to leave the room but turn back around, and for a brief moment, my heart swells at the sight of Talon lying there —helpless and hopeless. His shirt is tugged up and an array of raised bumps stem out like branches of a tree. Skin colored with a hint of pink where the injuries healed. Beneath them are blotches of brown-colored skin that look like the remnants of a bad burn. He might do some monstrous things, but he's not a monster. He's had to endure so much pain in his short eighteen years of life. It's no wonder that he looks at the world as a dark hole.

Stepping out into the hall, I shut the door, press my back to it, and close my eyes.

No regrets. Now is not the time.

Thinking for a moment, I shake off the unwanted thoughts. It has to be this way. Even if a small part of me might be getting attached to a small part of Talon, he's the reason that I'm in this constant state of worry. Because of him, there is evidence out there that could incriminate me in a murder. He's also failing to divulge any information on Josh's death. I still don't know how or why he died. All I know is that I have to look after myself. Because, in the end, I only have myself.

Shay is already three sheets to the wind, and she's giving a lap dance to a sophomore. Grabbing her by the arm, I pull her away from making a big mistake. Though, you'd think I just ran over her puppy with the look she's giving me.

"Let go of me. I like that guy," she snaps, and it's all too strange being on this end of the dragging. I've been dragged around for the past couple days by these guys, and it feels good to take back a little control.

Once we are away from the crowd, I release her arm. "Two words. Too young."

Completely changing the subject, she whines, "I miss my best friend. We used to talk every single day and now that you're running around with these guys, you're keeping things from me and it's like I don't even exist anymore."

"It's been six days. Things are just really weird right now." I pull her in for a hug and she doesn't fight me off. "I promise, things will get back to normal." That's why I'm doing this. They have to get back to normal. I'm just unclear of what normal looks like anymore.

Shay flashes a smile and pulls me toward the open French doors that lead to the pool. Blue neon lights are strung in the dark and the fluorescent glow of the pool is ambient. Music is blaring, and everyone is having a good time. Everyone except for Talon. I excuse myself when Shay picks up a conversation with a few girls from our class, then go back inside with the plan to leave out the garage door.

On my way out, I stop for a drink and make it an extra strong one in hopes of alleviating some of this anxiety. This whole situation is reminding me too much of last week. As the contents of my cup slide down, nice and smooth, I've already convinced myself that I'm skipping school tomorrow. I imagine half of the party-goers will be skipping too. It's typical when Talon throws these weekday parties.

The pool of liquor that's settling in my stomach has me welcoming the dark and quiet walk down the driveway. I stop at my car and look around before I grab the phone from underneath my seat and stuff it in my bra. The party can be heard in the distance, but it's nice to be by myself for once. I've spent so much of my life alone that being around these people and these guys all the time has become a day-to-day misery that overwhelms me.

I'm not sure when I transitioned from being a socialite to an introvert, but I was starting to like it there. Now, I'm forced to be within arm's reach at all times because someone thinks that I might slip up and destroy us all. They think I'm fucking stupid, but they don't know me.

Wyatt is parked right where I told him to be with his lights off. Another car pulls down the driveway, so I move to the side. Normally, I would discern that it was suspicious to have Wyatt sitting there, and he's probably shaking in his boots, but this liquid courage has my two fucks in my back pocket. I pull open the door and slide in, and before I can even shut it, Wyatt has the car running and we're speeding off, tossing gravel in our wake. "Woah Andretti, slow down. No one saw us." I go to tip back my half-empty cup, and he reaches over and grabs it. "Hey!"

"Come on, Marni. I know you're smarter than that. You're not drinking in my car while I drive."

Wyatt is as law abiding as they come. Well, he was until now.

Pouting, and missing my drink, I tuck one leg under the other. "So, what's the plan. Go to your dad's office and break in?"

"We're not going to the headquarters. We're going to the CEO's home office." He smirks.

My eyes light up. "Wait? Your dad has one at his house?"

"He does now. I may have paid him a visit earlier today and snuck into the manufacturing room and taken one."

"Holy shit." I chuckle. "Where is my strait-laced bestie and who the hell are you?"

"I might be strait-laced, but I also hate those douchebags and would love nothing more than to watch you take them down." Biting the corner of my lip, I nod in agreement. Though, inside, I'm so fucking terrified of what I'm about to find out.

We walk into Wyatt's house and I'm still reeling from the effects of the alcohol. "Your parents home?" I ask, as I head straight for the liquor cabinet. Some of the bottles are half water, thanks to Shay and I always tapping into them over the years. Wyatt's parents don't drink much, obviously, because if they did, these bottles wouldn't still be here.

"No, but they will be soon, so we need to hurry."

I twist the top off a bottle of Pucker and tip it back. The apple flavored liquor leaves behind a warmth in my stomach and a cloudy feeling in my head.

Carrying the bottle with me, I follow behind Wyatt as he leads the way into his bedroom. His room is a mess, as per usual. Kicking clothes under my feet as I walk across the floor, I flop my ass onto his bed. "Alright, let's see the device that made your daddy famous."

Wyatt bends at the waist and pulls open a drawer underneath his bed. I peer down and see the black box inside. It's much smaller than I thought. It's about the size of a Rubik's Cube and has two cords attached to it. One of which has about a dozen different connectors.

"Do you have a card?" I ask him.

Reaching into his pocket, he pulls out a small SD card and holds it up. "Like I'd forget the card." He slides it into the slot on the box and carries it over to the wall outlet where he plugs it in. "You sure you wanna do this?" he asks, as I give him the phone.

I tap my fingertips together deviously. "Absolutely." He plugs the phone in and powers it on. Then he hits a button and a green light comes on. We both watch quietly and minutes pass before a red light comes on and the device beeps. He unplugs the phone, turns it off, pops out the card and hands me both. "That's it?"

"Yep. Pretty awesome, huh?" He pulls open his drawer and puts the device back inside.

"So what now? I just put this into my computer and the data will show up?"

"Pretty much. I doubt you'll be able to read much of the data, but you'll be able to see phone numbers and any photos or videos he has."

"Perfect." I waggle my brows. "That's all I need."

16

MARNI

When I return, the party is still raging. Shadows of the swaying bodies dance off the walls in the dimmed living room. Voices carry through the kitchen and the splash of water and a girl squealing has me thinking that the peak of the party hasn't even hit yet. There are more people here now than when I left. Trying to blend in and make an escape upstairs, I spot Lars bent over the center island in the kitchen. His arms are folded in front of him against the granite and his eyes are plastered on yours truly. The look in his eyes isn't foreign to me, but it's not one that I care to see often. Pointing his finger at me, he bends it back and forth, calling me over.

I take a deep breath, roll my eyes and obey the command. Talon's phone is snug in my back pocket, and the SD card is tucked in my bra. Let's just hope he doesn't try to get touchy feely like he usually does. "What'd ya want? I'm tired."

"I bet you are. You've had a busy night."

Crossing my arms over my chest in an attempt to hide my third nipple, I pop my hip up. "You're right, I have. Now if you'd cut to the chase, I'd like to go to bed. I'm half-drunk and really fucking tired."

"Where's your bodyguard? Haven't seen him around. Now that I think of it, this is the first I've seen of you tonight."

"Talon's passed out and I've been laying low. I'm not exactly keen on the gossip going around about me right now."

I've heard the whispers. *She's screwing all four of them. She's only staying in that house because her dad kicked her out. No one wants the poor girl. Whore.* Fortunately, I have thick skin, and I've never cared what anyone thought of me. I also have no problem socking a bitch if she steps too far out of line.

With both hands, he pushes himself off the island and circles around it until he's at my side. "Fuck the rumors. They're carried by haters and accepted by cowards." With an index finger pressed to my chin, he tilts my head up. "We know the truth."

Yeah, we do. And I'm not sure whose truth I'd prefer—theirs or ours. "Are we done here?"

"We're done," he nods, "go get some sleep."

With squinted eyes of confusion, I leave. That was really weird. He didn't make any sexual innuendos, and he even tried to reassure me where the rumors were concerned. These guys are so damn confusing, but the more I get to know them, the more I'm starting to realize that they have some depth beneath the surface.

When I reach the top of the stairs, I walk toward my bedroom door. *My bedroom.* I never would have guessed that I'd refer to anything in this house as mine. Unease ripples through me when I notice that the door is ajar, though Talon is still right where I left him. Bending over, I stick his phone into his pocket like nothing ever happened. I struggle with whether or not I should try and wake him now, but it's probably best to just leave him and let him think that he passed out like this.

I shut the door behind me then strip off my clothes. Stepping into a pair of fuzzy pink pajama pants and pulling on a plain black t-shirt, I look at him again. My heart catches fire at the sight and I find myself on my knees at his side.

I wonder what the story is behind these scars. From the looks of them, it's not a pleasant one. My finger trails feather-like over the rough edges and my breath stills. He's so beauti-fully broken. Everything about his shell is perfect, even his scars. They're a reminder to the world that he's been through hell. It's the ones on the inside—the ones the world can't see—that serve as a reminder for only him. Those are the painful ones. I know; I have my own. Stretching over, I grab a blanket off of the bed and cover him up. For whatever reason, I press a gentle kiss to his forehead and whisper, "I'm sorry it had to be this way."

My head is still in a fog from drinking and sheer exhaus-tion, and I can't wait to climb into this bed and chase away reality. With only a flat sheet, since I gave Talon the blanket, I wrap it around me and settle in on my stomach.

Just as I'm about to drift away to another world, the door opens and light from the hall breaks through. A tall, dark figure appears, then disappears when the door shuts. Only, he's not on the other side, he's in my room.

Holding my breath, I listen for a sound that indicates where he is. It's when the mattress shifts and a hand slaps over my mouth that fear ensues. I gasp and squirm to get free, but he's strong. Much stronger than I am.

"Surprise, Little Thorn," he whispers in my ear. His words roll off his tongue sweetly and innocently, but they are laced with bad intentions. Zed isn't sweet. He's acidic and pungent, and I know that me going to sleep with a smile intact is not his end game.

His face is so close to mine that I can feel the brush of his skin on my cheek. My breath hitches, and my pulse races as I remain completely still. Zed's finger trails up my neck and around to my face as he traces the outline of my lips. Sweeping my hair to the side, he rests his chin on my shoulder. The full weight of his body is on my back as he lies flat against me. "Talon's in here. He'll wake up, and he'll be pissed," I say with no attempt to hush my voice.

"Talon. Talon. Talon. It's always fucking Talon. He's asleep, which you already know." His breath smells like cinnamon mixed with whiskey. "Don't you know that you should never drug a druggie."

Every fiber of my being is pulled out of me in that instant. Dizziness ensues and I feel like I just stepped off a merry-go-round while I'm still lying down. "He's ok. Isn't he?" I manage to choke out. It completely slipped my mind that Talon used to be addicted to pills. I have no idea what kind of pills, but if I would have thought for a fucking second, I would have realized that this was not the best approach.

"He'll be fine." He brushes it off like it's no big deal. "And, it gives us a chance to get to know one another, without him breathing down your neck." Cold air hits me, sending goosebumps down my arms. "Tonight, you get me."

"Can we turn on the light, please? I can't see you."

"What are you afraid of? Monsters? Ghosts?"

"Something like that."

"Ya know, when I was a kid, my dad once told me that it's not the things you can't see that you should fear. It's the things you can. My dad is also fucked in the head, so I would take what he says with a grain of salt. But, I always took it as him saying, 'be careful who you trust. Your best friend could also be your enemy.'"

The light of his phone flicks on right in front of my face. "You have to be careful who you let inside—your head, your heart, your pussy, and your room. Because the world can see this and all it takes is one little peak and we want the whole package." He taps play on a video. Not just any video.

It's me.

In this room.

Nausea returns with a vengeance. I don't respond. I just stare straight at the phone with my hands pressed firmly at my sides. Consumed with thoughts of nothingness. Unable to wrap my head around any of this.

"How did you get that video?" My words rattle, and it mimics my trembling body.

"Be careful who you trust," he repeats the words he said only seconds ago.

Your best friend could also be your enemy.

Talon is far from someone I'd consider to be a friend, but I felt a connection with him. In some ways, I trusted him. Obviously, I gave in to his wishes that night. But I never imagined he'd betray me to this extent. Recording me. Recording us and then sharing it with the guys. I'm still not sure that I believe anything Zed is saying to me. But the reality is, someone did record me and even if it wasn't Talon, I'm starting to realize I can't let my guard down.

"How did you get that?" My body begins itching as red waves of anger ripple over my skin.

"Surprised?" I can feel his body next to mine. "You shouldn't be. Talon's using you." He chuckles. "I mean, come on. He forced you to finger fuck yourself with a camera hidden in here. He's always watching you. Well," he pauses, "he *was* always watching. Until you stole his phone."

"But, why? What could I possibly have that he wants?" Why am I even asking Zed? He'll probably only feed me lies. He could be lying right now for all I know. He could have planted the camera. Attempting to lift my head, however far it will go, I look around the room for any sign of light from a camera.

Watching my every move through the light of the phone, it's like he reads my mind. "It's not on. I shut the cameras off." He grabs the phone from my hand.

"How did you shut it off? I thought Talon said he changed the password."

Flipping me over onto my back, Zed flicks on his phone's flashlight and holds it up to his face as he talks. "I've got my ways." The light reflects off of his shark-like eyes that are as black as coal, even with a beam of light hitting them. His legs cinch around my waist as he imprisons both of my arms at my side.

He must have watched me slip Talon the sleeping pills. All this time we thought he went rogue, and he's been lurking around watching us—watching me.

"Whatever you think is going on with you and Talon is all a facade. A dream preparing to take a twisted turn into a nightmare."

"Newsflash, *Zed*," I emphasize his name, "There is absolutely nothing going on between Talon and me. In fact, I hate him just as much as I hate you." My body reacts by shoving his body up and trying to squirm out from beneath him, but, as per usual, I'm too fucking slow.

"Lies. Lies. Lies. You think that I haven't been watching every single move you make." His legs swaddle me in, and his words suck all the air out of my lungs. "I know you, Marni. I know that you leave these curtains open when you sleep. I know that you sleep on your stomach and prefer to wear socks to bed with the blanket tucked all around you. Does Talon know these things about you? Does he even fucking care?" His voice raises with each word, and I lie there completely motionless. "No!" he shouts. "He doesn't know these things and he doesn't fucking care."

"How long have you been watching me?" I manage to ask, though my words are jutted and cracked.

"Ever since you got here. Every single day. Every single night."

I don't respond. I can't. My mind tells me to scream or to

fight him off, but something holds me in place and my tongue fails me when I go to speak. When his fingers trail up my shirt, my heart stills. I hold my breath and close my eyes. Taking every sweep of his thumb as it grazes the flesh of my cleavage. Something comes over me and it sure as hell isn't a desire for him. It's pure unadulterated hate.

His mouth crashes into mine, and I press my lips together firmly, while biting down on my teeth with immense pressure. But that doesn't stop him, he pushes so hard that I can feel his teeth through the skin of our lips. Tears well in the corner of my eyes and my body fails to even try and fight him off when he pulls my pants down. It could be fear, or it could be the fact that all of my life I have fought to feel wanted. I've struggled to feel comfortable in my skin. To accept the reality that I have no one. Mom is gone and she's not coming back. Dad loves his job more than his family. Axel is happy and in LA. Who do I have? Where do I belong?

Zed leans back and I lick my lips; the metallic taste of blood present. Strong hands clutch at my sides as I lie there without a voice. Just like when I was thirteen and that old security guard used to *visit me* in the playhouse. I swore that if any man ever touched me again without permission, I'd be the one to kill him. A couple weeks later, I told Axel about it and the next day the sorry bastard went missing. I'm still not sure if Dad did the job or if Axel took matters into his own hands. Either way, here I am. Getting the attention I've always craved. I have no one to blame but myself. I put my body on display and reeled in these fucked-up men.

Wispy strands of hair tickle the insides of my thighs as Zed presses his lips to them, sucking the skin into his mouth so hard that I can already feel the bruise come to the surface. Again. And again. And again.

"No one was supposed to touch you outside of that one video. But Talon did, didn't he?" He growls as his teeth clamp down on the flesh of my side. I go to sit up, but he pushes me right back down.

I gasp when his fingers slide inside me. Twisting and turning, poking and prodding. Rough and unwanted, but here I lie. Quiet as a mouse.

Sliding up my body, his fingers remain in me and his thumb rubs aggressively over my clit. I fight against the rush that courses through my body, begging myself not to give in. "How do you know all of this stuff about me?"

"I'll tell you," he sucks my earlobe into his mouth while his teeth graze my cartilage, "but not until I finish you off. I want you to come so fucking hard that it gushes."

Shutting off my mind, I escape this room. I unfeel his fingers sliding in and out of me. I pinch my eyes shut and carry myself away to another time. I picture my family at Thanksgiving dinner when I was seven. When Dad kissed Mom on the cheek and she accepted it because she wasn't whoring around just yet. A life before the affair she had. Before cancer struck and took her away from us. Though we didn't see Dad much, he used to smile back then. Axel was still a little jerk, but never to me. If he knew what these guys were doing to me, there is no doubt in my mind that he would kill them all. That's why he can never know.

He can't know that I'm letting Zed have his way with me all because I'm weak and pathetic. Because I want answers. It's a sad truth that if you want something from a man then you either show some skin or spread your legs. All I've ever wanted is to be wanted. I just want someone to touch me like this and stay when it's over.

"Come for me, Marni. I know you want it."

I can't.

I don't.

He sits up, straddling my legs, and as his intensity slows, I begin to question myself and how disconnected I am from my body. Two fingers slide in and out at just the right speed, while he uses his other hand to rub against my clit. A suppressed moan unleashes and my back arches as my chest rises. Trying to regain my focus on something other than the way my body is inviting him in, I think of Talon. Lying there on that floor with no clue what is going on. As much as I hate him for what he's done with that video, I need him to wake up.

Wake up and stop this, Talon.

I close my eyes and don't allow myself to feel anything other than the glide of his fingers and the adrenaline that floats through me. I let out a breathy exhale and clench myself around his fingers, bucking my hips up and forcing myself into oblivion. *I want this.* I lie to myself.

His face is right in front of mine, and I know, without a doubt, that he's watching me intently. It's pitch-black, but I can feel his eyes burn into my skin. Leaving an imprint that I'm not sure will ever fade. This memory will forever be etched in the back of my mind. One day when I'm old and depressed and have to seek counseling because of PTSD, this sin will be my first confession. I let the devil have his way with me, not because I was scared of the hell he was dragging me into, but because I liked the way it felt.

"You like that don't you?" he says with a raspy pitch.

"Don't fucking talk," I hiss, bucking my hips higher to gain momentum.

How can something this unwanted make my body feel this damn good?

His pace picks up, and this time, I embrace it. Taking everything he's giving me. He wants to make me feel good. He's hungry for it. So much so, that I firmly believe he will go mad if I don't give him the satisfaction of making me come.

"Oh yeah," he moans, "you're soaking wet for me. Just for me."

"You're fucking sick." I groan as my body is taken over by a warm current that spills out between my legs. Reality slaps me in the face as soon as I come down.

Zed's body drops down onto mine and I turn my head to the side to avoid him kissing me. Pressing a chaste kiss to my cheek, he whispers in my ear, "I am sick, but you drugged the guy you care about and let me shove my fingers in your pussy while he slept on the floor." I squirm out from underneath him and get to my feet.

"I don't care about him. I hate him and I hate you." My arm stretches back and I swing my open palm, just hoping and praying that it lands somewhere on his body.

When my hand meets his face, I smile. "You fucking bitch." He spits.

Digging around on the floor until I find my pants, I untuck the leg sleeves that were turned inside out, then slide them on.

Before I even have them over my hips, Zed is gripping both of my wrists. "I'm not above hitting a woman who hits me first. Next time, I'll fuck you and choke you at the same time. Then again," he chuckles, "you'd probably like that, you little slut."

Jerking my arm away, I stumble over Talon's comatose body and almost fall to the floor, but I'm stopped by the wall that I slam into. Pushing myself off, I grab hold of the handle, just as I pull it open and light shines through, his breath hits my neck again. "What just happened in here is our secret. Unless you want Talon to know you took his phone, drugged him, and had this made." I turn around and see the SD card.

"No!" I cry out as I try to take it from him. "That's mine."

That's fucking mine. I worked my ass off for that card. That's my escape from this hell. It's my proof and my only chance to hold something over their heads.

"It's mine now. I might not care what happens to your boy right there," he glances over his shoulder then returns his gaze to me, "but I refuse to go down because he's too stupid to know when he's being played. You did good. I'll give you that. But you can't have this card. You can never know what's on it." He pauses and tugs his bottom lip between his teeth. "You couldn't handle the truth. It just might kill you." With that, he finally leaves.

My legs turn to jelly as I brace my back against the wall. I'm unable to move out of fear that I'll fall to the floor. He's evil. Pure fucking evil, and for whatever reason, he has a vendetta against me.

Unless…Unless, it's Talon he's after.

He may have taken the card, but after what these guys have done to me—Talon and Zed in particular—I'm not backing down. I'm ready to fight, and I'm dragging these sons of bitches straight to hell.

17

TALON

Throwing Marni's bedroom door open, I shout, "Wake your ass up. You have school."

"Fuck off," she mumbles, without even rolling over to face me.

She's had this sour attitude ever since the party last week. A party that I can't even remember. I woke up on Marni's bedroom floor with my phone in my pocket. She claims that I must have stumbled in there while she was asleep, but I'm not buying that bullshit story. I'm also well aware that she stuck my phone in my pocket, but getting her to admit that is about as hard as my dick is right now. She's sprawled out on the bed in just a sports bra and a pair of skimpy shorts, her ass is practically screaming for me.

"Dude," Lars comes rushing into the room. "They found Josh's car." He's out of breath with a mask of panic on his face.

"Ok," I shrug it off, "we knew they would eventually. Keep calm and don't draw attention. That's all we have to do."

Marni stretches her arms up and then gets out of bed. "You guys, not draw attention? That's laughable. Now if you wouldn't mind getting the hell out of my room, I have an education to get so that I can become more than a trust fund brat and pothead like four guys I know." She smirks.

Lars and I share a glance, and I just nod my head in agreement with whatever he's thinking because I suspect it's along the same lines as my thoughts. *This girl is a royal pain in the ass.*

Shrugging her shoulders, she glowers. "Fine then. Don't bother me none. Not like all four of you guys haven't seen what's underneath these clothes." She pulls her sports bra over her head and her tits flop out, stunning us both. I have no idea what the hell she's talking about or why she'd assume that Lars or anyone else has seen her naked. Her shorts drop and to my surprise, she's not wearing any underwear. Standing completely naked in front of me and Lars, she places her hands on her hips and narrows her eyes. "Well, like what you see, assholes?"

Glancing over, I remember that Lars is still standing there. If his mouth was opened any farther, I might trip over it. "Get the fuck out." I spin him around and give him a shove out the door then slam it shut.

When I look back at her, her scowl has only grown. "Is there a reason you're still here?"

Tilting my head up, I force myself to maintain eye contact with her. "What the hell is your problem lately?"

"Hmm. Let's see," she taps her finger to her chin then shouts, "I fucking hate you! All of you! But especially you!" Bending over, she grabs a pair of underwear from her open bag then shuffles around until she pulls out a pair of jeans.

"And what did I do to earn that extra helping of hate?" I continue to watch her as she gets dressed. She's a handful of beauty and she's bound to be my downfall if I keep thinking these dirty thoughts.

"If you even have to ask, then you have no business even talking to me right now."

"Ever since the party last week, you've been throwing out

these hints of accusation and unless you're ready to tell me what the fuck your problem is, cut this shit out." I snatch up her dirty clothes and toss them in the laundry basket then hand her the brush on her dresser like some kind of servant.

She looks at the brush then back at me. Thinking for a moment before grabbing it. Her tone shifts, and her eyes harbor a glimmer of hope behind them. "Thanksgiving is next week. I'd like to go home and see my dad and my brother."

"No," I quip.

Don't even need to think about it. No and hell no.

That hopefulness in her baby blues is quickly diminished.

Swinging her arm around with the brush in hand, she comes close to smacking me with it, but I'm faster and more aware of her spontaneous outbursts. Grabbing her by the wrist, I twist it and hold it up to her head. Moving it up and down as the brush weaves through her hair. "It's a brush, not a baton."

Menacing eyes stare into mine while I continue to help her brush her corn silk strands. "I hate you with every bone in my body, Talon Porter. And one day, I will make you pay for what you've done to me."

When I drop her hand, she gives the brush a toss onto the bed. My hands smack her hips and I give them a firm squeeze, "Make me pay, baby, because I like to be punished." I give her a wink and a sinister smile raises her cheek bones.

Her hands raise to my cheeks then slide around my head. "Oh, I will. And I plan to enjoy every fleeting moment." Firm lips slam into mine and nails dig into the skin of my neck so hard that I'm ninety-nine percent sure they just pierced the skin. As she drags them around to the front, I don't recoil. My mind is focused solely on the taste of her cherry Chapstick and the warmth of her full mouth. Our eyes are both wide open, burning into one another. While this kiss is turning me on to the fullest extent, she's getting off on the pain she's causing me with her nails beneath my flesh. She stops digging them into me, pulls back and looks down at her bloodied nails. "Now look what you've done."

Taking her hand in mine, I examine her red-tinged fingers. She probably hoped I would shriek and beg her to stop. To wince due to the sting of pain. She doesn't know me, and nothing she does can hurt me.

With my free hand, I clench her cheeks between my thumb and forefinger and force her mouth open. "Not so funny now, is it?" I tsk. "I'll play your game, but you'll play mine." I take her hand and shove three fingers inside of her mouth while still holding it open. "Does it taste as good as it felt?"

Her eyes widen, and when she tries to fight back, I squeeze her cheeks hard. Gags, gurgles, and whimpers sound in my ears, but all I hear is triumph.

When I think she's had just about enough, I release my hold on her. Spit flies in my face, and I take it. "You are deranged." She coughs and chokes while spitting repeatedly on the floor.

That I am. My fingers graze over the raised ridges of the scratches on my neck. I might have finally met my match.

∞

I'VE BEEN DRIVING Marni to school, and every morning, her face is stuck to the passenger window, just so she can avoid looking at me. Today is no different in that aspect, but I'm certainly about to throw a wrench in her plans.

Her head perks up. "What are you doing?" she asks when I drive straight past the drop-off line and pull into the student parking lot.

"Oh shit, I forgot to tell you. I'm going to class with you today." I shift into park and turn the ignition off.

I didn't really forget to tell her. It was just determined this morning while she was taking her time coming down stairs. After talking with the guys, we figured it would be a good idea to keep her at arm's length, considering there's been a break in the case and Josh's car was found by divers last night.

"No, you're not," she spits. "You're not a student here."

"Just because I choose not to attend classes in person doesn't mean I don't go to this school."

Technically, I'm not supposed to be here, but I called Principal Burton and told her that I needed some detailed instruction for a few assignments and requested to sit in on some classes—all Marni's classes. With a little persuasion, she made it happen.

With a long drawn out huff, Marni grabs the handle and gets out so quick that she drops her opened backpack and the contents spill out on the pavement. Of course, I laugh.

"I hate you. I hate you. I hate you." She repeats over and over as I try to help her pick up the dozen pens and pencils. Slapping my hand away, she stuffs everything inside the bag, but I reach in and snag one of the pencils.

"Thanks. I'm gonna need that." I stick the pencil behind my ear. "Probably some paper, too."

Swinging the bag over her shoulder she stomps off. "Like you plan on doing any work, loser," she shouts with a flip of her middle finger over her shoulder.

Cupping my hands around my mouth, I shout louder, "Maybe I wanted to write you a love note...honey." I laugh, but she just picks up her pace.

This is fixing to be a hell of a good time. I'm not sure why I ever stopped coming here. The place is swarming with babes. They've really filled out since I left. Tits and ass everywhere.

Marni's walking about six feet ahead of me when I jog up to her side and throw an arm over her shoulder. "What's the matter? Embarrassed to be seen with me?"

Pulling my arm off of her, she makes an abrupt turn

straight over to the lawn where her friend, Shay, is talking amongst a group of guys from the varsity football team. I stop walking, watch for a minute, and contemplate whether or not I'll allow her this space. But when Jordan Wells, the varsity quarterback, winks at her and flips the front of her hair with lust-filled eyes, I eat up that distance.

"Yo, Wells," I shout, "Touch her again and I'll shove my foot up your ass."

A few eyes watch as I walk over. Confusion written all over their faces. "Miss me, fuckers?" I say to the guys. A couple of them are at my house practically every weekend, just for a free space to party, but none of these assholes are friends of mine. Not anymore. When I fell down the drain of addiction and left sophomore year, they found humor in my downfall.

I wrap my arms around Marni from behind and rest my chin on her head. "Carry on. Didn't mean to interrupt." I smirk.

Marni doesn't make a move, but Jordan is looking at her with puzzlement. "Are you two—?"

"No!" she blurts out, "we are not."

Tipping my head back, I mouth, "We are," but only he catches it. It's complete bullshit, but everyone may as well assume she's off-limits, because she is.

"We were just inviting the girls to a bonfire this weekend. You're welcome to come, too." Keegan, the nicer of the guys, says.

"He's busy." Marni turns around and grabs me by the arm, pulling me away before I can respond.

"Hey, I was just about to make friendly conversation with your friends. What's with the dramatic exit?"

"Nothing you say is friendly," she mutters, while continuing to pull me toward the steps of the school.

The crowd out front begins to thin out when the warning

bell rings, but Marni stands there with her arms crossed over her chest. "You can leave now. I have class."

"Oh," I laugh, "you thought I was joking?" I shake my head. "No, babe. I'm staying here. All fucking day." I walk up the stairs and turn around. "Come on, I don't like being tardy." That's a lie. In fact, I can't think of a day that I was ever really on time for class. Not on purpose, I'm just a slacker and naturally walk slow.

Nothing has changed inside the walls of this place. You still have your jocks, your stuck-up bitches, the stoners, the geeks, and the inbetweeners who still don't know where they belong. You know the ones—we've been around for eighteen years and still have no idea who we are, where we fit, or where we're going.

Following behind Marni, I catch all the deplorable looks from my former classmates. They're probably wondering what a catch like Marni is doing with a guy like me. They have no clue that my presence in her life is not wanted in the least.

"I'm not sure how you pulled this off, but just so you know, you're not sitting by me in class if that's what you're thinking. In fact, the only available seat is in the back of the room next to Allergic Alan." The corner of her lip tugs up with the thought.

"Don't you worry about me."

We make a quick stop at her locker then head to her first class. Her arms are loaded with a textbook, a Chromebook, a notebook, and a folder. Grabbing them from her hands, in an attempt to carry some of the weight, she retorts, "Don't touch my stuff."

"Dry your panties, girl. I'm just trying to help." I grab at them again and somehow, we engage in a tug of war contest as we walk down the halls, warranting more looks and snickers from the onlookers.

"If I wanted your help, I'd ask. Now give me my damn

stuff," she hisses as I hold tightly to them and pick up speed, booking it to her first class of the day.

Just when she catches up, I slide into the half-open door. Everyone is in their seats and all eyes are on us.

"Mr. Porter. It's good to see you." Mrs. Tate, the astronomy teacher, lies to my face. She fucking hates me. I may have flipped up her skirt because of a bet, just to see what kind of panties she wore. Some might call it sexual harassment; I looked at it as a way to win a bet.

Solid white hip huggers. Also known as granny panties.

"I'm sharing material with my good friend, Marni. So, if you wouldn't mind, we'll need to sit next to each other." My comment warrants me a massive growl and a double eye-roll from Marni.

Mrs. Tate's eyes question Marni's safety, and quite possibly her sanity.

"Tell her, babe." I give Marni a nudge and bite back a smile. I love getting under her skin, and right now, I'm sure as hell doing just that. The entire class is watching while she nods her head nervously in agreement. "It's settled then." I smile at Mrs. Tate.

Marni heads to her seat and I follow. When she sits down, I narrow my eyes on the douchebag with highlights in his hair who is sitting next to her. "Get up," I demand.

He looks from me, to Marni, and then to Mrs. Tate, who is standing at the front of the class tapping the toe of her shoe to the floor. "James, could you please sit in the back with Alan. Talon will be sitting in with us for the next couple of days."

Alan begins a sneezing fit in the back row, and James huffs, "Seriously?"

"'Fraid so." I smirk as I begin stacking his belongings up. When he stands up, I shove them into his chest. "Thanks, bro." Marni drops her face in her hands to hide her blush-colored cheeks. I lean over and whisper in her ear, "You're cute when you're mad."

She grabs a piece of paper and snatches the pencil from behind my ear and scribbles out in all caps letters, FUCK YOU.

I grab the pencil from her and return the gesture. LATER.

She fights not to smile, but I feel it.

18

Somehow I managed to make it through the school week with Talon breathing down my neck—literally. All except for first period, he sat behind me. In the lunch line, he stood behind me. And today, while we stood there in line waiting for our turn, he placed his hand on my waist as he talked to Tommy and his crew. I'm not even sure if he realized he did it. I'm not sure how he didn't though, with the way my body trembled at his touch. All the blood inside of me rushed to that one spot, and I'd swear there was a heartbeat beneath his fingertips.

The rumor mill has been in overdrive this week. Most assume that Talon and I are an item. Neither of us has validated nor denied those claims, particularly because it's better to let them believe the rumors than the truth.

It's been a struggle not to lay it all out there for Talon. The fact that I know someone recorded me, Zed coming in my room and touching me—me letting him touch me. If I wanted Zed dead, this would be my golden opportunity. Yet, I've kept my mouth shut. Though, my heart still feels the sting of it all.

My hand hovers over Axel's name while I stand outside.

My eyes shooting in every direction to be sure that no one is about to pop out, shout, or attack. I've gone back and forth for days on whether or not I should call Axel. I know he'd be here in a heartbeat if he knew that I was in trouble. He'd help me make an escape from the hold that these four guys have on me.

The sad part is, there is one that I'm not sure I want to run too far from. There is this magnetic pull between Talon and I and every time we're drawn together, we force ourselves apart. He's controlling and bossy and he drives me batshit crazy. We fight constantly, and most days, I want to beat him over the head and bury him next to Josh. But then I look at him when he's not watching and I see a guy who has never been loved by a single hand that's touched him. I see a person who longs to feel alive and for some screwed up reason, he awakens life inside of me, too.

He hurts me, but he also protects me.

Maybe I'll call Axel tomorrow.

Sliding the door closed quietly behind me, I tiptoe up the stairs, hoping that the guys are too involved in their game to notice me. When I reach the top, I immediately spot Talon at the end of the hall. His back is pressed to the wall with one foot kicked up behind him. A few wispy strands of hair hang over his left eye, but the other one is zeroed in on me beneath a cocked brow. "Where the hell were you?"

"I needed some air." I walk toward my bedroom door, but his thunderous strides in my direction have me halting.

"Or some privacy?"

Yep. Though, I don't say it. There's no way I could even attempt to make a call in this house with all the eyes and cameras. I found the hidden one in my room stuck to a painted picture. It was about the size of a pencil eraser. I tore that sucker down and flushed it down the toilet. Even if I got that one, I can't be certain there aren't more.

"I'm not in the mood to argue. It was an extra-long day at school today."

"That must be why I'm so exhausted." He pats his mouth and fakes a yawn. "I couldn't figure it out, but now that you mention it, school is alotta work." There is something different in his tone. He's not being abrasive or domineering. There are no crude comments or sexual innuendos.

"So go to bed."

His eyes land on my lips, and chills dance down my back when his index finger trails along my cheekbone and down to my mouth. He leans closer and whispers, "Come with me."

My heart skips a beat. "I don't feel like playing your games tonight. I'm just gonna shower and go to bed." I twist the handle behind me and the door gives way.

He shakes his head. "No games." His body walks into mine, and we push through the open door. Wrapping his hands around my waist, he pulls me close and those chills only multiply, sending my heart and my head into a frenzy. He tugs the lobe of my ear between his teeth and grazes the skin ever so gently. "Grab your clothes. You can shower and sleep in my room tonight."

Effortlessly, my head tilts to the side. "Why?" My eyes close and I take in every exhale of his breath on my skin. "I thought you didn't let anyone sleep in your bed?"

"You're not just anyone. Besides, you've already slept in it."

"You're right, I'm not. I'm someone you claim to hate. So, tell me why?" I take a step back so that I can see his face. I need to read his expression because his words lie.

"Because I wanna be near you."

Wide eyes and pouty lips look back at me. A solemn expression with no hidden agenda. I shouldn't, but I believe him. I always knew that somewhere deep inside, buried under the rubble, was a heart that ticked with more than hate. He feels the pull between us, too.

Once I have my bag packed with my bathroom stuff and some pajamas, I follow Talon up to his room. It feels weird. Really fucking weird. I slept in his room before, but I wasn't given a choice. Now here I am, of my own freewill. Gripping my bag tightly to my chest, I swallow down any notion that this is a trap. I hate that I feel so on edge around him. I'm so afraid to let my guard down because I fear he'll use it against me.

Reaching into his pocket, he pulls out his keys and drops them on the dresser. Followed by the thud of his wallet and his phone. "Shower's yours. Towels are in the closet."

Taking my bag with me, I go inside the bathroom and begin searching for cameras. I pull open the cabinet mirror on the wall, over the sink, and see a bottle of pills. *Zepro.* Which is a mood stabilizer. One of the many that Mom used to take. I pick I up and read the expiration date. September, and the bottle is still full. Hmm, maybe he stopped taking them.

I set the bottle back inside the cabinet and continue my search. There's the typical male necessities. Shaving cream, a few bottles of high-end cologne, a tube of toothpaste. Boring stuff and nothing that screams *he's watching me.* I scope out the walls and the corners and each step has my stomach filling with anger that I have to even do this.

The door swings open, and my heart jumps into my throat. "Everything ok in here?"

"Geez, Talon, I could have been naked." I unzip my bag and begin pulling out my shower supplies.

"You should have been. You've been here in for ten minutes and you haven't even turned the shower on." His hand presses against the doorframe. "Were you going through my things?"

I could lie. But I don't. "Sure was. Just making sure that the guys downstairs aren't streaming a live feed of me getting undressed in your bathroom." Regardless of *who* recorded me, someone did, and right now I can't trust anyone in this house.

"Even if there was a live feed, which there's not, I wouldn't share."

Liar.

I fight the urge to scream it at him and demand the truth along with answers to every fucked-up thing that has happened.

Here I am falling for this guy, at least that's what it feels like, and he's been using me. And I've let him! I've let them all do whatever they please with me. I can't imagine how pathetic I look. I bet they laugh at night when I'm sleeping because they have me right where they want me.

This was a bad idea. I never should have agreed to spend the night with him. Being here like this, it's wrong. This isn't us. Talon and I yell and scream at each other until an insatiable hunger consumes us. One so strong that we are forced to satisfy it. This whole scenario feels too intimate. Far too intimate for a guy who is mind fucking me.

"I couldn't find my toothbrush." I grab it from the bag and hold it up.

Without a word, he walks out the door and closes it behind him.

Before I get in, I let the shower run for a few minutes and when I step inside, I do what I've done during every shower for the last year. I cry.

Full on snot nose, heaving sobs. I cry for my mom. I cry for my dad. I cry for the life that I had that was ripped away from me by the cartel that sucked my dad in. For the cancer that took my mom. For the sleepless nights and tired days. For the body-numbing anxiety, and just plain old fucking life. This dark hole that has sucked me in and no matter how hard I try to climb out, I keep getting pulled deeper into the pit.

Then there's Talon. A guy who screams dominance and

hostility to the entire world, but shows me a sliver of conviction and I hold on so tightly to it because I'm the one who gets to see it. Not the guys, not the girls from his past. Me. He let me touch it. Balled up in my hand and stuffed inside my heart, I take it out as a reminder every time he does something hostile. Because I *know* that somewhere inside of him, there is a fire that burned out when he was a kid and he so desperately wants to rekindle it. And I want to be the one to light that flame and shield it from the wind.

Minutes pass and the tears have stopped. I wash myself up as if I didn't just have a complete breakdown and I step out to grab a towel, feeling slightly less burdened. My hand wipes over the fogged-up mirror, and I stare back at my swollen eyes, knowing that I can't leave this room until they've settled.

When the bathroom door flies open, I tug the towel around me firmly and avoid looking at him. "Seriously? Again?"

"Damn woman, do you always take hour long showers?"

"As a matter of fact, I do. Now if you don't mind, I'd like to get dressed."

My entire body is now turned to the wall opposite him, and when I sense him coming closer, I tense up.

"Turn around," he says, as he stands directly behind me.

I shake my head no. "Just get out!"

Placing a hand on my shoulder, he turns me around. "Why are you crying?" he asks, all too calmly. As if he's asking me if I want a glass of water.

"I'm not." I lie.

His thumb sweeps under my eyelid. "You were."

Shoving his hand away, I clear my throat. "Talon, just get out! I need to get changed. I'm tired."

"Then get dressed. You had no problem stripping down last week in front of both me and Lars. What's the difference?"

The difference is, I was doing it to prove a point. Now, I'm feeling a clusterfuck of emotions that have me second guessing every stupid thing I've ever done. But, I don't say that. Instead, I swallow my pride and drop the towel. "Fine." My lips curl into a sarcastic smile meant just for him.

I bend down and grab the lotion from my bag, all while watching him. Even as I stand here completely naked, his eyes stay fixed on mine. Squeezing a dollop into my hand, I slop it on my body much quicker than I normally would. As I bend down and rub it on my feet, I'm eye level with Talon's semi that's peeking through the fabric of his grey sweatpants. Gulping, I pick up an oversized t-shirt from my bag and pull it over my head hastily, then slide on a pair of underwear.

I toss my hands out. "Satisfied?"

He looks my entire body up and down. "Hardly, but I'm definitely intrigued." His brows waggle as he takes me by the hand and leads me out of the bathroom.

Beads of water trail down my back from my tangled, soaked hair. I don't even care. I'm too focused on him—on this.

Untucking the blanket from the neatly made bed, I climb under it and tug the silk comforter up to my chin. Talon stands there, watching me, studying me.

"Why were you crying?" he asks again, as he climbs on all fours and crawls toward me.

I shake my head. "I wasn't." My voice cracks, and I know that he's seeing right through the tough facade I'm putting on for him.

"I don't like when you cry."

A bout of laughter rolls out of me. Cynical and breathy. He doesn't like when I cry; yet, he's keeping me here as his imprisoned pet.

One hand presses into the mattress by my rib cage, and the other by my hip, as his face lingers over mine. "Why is that funny?" Feathery strands of hair cascade down his forehead and touch the tip of his nose.

"Because you're the reason for my tears. Isn't that obvious?"

He shakes his head no. "Not all of them. You've been different. What happened?"

Tugging the blanket up further, I roll over to my side and face the wall away from him. He's forced to reposition and does so by lying directly behind me. In my peripheral, I can see his hand levitating over my body. As if he's unsure where to put it. At war with his mind on whether or not he wants to touch me out of something more than loathing. When he drops it to his side, I breathe a sigh of relief. It's not that I don't want him to touch me; I just don't want him to try and comfort me. I don't like being coddled, and something tells me that it would be just as awkward for him.

There's an interval of complete and utter silence.

Until he breaks it. "Who else has touched you."

I roll over on my back and his head shoots up. I look into his eyes. "Why are you asking me this?"

"I need to know. I have to know every man that has ever touched your body sexually."

My brows pinch together and I huff out, "That's not your business!"

Narrow eyes and a twisted expression stare back at me. "It's not, but for my own personal sanity, I have to know. It's eating away at my insides, knowing that there are other men out there who have touched you—tasted you—and felt you from the inside."

Throwing the blanket off from me, I go to get up. "I'm going back to my room."

Strong fingers press to my stomach. "I'm sorry. Please stay." He throws his head back into the pillow, lying completely on his back. "Fuck, Marni. Don't you see what you're doing to me?"

"No. No, I don't. But I think you need to tell me because you're acting even more fucked up than usual."

In one breath, he's on top of me. Clenching my cheeks into his hands and his eyes...they're glistening with dampness. "You're slowly killing me, Marni. I'm so beyond fucked up and each day that you exist, you're slowly slaying my heart."

Opening my mouth to speak, nothing comes out. "I—"

"Something keeps flickering inside of me. It's like a child toying with a light switch. Flicking it up and down and the damn thing either needs to be on or off. It's you. You're fucking with it."

"But I'm not doing anything. Only what you've asked of me."

I have no idea what he's talking about or what is happening right now. I've never seen this side of Talon and I'm not sure what to think. Could it be that he's having regrets? That he feels something for me that has nothing to do with the reason I'm here?

His thumb glides over my lips as he watches the movement. "I've done something, Marni. I had to fucking do it. It was the only way."

My body stills. "What did you do?" His eyes shoot up to mine and something whirls around inside of me that has my heart palpitating. "What the hell did you do?"

"I brought you here as a sacrifice. A pawn in my game of revenge." His head tilts forward as his lips linger over mine. "And now, I have to let you go."

19

TALON

Aggressively, she tries to shove me off of her, but I'm not having it. Not yet. I have one more night with her— one chance to change things, and I'm not about to lose that time.

"Get off me," she bellows, as her fists knock at my chest. "You're freaking me out, Talon. What are you talking about? Sacrifice? Pawn? Have you lost your damn mind?"

I can't get up. She'll run. I have to keep her here and make her understand. To try and rectify what I've done. My head sways back and forth as I linger over her. "It wasn't supposed to be like this." It wasn't, damnit. I wasn't supposed to fall for her.

"Like what?" She screams, "Talk to me. Now!'

Lifting my head up, I look at her. Her big, beautiful blue eyes. Something bites my insides. Something that has no business being there. It's a feeling of...I'm not even sure what it is, but it has my heart feeling like it's doubled in size and it's requiring more of my blood to pump each beat. All I know is, I don't like that look on her face and the sadness in her eyes.

"We had a plan. You were only here as part of it. Get the video, start the conversation and lure him in." I'm not sure why

I'm telling her this. It could ruin everything, but the words spill out like liquid ink. "But you slowly started filling up a space inside of me that has been empty my entire life. I began to feel my pulse and see the sun and damnit, Marni, I felt remorse. I hated what I was doing to you. And I've never regretted anything before this."

Cold fingertips sweep across my forehead, brushing the airy strands of hair from my face. "Does this plan have anything to do with the video you recorded of me?"

Something snaps inside of me. "How the fuck did you know about that?" I watch as she swallows the hard lump in her throat and fear settles in her eyes. "Tell me, damnit!" I shout.

"Zed showed me." Tears well in the corner of her eyes and a new level of rage ensues when one slides down her cheek.

It's not the video. It's something bigger than that. "Did he touch you?"

When she doesn't respond, I have my answer.

My steps reverberate beneath me as I tear open the door, unsure of the interval between lying in bed with her and hurtling down the stairs. Completely oblivious to the words flying through the air that she spews behind me.

I'll kill him with my bare hands.

He's dead.

He's so fucking dead.

"Talon, stop!" she cries out.

I bee-line straight for his door and kick it in. My foot gets tangled in the slivers of separated wood and I rip it out, paying no attention to the chunk burrowed into the skin of my tugged-up pant leg.

I thrash onto the bed and tear through the blankets. *Where the hell is he?*

Spinning around, she's there. Beautiful tears spread down her face like wildfire. "Talon, please. Just stop."

"Where the fuck is he?" I scream at the top of my lungs. Every vein in my body throbs and threatens to pierce through my skin.

I push past her and rush downstairs to where I left them playing video games. Tommy jumps up from where him and Lars are sitting. I see blood red as I lunge at him and take him straight down to the floor. "Where the fuck is Zed?"

"Dude. What the actual fuck?" Lars says, as he lifts me off of Tommy.

"Did you assholes know about what he's been up to?" I shout, "Did you?!"

Marni is still mumbling off something to try and calm me, but I pay no attention. I need answers.

"What are you talking about? What who has been up to?" Tommy asks, as he brushes himself off.

"Zed! He showed her the video and—" I can't even say it. For one, I don't even know what he did to her, but I know he did something. Second, if the words escape my mouth, my entire body will combust.

"Zed left after you went upstairs. Said that he wanted to start the first phase of his plan."

Pointing at Marni, I scream, "She's his plan."

The son of a bitch. I knew he couldn't be trusted.

Marni steps closer, joining the circle we stand in. "Would someone tell me what the hell is going on right now before I run out of this house and never come back."

"I need a minute." I walk away abruptly into the kitchen and out the back door. I slam it shut behind me and it ricochets open a couple inches. The fresh air hits my face and I can slowly feel my heart return to a somewhat normal rhythm.

When the door slides back open, I spin around ready to take action, but it's Tommy. I pinch the bridge of my nose. "Sorry, man. Didn't mean to come at you like that."

"It's fine. Just fill me in. What the hell happened?"

I point into the night, even though Zed isn't around. "That sick bastard has been playing her behind our backs." My voice cracks. "He fucking touched her, Tommy."

Tommy's eyes widen. "He what?"

"Yeah. And he showed her the video. I haven't gotten the full story, but I know exactly what he's doing."

"I think I'm his act of revenge. Think about it. He's using her to get to me."

"Nah," Tommy sweeps the air with his hand, "that's old news. You two moved past that a long time ago."

"Did we? Or did we just sweep it under the rug because it was easier that way? Come on, would you forgive one of your best friends if they supplied the pills that killed your mom?"

Tommy doesn't respond, but the look on his face says it all.

A gust of wind tears through, sending an eerie feeling into the night,

"We need to call this thing off. I'll find another way. It'll take some time, but I'll figure it out," I tell him. There will be more opportunities. Maybe not now, but someday, I'll get my vengeance.

"You're sure you wanna end it? You've worked hard for this. You deserve it."

"Do you not see that girl standing in there?" I turn and look through the glass door. "She's been through hell."

"Don't get me wrong, I'll gladly step aside and let you stop it all, but wasn't that the plan? What's changed?"

"Everything." Everything has changed.

Through the door, Marni comes into view, and she's not pleased. Her sassy steps lead her out here and I know she's loaded with questions. "We need to talk." Her arms cross over her chest, and her eyes threaten more tears.

My hand lands on the small of her back. "Not out here. Come on." Glancing back at Tommy, I nod. "We'll find another way."

Once we're back in my bedroom, Marni sits on the bed with her feet on the floor. Her eyes stay fixated on her fingers as she picks at her nails.

Pacing the length of the room, I begin chewing on my thumbnail. "I know this is confusing as hell for you."

Her head lifts. "Ya think?"

Just when I go to speak, her phone sounds in her hand. "Who is it?" I rush over to her side.

She ends the call and drops her phone back down. "Just my dad."

Dropping to my knees in front of her, I rub both hands up and down the top of her legs. I could sugarcoat this shit. Sprinkle in some lies and put a bow on it, but instead, I just lay it all out there. "When I was thirteen years old, I watched my dad drag my mom across the kitchen floor by her hair, leaving a trail of liquid. Only it wasn't blood, it was her own urine. The blood was still caked in her hair and drying by the time he was finished with her." I don't look up as I continue. I can't look at her out of fear she'll see him inside of me. "He beat her so bad that she passed out and pissed herself. I didn't even care. Her eyes were rolled into the back of her head and she could have been dead for all I knew. Yet, I felt nothing."

"Talon—"

"Let me finish." I hold up a finger as I continue, "They say that somewhere deep down all parents love their children, but my mom and dad weren't like others. They were incapable of love. When I watched him pull her away, do you wanna know what I said?" I finally look up at her. "I asked him if he needed help." Her expression isn't fearful or calloused. The eyes I'm staring into are laced with pity.

"I craved his acceptance and his love. It's all I ever wanted."

A tear drops onto my hand that's still rested on her leg. Sweeping it away, I muster up the courage to get to the point.

"His cold eyes sought me out and he dropped Mom's head to the floor with a thud and strutted toward me. She was finished off for now—alive, but no fight left in her—I was his new target for the remainder of the night. He was a monster." I recant that, "He *is* a monster. And he deserves to pay for the misery he inflicted on me and my sister. We are forever fucked up because of him." Getting to my feet, I begin pacing again. "That night I made a solemn vow that, one day, I would kill the mother fucker. That day was supposed to be tomorrow."

What started as a void inside of me, when I started telling her my truth, has blossomed back into rage and an overpowering desire to carry out my plan, even if it doesn't involve Marni anymore. One day, he will pay.

I'm looking out the window into the night of nothingness when she walks up behind me. Comforting hands wrap around my waist and her head rests on my back. It feels foreign. To have someone pacify me out of sheer concern.

"You shouldn't try and comfort me. Because there's more."

She doesn't budge. "Tell me everything."

I could let this all go right now. Tell her a lie and keep her in my life until she's sick of me and wants to leave. Or, I could tell her the truth and set her free.

"I never heard of the WatchMeNow app until I was packing up my things in the old house and found a box of papers my dad left behind. It had his username and password on it. I downloaded the app, logged into his account and searched through his entire history. I talked to so many random women before I found you."

Her hands drop, and she takes a step back. Her displeasure shows in the reflection staring back at me through the window. "You found my profile on your dad's account? Please tell me, he wasn't—"

"No," I spin around. "He never talked to you, at least not then. I did an area search and found Josh. I was desperate to find anyone in Redwood who had connections to the app and to him. I wanted to find him, Marni. I wanted to find him and kill him. So, Josh and I met up. Most people don't list their location, because most people are smart—like you. Josh was an idiot. Anyways, he ranted and raved about a girl from Redwood who bared all on there. He said she was in the top ten for most *interactive*." I quote with my fingers.

Marni's hand slaps over her mouth, but I keep going. "Josh didn't just watch you on the app. He watched you at night from outside your window. He was fucking obsessed with you."

Color drains from her face, and I extend an arm when I think she might pass out. Instead, she shoves it away and rushes to the bathroom. "I'm gonna be sick."

Heaves and sobs come from the bathroom as I stand here looking at myself in the reflection of the window. All of this is my fault. Zed would have never touched her if I didn't lure her in. I practically fed her to him on a silver platter.

No. This is *his* fault. All of this is because Dad fucked up my life and created a monster inside of me—a monster that is meant to be unleashed on him.

When the sounds from the bathroom stop, and she doesn't return, I knock on the door. "Marni?"

Still nothing.

That's to be expected. She fucking hates me. Why wouldn't she?

"Please, let me finish."

"This is all too much. Josh, your dad, everything your dad did to you."

Sliding my back down the door, I can feel her on the other side. "You hearing us in the room that night wasn't an accident, it was strategically planned. We saw an opportunity and we took it. Paid some random chick five-hundred bucks to wait for you to use the bathroom then send you upstairs. We watched every step you made through the cameras. We needed assurance that we could force this on you and leave you with no choice. That's why we gathered evidence that could incriminate you. Because this whole time, our end game was getting you to meet my dad, and I was prepared to use the evidence against you if you didn't."

It sounds so much worse saying it out loud to her. Talking it over with the guys felt like child's play. Adrenaline rushed and excitement roared. We were all in. Ready to drag Marni through hell and back, so I could kill my father. I just never expected whatever this is. And I sure as hell didn't expect Zed to turn on us.

"Did you plan to kill me, too?"

"God no. Never, Marni. That was never the plan."

"What about Josh's death? How did it happen?"

Dragging my bottom teeth between my lip, I bite down. Fuck. I can't go there with her. I just can't. That's one topic that's off-limits.

"It was an accident. That's all you need to know. Please don't dig any further because it will only make things worse."

"Fine. What happened with the app?"

"That night at Briarwood, I changed your password on the app. I've been pretending to be you while I talk to him in a private chat window. I used the video of you as bait." I stop talking to see if she has anything to say. When she doesn't, I go on. "It worked. He's prepared to meet you tomorrow."

It's quiet. Far too quiet.

"You changed my password?"

"I assumed you'd figure that much out by now."

I can hear the handle turn, so I jump to my feet. The door opens, and she's standing there with a bunched up tissue in her hand. "I haven't logged into the app in weeks. RebelSin was the only reason I even bothered with it anymore."

"What about the other guys?"

"There were others in the beginning, but it was just a few

shots and live feeds for fun. In the end, there was only you." She steps closer, surprising us both. "Would taking your dad's life give you yours back, Talon?"

I nod.

"You're sure?" Her brows raise. "Because once it's done, it's done."

"He needs to pay for what he's done. Not only to me and Blakely, but also for Jasper's mom. She died because of him. So yeah," I nod again, "I'm sure."

Her hands wrap around my neck and that foreign feeling returns. "Then let's make him pay."

20

MARNI

There is no way I can begin to fathom what Talon has been through. I've basically lived my life as an orphan, but my parents do love me. Dad might love his job more, and Mom may have had an odd way of showing her love, but it existed. I could lie and tell Talon that deep down his parents did love him, but I truly don't think they did. His dad is the devil incarnate, and I'm not above an exorcism that sends his soul straight to hell. I've never killed anyone, and I don't plan to now, but Talon deserves a shot at life. He can't rest easy until his dad can no longer touch him or anyone else.

I don't look at it as murder—I call it justice. The death penalty that he deserves.

"What are you thinking about?" I say to Talon, as my head rests on his chest. He's been quiet ever since I agreed to help him. There is so much more that I need to know, so many unanswered questions, and as soon as this is over, I will demand answers.

"You'll be the first person I've ever shared a bed with."

I look up at him, resting my chin on his chest. "Really? No ex-girlfriends or one-night stands?"

His chin tucks as he tries to look at my eyes. "I don't usually like sleeping next to others. You'll probably laugh at this, but I've never even cuddled with a girl before."

"I would never laugh at that." I sort of understand it. He rejects affection because he's not used to it. It's like caging a lion and expecting the wild animal to let you pet it. It takes time. "But, why me?"

"Don't know. I keep asking myself the same thing. Aside for the obvious, you're sexy as hell, but you also do something to me that I can't explain. It's this overpowering need to be near you. To protect you. To touch you." His fingers trail up and down my arm, leaving behind a path of goosebumps. "Now you get to tell me why you're still here? Why stay in my darkness?"

My shoulders shrug. "Maybe I like your darkness. It ignites a flame in my lightless world."

Talon begins to scoot up, taking me with him. With his back pressed to the headboard, I do the same. "I need to know what happened that night?"

I knew this was coming. I'm just not sure I'm ready to talk about it, yet. Talon is furious with Zed, but there's a part of me that worries he'll blame me for not stopping it. I drop back down and roll over to face the wall. I can't look at his face when I explain.

"Please, Marni. I need to know, or it will continue to eat through me until there is nothing left."

"I really don't think you wanna know. We should just let it go."

"Not a chance in hell."

He has no idea what he's asking for. He knows Zed touched me, but he doesn't know it was on the inside or that he was sleeping on the floor—because I drugged him.

"You know how I took your phone?"

"Yeah."

There's a shift in the mattress, and I know he's peering over to look at my face, but I pinch my eyes shut. "I needed to transfer the data to a SD card, but you were everywhere I went. So I did something."

"Wait a minute. You have a card with my phone data on it? What kind of data?" His body shoots back to the headboard hastily as it crashes against the wall.

"I don't have it, but there's more."

"What happened?" he quips.

"I put a sleeping pill in your drink." My lips press together and I clench my eyes shut. Opening one eye, I expect him to make a move, but he's still in the same spot.

"You knocked me out?" He laughs. He actually fucking laughs.

"I'm sorry. If I'd thought for a second about your history with pills, I would have never done it, but it slipped my mind and I was desperate."

"I suspected something along those lines happened." He pauses. "Ok. I can forgive you for that. After all, I've done worse."

"I got you upstairs before you completely passed out and you pretty much fell to the floor in my room and went to sleep. Then I snuck away and transferred the data."

"Why the hell didn't you just turn my phone on and snoop?"

"Well, there's the passcode block. I also worried you were tracking it, so I only turned it on to transfer the data then shut it right back off."

"Ok, that's not important. Where does Zed fit into all of this?"

Tugging the blanket up over my shoulders, I attempt to hide the chills that have washed over me. "When I got back, you were still sleeping on the floor. I covered you up and crawled into bed. A couple minutes later, he came in."

Talon leaps off the bed. I don't turn around to see what he's doing. I just get this over with. "He got in the bed with me. Showed me the video and tried to turn me against you. Which, at that time, wasn't difficult."

"Did you fuck him?!" he blurts out, gruff and unmannered.

My body shoots to a sitting position in a knee-jerk reaction. "No!"

"Then what the hell happened, Marni? You just laid there and cuddled all night while bashing me?"

I shake my head, dropping my tone. "No. He took my pants off and..." My words trail off.

"And what, damnit?"

"He fingered me."

Shivers roll through me and my body jolts up when the lamp on his dresser is torn from the outlet and thrown across the room. Black splinters of ceramic coat the floor, leaving the wall with a dented smudge. His jaw ticks with ferocity. "And you fucking let him?"

Tears slide down my cheeks, and I swipe them away. "I was scared." Curling my legs up to my chest, I secure them in a hug. "I didn't know what to do. I froze up and I just let him have his way with me knowing that it wouldn't last forever."

Talon storms off into the bathroom, and the door slams shut. Breaking out in a full-blown ugly cry, I bury my face between my legs. Wet drops of tears slide down my legs and my heart writhes into a million little knots.

I didn't want that. I didn't ask for Zed to do that to me. But I let it happen. I'm weak. Even if I can count on one hand how many men I've slept with, I still feel like a whore.

Minutes pass and Talon doesn't come out. He just needs a few minutes to cool off. So I give it to him.

Five minutes later, he's still not out.

Tossing the blanket over me, I walk over to the door.

"Talon. Can I come in?" I give the handle a turn, and to my surprise, it's not locked. "Talon," I say again.

My heart falls from my chest. "Oh my god, Talon. What in the hell are you doing?" I hurry over to where he sits with his back against the bathtub while blood trickles down his side.

"Get the fuck out!" he screams. So loud that I can feel the echo through my entire body. "Out!" he shouts again, pointing the bloody razor blade at the door.

Completely ignoring him, I grab him by the wrist. 'Why are you doing this?" I cry out. The blade drops to the floor, and I kick it away, watching as the blood smears a line across the white marbled floor.

"I have to. I have to cut out the burn," he mumbles.

I gasp. That's what the scars over the burn are. He cuts himself there.

Talon's head drops, his chin falling to his chest. Grabbing the hand towel off the sink, I lift his shirt and hold it in place. Then I just hold him. I have a lifetime to get answers.

Right now, this is what he needs.

He needs me.

∞

WE SAT on the bathroom floor for over an hour in complete silence. I've never seen Talon in that state—I've never seen anyone like that before. It's like his mind was paralyzed. When he finally snapped out of it, he was humiliated. The cuts were just on the surface, so all he needed was some bandages, but he wouldn't let me help. Instead of being too overbearing, I laid down in bed and gave him some privacy.

A few minutes later, he joined me and asked that we never speak of it again. I agreed, for now. Sleep didn't come easy, even though Talon held me all night long. Maybe that was the problem. Neither of us is used to bodily contact when we sleep.

When I woke up this morning, Talon was already preparing for the day. I just joined them downstairs, and I'm attempting to mentally prepare myself for what's coming.

Lars stuffs a few water bottles into his backpack then zips it up. "You ready for this?" he asks Talon, who's tapping into his phone.

"More than ready. I'm fucking pumped." He howls.

Apparently, we are driving four hours to San Diego to meet up with his dad. I don't know the full details, and I don't care to. All I know is that I have to stand outside of some park, so he can see that I'm real, before texting me the address where we'll be meeting.

My nerves are shot. Anxiety is at an all-time high, but I'm ready to take this fucker down. This sick and sadistic man has tortured so many lives. I'd bet my life that he still is. He's willing to meet an eighteen-year-old girl because he thinks he's gonna get a piece of ass. His mind is twisted, and it's apparent that he never learned right from wrong. Sadly, his son still needs to learn. But there's still time for Talon, and I've seen a side of him I'm not sure anyone else has ever seen. There is good in him.

After Talon stuffs his phone in his pocket, he comes to my side. "Are you sure *you're* ready for this? You can still back out."

Without even giving it a second thought, I tell him, "I'm all in."

This morning feels so different. I'm not sure what to make of it. It's not like a relationship bloomed in just twenty-four hours. Besides, Talon's not the relationship type, and I'm really not either. He and I together would be a fucking tsunami. All we do is bicker and fight. He likes to crawl under my skin, and I like to dig my nails into his.

"Alright. Let's hit the road." Talon smacks my ass. I bite back a few choice words and just walk away.

"Anyone heard from Zed?" Tommy asks, as we walk out the door.

Talon responds, "If he knows what's good for him, he'll never show his damn face in this town again. We had a pact, and he stepped over the line and double-crossed us. It wasn't just her and I. It was all of us." His voice grows louder and louder with each word until he's screaming. "He tried to fuck with my plan, and he's trying to fuck with me."

"Chill, man. We've got your back." Tommy holds up his knuckles in front of Talon as we walk. "Start to finish."

Talon bumps back. "And all the in between."

Lars is being abnormally quiet as he shadows behind us. Maybe he's having doubts about this. I could understand that. It's not like we're taking a road trip to the beach. Knowing what's coming definitely has me feeling uneasy. But, this isn't about me, or Lars, or anyone else. It's about Talon finding the peace to move on with his life.

We get to Talon's truck parked in the middle of the driveway, and I open the back door. Talon's hand slaps it, forcing it closed. "Get in the front. They're driving separate."

"Aren't we all going to the same place?"

"We are. But we need the second vehicle, and I wanted some alone time with you." He peers down at me with hooded eyes. "Gotta problem with that?"

Arching my brows, I shove him playfully. "No. No problem at all." Our eyes stay locked until I round the truck and climb in.

Once he's settled in the driver's seat, his hand makes its way over to my lap with the other on the steering wheel. He catches me looking at it. "Is that ok?"

I bite back a smile then tangle my fingers in his. "Is that ok?"

He chuckles. "Yeah, I think I can handle that."

This is strange. So damn strange, but I'm loving every minute that he makes me feel alive. Even if we are on the road to mass destruction.

I'm unsure how long we're into the drive when I lift my head and rub the sleep from my eyes. "How long was I out?" Glancing down, I notice we're still holding hands, and my stomach does a little flip.

"Couple hours. We're halfway there. Tommy just called and they're stopping at the next rest stop."

"Good. I need some coffee."

"Didn't sleep well last night?" he asks, with his eyes still on the road.

"You could say that. You, on the other hand, slept like a baby."

Smirking, he looks over at me. "I always do. Especially when I'm knocked out with sleeping pills."

We pull into the rest stop and Tommy is hanging out the driver's side window with his arms in the air. As soon as Talon rolls my window down, Tommy shouts, "Bout fucking time."

Lars has his seat reclined and a ball cap over his face. Talon leans forward with his arm draped over the steering wheel and nods at Lars. "Has he been sleeping the whole ride?"

"I think he's sick or something. Hasn't said a damn word." Tommy shrugs. "Hurry your asses up. We need to get back on the road, so I can get him outta this car before he vomits."

"Alright then," I say, "I have to use the bathroom and then I'm hitting up whatever coffee vending they have in there." God, I hope it's not actual vending machine coffee.

"They've actually got a couple fast food places inside. Pretty decent rest stop," Tommy says.

I look over at Talon. "You coming?" He gives me a nod, and we both get out.

"Make it quick," Tommy shouts as we walk away.

When we get inside, I turn toward the ladies' room and expect Talon to go in the opposite direction to the men's room. Only he's right on my tail. I turn around and begin pushing him out. "What are you doing? You can't come in here."

"I sure as hell can. And I will. There's no fucking way I'm leaving you alone in a place like this."

Taking a step back, I cross my arms over my chest. "It's a bathroom, Talon. People generally use them alone."

"Most people do. You do not." He grabs my hand and pulls me into the double-sized stall.

I huff. "Talon Porter, get out of here right now."

Shutting the door, he slides the lock across then places both hands on my waist. My head tilts when his face nuzzles into the fold of my neck. "You looked so damn sexy while you were sleeping with your mouth wide open. All I could think about was filling it with my cock."

Quivers descend down my side where his hands rest, sliding down my thighs and settling between my legs. "We can't. Not here," I mutter under my breath.

"Sure we can. I'd take you on the hood of my truck in the parking lot if I wanted to. Unless you'd rather suck me while I drive."

Cold fingers snake up the sides of my shirt, and my eyes close on impulse. Grazing beneath my bra, Talon cups both breasts in his hands, before rolling my nipples between his thumb and index finger.

"Alright. Guess we'll wait until we get back home tonight," he grumbles in my ear as he teases my nipples.

I can feel my arousal dampen my panties and while this isn't the most desired place, or the most sanitary, I don't think I have the strength to walk out of here unsatisfied. "No," I say in a breathy moan.

"That's what I thought. Now drop your pants." I do as I'm told but let them linger around my legs, without taking them completely off. "Turn around." His pants zipper slides down and his keys clank together when they hit the floor through his jeans.

With my hand pressed to the inner wall of the stall, I roll my hips to give him easy access, but he grabs my leg, takes off my flip flop and frees one leg from my leggings. "What are you doing?" I twist my head to catch a glimpse of him. His mouth is agape and his glazed eyes stare back at me. Instead of answering me, he slides my flip flop back on and hoists my leg up with one foot on the toilet that sits to the right of me.

The silky head of his cock begins probing at my entrance in a circular motion. "You've been a naughty girl." Fingers tangle in my hair. Wrapping around them like a rubber band. When he tugs the bunched-up mess, my head jerks back. "You drugged me, snuck out of my house, and let another man touch you while I slept on your bedroom floor." Unease curdles in my stomach like sour milk. "It's time for you to be punished." His dick slams so hard into me that my forehead ricochets off the metal stall.

I gasp and moan and curl my toes as he fucks me from behind. "Oh my God," I choke out with a pent-up exhale. Unyielding strokes have him claiming my pussy like it's his and his alone.

"Did you like it when he touched you?"

What?

My body tenses up, and I clench my walls around him. I go to move my leg off the toilet, but he puts it right back in place, like that too belongs to him.

"Answer me, damnit. Did you like it?" When I don't respond, he pulls my hair so hard that It feels like my scalp may peel off. With my head hanging back and his grip holding it in place, his eyes look into mine. "This pussy is mine. If anyone ever touches it again, I'll sew it shut. Got it?"

Blinking, I agree with a nod. Once my hair is released from

his fist, his hips roll in a clockwise motion, while his dick stretches me to the fullest, making me cry out in pleasurable pain.

When his groin begins vibrating off my ass at an impetuous speed, I lose complete control of my body and any sounds that escape. "Fuck!" I slap one hand to the wall. "Holy shit, Talon." He hammers me from behind and just as I'm about to explode and soak the floor of this stall, I hear the creak of the rusted-out hinges of the bathroom door open. My body freezes.

Talon leans over, his chest pressed to my back. "Shh," he whispers, as his hand curls under my legs, and he begins circling my nub while my foot is still perched on the toilet.

My body trembles, and when he slides his dick in and out of me, while flicking his fingertips against my clit. I watch as the beige loafers inch closer to the door and follow them until they are out of sight. An impalpable, uncontrollable, and undeniable sensation overwhelms me and I can't contain myself when I whimper in pleasure. "Oh, God."

"Shhh," he whispers again, but I know he's fucking with me, trying to make me scream.

An electric shock courses through my veins. Pulsating around his cock, I explode in a frenzy and feel the remnants of my orgasm drip down my leg.

Without letting up, he rides me through my orgasm and grabs me by the hips. Bouncing off of my ass, one final thrust has him releasing and spilling his cum all over my back and dribbling down my side.

"Sick. That's what y'all are. Just sick." I hear the squeal of an elderly lady as the beige shoes walk past the stall again. I laugh. "We're sick? She didn't even wash her hands."

Completely ignoring my presence, Talon turns his body to the toilet and lets his softening dick linger over it. He looks at me and catches my wry look. "What?" He shrugs. "I told you I had to piss."

Shaking my head, I unroll a wad of toilet paper and begin cleaning myself up. Once Talon shakes and tucks then zips his pants, I cross my arms and nod toward the door. With a sigh, he flushes the toilet and exits the stall, so I can pee next.

I'm not surprised to see him when I walk out of the stall. Legs crossed at the ankles, back against the sinks with his phone in hand. "Someone is all too eager to meet you." His eyes perk up.

Rolling my eyes, I walk to the sink and wash my hands. "If only I could reciprocate his enthusiasm."

Talon walks up behind me and begins kissing my neck. "Don't worry. I'd never let him lay a finger on you. You trust me, right?"

He spins me around, and I pat my wet hands on his t-shirt. "I don't know yet." I pause. "Do you trust me? Because after the things you said in that stall, I'm not so sure you do."

"What aspect of trust are you talking about?" He cocks a brow. "Because relationship trust and basic trust are two different things, and we're not in a relationship, Marni."

I can feel my face flush. Not out of embarrassment, but anger. "I never said we were." I push off from him and head for the door.

He eats up the space between us quickly. "Then what's the problem?"

"For the record, I don't want a relationship with you either, but you don't have to be such an ass about it."

He chuckles, and it makes me wanna shove his face in the pile of dog shit we just walked past. "How was I being an ass. I was just stating the facts."

"Jesus Christ, did someone fall in the fucking toilet," Tommy says, as Talon and I walk straight for the truck. Ignoring him, we both open our doors and get in. "And where the hell is your coffee?" he shouts even louder.

Damnit. I knew I left more than my dignity in that building.

"Tell me how I was being an ass?" He repeats himself, as he revs up the engine.

Resting my hand on my cheek with my elbow on the door ledge, I let out a deep breath. "When aren't you an ass?"

Talon and I argue on a daily basis, but my lips threaten a hint of smile when I realize that this is our first argument about *us*. Technically, there isn't an us. And even though I feel like socking him right now, there isn't anyone else I wanna have fights with after fucking in the bathroom stall at a rest stop.

I sneak a peek at him, letting my pride take a back seat, and he flashes me a smile. "What?"

"Nothing." I smile back.

21

TALON

When you feel like you'd rather be on the edge of a cliff, ready to plunge to your death, than turn around and face another day, you know it's time to make a change. That's when I set this plan in motion. I went to the guys and I told them I needed their help and, naturally, they stood in my corner. We swore we'd take on this quest together. Zed, of course, perked up and asked what was in it for them. That's when we made the pact. Four acts of revenge - one shot each.

We lost one, but he's been replaced by someone better.

Tucking a chunk of Marni's hair behind her ear, I force her scared eyes on mine. "Do you trust me?" I ask again, because last time I didn't get the response I wanted.

"I want to." Her voice is shaky, yet calm and collected.

"The stuff I said in the bathroom stall, that was just fore-play. Gets me going. It wasn't my way of trying to belittle you. You know that, right?"

She nods. "I get that. I just wish you wouldn't bring it up, especially like that."

"Won't happen again."

"And Talon…" Her tongue darts out to her lips, wetting

them as she prepares for what's coming. I know that tone enough by now to know she wants something. "I won't talk about what I walked in on last night...after this."

My head shakes. "Don't."

"I need to know why?"

I drop my hands and rest my back against the seat. Staring straight ahead at the park across the street, I notice a little boy running while a golden lab chases after him. He's eight, maybe nine years old. There's no hiding that happiness. He looks back, feeling the security of having his parents nearby.

"I got a burn when I was a kid. Got some cuts on it. No big deal." I lie. She looks at me with that pitiful look again. "It's just an ugly scar. Drop it!" I can feel myself getting angrier as each second passes.

"Your scars aren't ugly, Talon. They're beautiful."

I laugh. "What the hell could possibly be beautiful about a scar that spreads the length of your side and your back?"

"Because it's yours. It's your story. It's your past and your redemption." She shrugs a shoulder. "I happen to like it."

"You wouldn't like it if it was your story."

"We all have scars."

She's still lingering between the two seats when I grab her by the waist, pick her up, and bring her over to my lap. Once she's adjusted, with her legs wrapped around either side of me, I graze my fingers under her shirt, lifting it up and admiring her flawless skin. "Looks like a good life to me."

"Just because you can't see them doesn't mean they aren't there."

Gripping both sides of her head in my hand, I press my lips to hers. Effortlessly, passionately, and totally mind-numbing.

I'm beginning to welcome that feeling that trickles through me time and time again when she's near. The backside of her hand sweeps up and down my neck over the scratches she left behind. "Show me your scars and I'll show you mine," I mutter into her tantalizing mouth. She seduces me without even realizing she's doing it.

Methadone has nothing on this girl. She's my own personal drug, an addiction I have no intentions of detoxing.

A knock on the driver's window startles both of us. Marni climbs off of me, and I roll down the window. "It's showtime," Tommy says with wide eyes.

Looking over at Marni, I search for her consent. Anything that tells me this is what she wants, even if she doesn't. No one wants this. No one but me.

She fakes a smile. "I'm fine. Let's do it."

Reaching over, I fluff her hair out for her, pick a speck of fuzz off of her black shirt, and grab the lipstick from the center console that she brought. I hand it to her and she takes the top off, smearing the red wax across her lips and smacking them together.

Ignoring that fact that I'm primping the girl I've recently started to tolerate, which says a lot because I don't tolerate many, I give her a once-over. A crop top that has her tits popping out of the v of her neckline. A pair of tight skinny jeans and black ankle boots that add an extra couple inches to her height. "

You're so fucking sexy." I lean across the center console and kiss her ruby red lips. Swiping my finger beneath her bottom lip, I wipe the excess then do the same to mine.

"There's time for that shit later. Let's go," Tommy barks from the door.

"Take this." I hand Marni my phone with the app open. "When you get to the bench just sit there and wait. He'll message you an address. Screenshot it and send it to Tommy's phone. When I give you the ok, walk casually over to Tommy's car." I point to the opposite end of the parking lot where Lars is walking toward us. "The keys will be inside. Get in and drive it out front of the bowling alley and Lars will be waiting there for you. He'll drive you to the hotel. I'll have my eyes on you the entire time. I promise."

"And I won't see you until it's done?"

"It's best if you aren't there. You don't need that shit on your conscience."

A smile tugs her mouth upward. "I trust you."

I don't deserve those words. Not by a long shot. As much as I want her trust, she really shouldn't give it to me.

Watching as she walks away, I feel a sense of relief that this is coming to an end.

"She's gonna be fine," Tommy reassures me, as he leans against the window.

"Yeah." I nod. "I appreciate you coming with me. But I meant what I said, you don't have to be there. I can do this alone. I *should* do this alone."

"No. You shouldn't." He taps the tattoo on my forearm. "I've got your back."

22

MARNI

Wind gusts, causing particles of sand to pelt the bare skin of my arms. My eyes stay focused on the bench as I hug myself tightly. Nausea creeps into my stomach, and I begin to feel lightheaded. I attribute that to the extra blood flow to my heart as my beats kick into overdrive.

There are so many eyes on me right now that I'm not sure how I'll ever be able to sit down and pretend everything is normal. It's not just Talon, Tommy, and Lars—it's Talon's dad. I don't see him, but I can feel him watching me with motive and intent. I'm not sure what he has planned, and I don't wanna know. But just the idea of what he could potentially do to me if this wasn't a set-up sends a wave of panic through my entire body. Drawing in deep breaths, I remind myself that this *is* a set-up and I'm not alone. The guys are here and they won't let anything happen to me.

I sit down on the cold metal bench and my hands tremble as I hold out the phone and wait for his message. I set it on my lap and tuck my hands beneath my legs to try and stop them from shaking, then I look around. Tommy's car is within eye sight, but Lars is long gone from it. At least I have the safety net of the guys watching. Talon would never let anything happen to me. In that respect, I do trust him.

When the phone vibrates on my lap, I jump back so forcefully that it falls to the ground. Bending down to pick it up, I tap the app to open it and read the message as I lean back against the bench.

SugarDaddy11: You're even more beautiful in person.

Ew. Gross.

SugarDaddy11: Look up. I want to see your eyes.

Holy shit. How close is this man?

I pick my head up and look around. Then direct my attention back to the phone.

SugarDaddy11: Are you ready to suck on my big cock before I fuck you in the ass?

My stomach turns. I draw in a deep breath, and suddenly, I'm not cold. I'm sweating so badly that my feet feel like they're suffocating in these boots.

Play along, Marni.

SugarDaddy11: Two-thousand dollars should cover that and I'll even suck your pussy in return.

NotYourAngel: If you've got the money, I'll do whatever you want, baby.

SugarDaddy11: That's my girl.

NotYourAngel: Obviously we can't do that here. Tell me where to go. I can't wait to finally touch you.

There's a pause between messages that has me scoping out the park again.

SugarDaddy11: See the black Suburban with the tinted windows by the restrooms? That's me. Why don't you just walk on over here and I'll lay the seats down and fuck you from behind.

My eyes shoot to the restrooms. Sure enough, there he is. He's supposed to give me an address. This wasn't the plan.

Fuck. What do I do?

I turn around to look at the bowling alley parking lot, making sure Talon's truck is still there, but it's too far away and there's traffic on the road that separates us.

Swallowing hard, I take matters into my own hands.

NotYourAngel: Do I look like a cheap fuck? I want a bed and a shower to clean up after. Give me an address that will provide those things or the deal's off.

Another brief pause and then it finally comes through.

SugarDaddy11: Hilts Landing Hotel. Take the elevator to the eighth floor. Room 811. I'll be waiting for you.

Bingo.

NotYourAngel: Can't wait.

Gagging, I screenshot the address and send it to Tommy's phone. Seconds later, he responds.

Tommy: Alright, we're heading out. Don't worry, this is almost over.

Must be Talon I'm talking to. Standing up, I keep my eyes on the Suburban. He still hasn't moved. Before I even realize it, I'm practically running to the car. Slowing my steps once I'm closer, I look over and see that his brake lights are on.

Shit.

With an uncontrollable shake to my hands, I rip open the door, glancing behind me the entire time. Once I'm in, I slam it shut, start the engine and kick it into reverse. The Suburban inches closer and closer, so I toss the phone in the passenger seat, shift the car in drive and peel out of the parking lot. I don't even know where the hell I'm going. My entire body is trembling, and my thoughts are a scrambled mess. Traffic is chaotic with cars coming from both directions, but when I look in the rearview mirror and see his face in the reflection, I pull out. Cutting off a minivan that begins laying on their horn.

White knuckling the steering wheel, I keep heading straight. My eyes migrate back and forth from the road in front of me to the mirror, and I'm pretty sure I lost him, which finally allows me to take a calming breath. I grab the phone and the entire screen is filled with text messages from Tommy's phone. I need to turn around for Lars, but I'm scared he'll follow. Instead, I keep heading straight.

Turning left down a side road, I turn into the back of a gas station parking lot. Twisting my head every which way, I don't see him. I grab the phone and my finger hovers over Lars' name. As I sit here—alone—with no eyes on me, it hits me that I have Talon's phone. Only days ago, I went to hell and back trying to find out what was on this thing. And now I have it—unlocked. I could just trust that I know all I need to know. But as Talon mentioned, there are many aspects of trust, and in this aspect, he hasn't earned it yet.

Starting with text messages. Nothing, just Tommy. Next, I go to his call log.

Fuck. Nothing.

Contacts. There's about a hundred of them and I wouldn't even know where to start.

Facebook? Nah.

Instagram? He doesn't have one.

Damnit.

I almost give up, until I realize that the WatchMeNow app is what started this all. I open it up and, of course, it's logged in as me. But—RebelSin has his log-in information saved. I switch profiles and tap into his search history. Just NotYour-Angel and one other. It's a name I recognize, one of my clients: iPlayDirty.

Clicking on the private chat button, the screen fills with exchanged messages between Talon and this guy. Only it's not just any guy.

It's Josh.

Chills slither down my spine.

I scroll to the very top and sink into the driver seat comfortably as my eyes skim from the phone to the parking lot, just to be sure I'm still alone. The start of the conversation is just a real name exchange, nothing too incriminating.

October 26.

RebelSin: I don't want you talking to her anymore. You're done.

iPlayDirty: I think we should let her make that decision.

RebelSin: I made it for you. Now delete your account or there will be hell to pay.

iPlayDirty: Make me.

RebelSin: Seriously? What are you ten? Leave her the hell alone, you fucking psycho.

iPlayDirty: I bet I could pay her thousands to come over here and lick my dick right now. Money talks, Porter.

RebelSin: My fists talk, too. And you'll be having a long conversation with it if you go near her house again.

iPlayDirty: Now who's the stalker. You wouldn't know that I was at her house if you weren't snooping around yourself.

Holy shit.

All this time these two were fighting over me on this app and I didn't even know who the hell they were. How did I miss this? How was I so naive?

RebelSin: Tommy's house is a three-minute walk to hers and you parked your car in front of his house at one o'clock in the morning, dumbass. When it was sitting there empty for over an hour, I knew exactly where you were.

iPlayDirty: Yeah, she was making a video for me. Good times.

RebelSin: Lying son of a bitch. She was talking to me. I walked down the road talking to her in the private chat.

iPlayDirty: Did it ever cross your mind that she had two chat windows open? Now who's the dumbass?

RebelSin: You're as good as dead if I catch you out there again. Hear me? Dead.

The phone drops into my lap and my hand claps over my mouth. That's why Josh is dead? Talon killed him over me? No, that's not right. It can't be.

It was two days later that I was at Talon's house and over-heard the guys talking. Technically, I didn't overhear them because it was a setup, but this conversation could put Talon in prison for murder. Without even hesitating, I delete it. I have no idea why he hasn't done this already.

Just as I swipe out of the app, a thud on the driver's window sends the phone flying into the back seat.

"Fuck!" I shout, as I roll the window down. "You scared the hell out of me, Lars. Where did you even come from?"

He stuffs his hands in his pockets and his back steels. "Let me in. It's fucking cold." I hit the unlock button, and he walks around to the passenger side and gets in.

"How'd you even know where I was?" I ask him, as he closes the door.

"Tracker. We all share locations, and you have Talon's phone. I've been calling, but you must have been preoccupied. I've been following behind you in an Uber."

"Oh," I look around for Talon's phone, but it must have flown into the back seat. "Yeah, Talon's dad scared the shit out of me so I pulled over to call you, but I got sidetracked."

"All good. I know the way. Let's get the hell outta here." I shift the car into drive and make a sharp U-turn to get out of the parking lot. "Take a left here."

Glancing over at Lars when he goes quiet, my heart drops into my stomach, and I gasp. "What are you doing?"

"I'm sorry, Marni. I don't wanna do this. But he gave me no choice," Lars says, as he holds the gun low in his lap, pointing it right at me.

My entire body tenses up, and my palms begin to sweat as I

grip the steering wheel. "Who?" I choke out. The long pause of silence between us is deafening. My heart hammers so violently that I fear it will explode, or I'll pass out before it does. "Who?" I repeat again.

He looks over at me. Sheer displeasure written all over his face. "Zed."

23

TALON

I toss the license plate that I've had sitting on my lap the entire ride in the back seat. No plate, no tracking.

We made it to the hotel with time to spare. My fingers tap continuously on the steering wheel while we wait for him to pull in. Tommy's been trying to check in with Marni to make sure she made it to the hotel ok, but she has yet to reply. "Where the fuck is Lars? And why isn't she answering my damn phone?" My palms smack forcibly against the steering wheel.

"You don't think your dad—"

"Don't say it." I twist my head wryly. "Don't even go there." She's a small-town girl driving in a big city. She probably took a wrong turn and had to reroute.

Tommy's hand slaps at my shoulder. I catch the bob of his head in the direction of the entrance, and my eyes shoot over. "There he is." He's really here, and this is really happening. I've waited my entire life for this moment. This plan has to go accordingly, so I don't even have a minute to mentally prepare. "Stay put until I wave you over," I tell Tommy, as I pull the black hood up over my head and slide on my black leather gloves.

Tommy pulls up his black mask, showing only his eyes. "You sure? I can come."

"I need to do this part alone." I need this moment to be just between me and him. His death is only part of this process. I want to kill him slowly with my words. Force him to feel some sort of regret for the way he treated us.

My feet hit the black pavement, and I keep my sights on his vehicle. The windows are tinted, so I can't see his face, but I know he's in there. When his driver's side door opens, and his legs creep out, I pick up my pace and make it just in time to slam it back shut. Only it doesn't close. It catches his shins and squeals come from the other side of the door.

"Talon?" I hear him say, as I press firmly on the door with his legs floating off the ground. "You're gonna break my damn legs!" he shouts.

I retract and give him some leg room. "Get them back in the fucking vehicle now or I'll shatter every bone in your body." My adrenaline is pumping so vigorously that I feel unstoppable, like I could do just about anything to this man and fail to feel even an ounce of remorse.

Once his legs are back in, I close the door all the way. "Crack the window," I demand. He rolls it down, leaving about two inches of open space from the top. "Surprised to see me?"

"My leg, Talon. I think it's broken. I think I need to go to the hospital." He cries out like a fucking pussy.

I hold my composure and keep my tone casual. "Don't worry, in just a minute, you won't feel a damn thing." I lean closer to the window and his eyes hover over the top through the open space. They're still just as empty as they were the last time I saw him. Soulless and harrowing. "Do you remember that time I broke my arm? I was eleven years old. Fell out of the tree house and laid there crying while Blakely ran inside for help. You stumbled out the door about twenty minutes later—drunk off your ass. You walked over to me, lingered over my body, then you kicked me in the side and told me to toughen up." Fire radiates through me and my chin begins to tremble out of anger.

"Did you track me down and come all the way here just to revisit the past?"

My jaw locks. "You're a fucking monster. You beat the shit out of me and Mom. And while I'm not her biggest fan, she didn't deserve a goddamn second of it. You verbally beat Blakely down and you turned our house into a living hell. You killed a woman and you're still roaming free and trying to shack up with teenage girls." My words keep spewing out with no self-control. "And let me tell you, it's taking everything in me not to chop off your dirty dick and shove it up your own ass."

Taut brows and a pleading look lurk in his expression. With menacing eyes, I stare him down. There is so much I want to say, but he's not worth the breath. I had every intention of drilling my demons into him before he took his last breath. But now, now I can see it would be a waste of time.

I glance over to Tommy and give him a look of approval. Seconds later, he's grabbing the gas can from the bed of the truck. Snapping my right glove at my wrist, I quip, "Roll it down."

"Get lost, son." The window begins to slide up, but my hand grabs the handle and wrenches the door open. My entire body is numb as my hands wrap around his neck and squeeze with as much force as my body will allow—which is everything I've got. "Toughen up," I grit through my locked jaw. The tips of my fingers dig into his skin while my thumbs press against his Adam's apple. "I'm not your fucking son. Your life was so damn boring that you thought you'd take on a family to terrorize. Congratulations, you succeeded. You did this to yourself, always remember that."

I'm not even sure when he stopped squirming and fighting to free himself from my clutches. It was likely the moment right before his eyes bugged out and the gurgles stopped. I don't even know if the bastard is actually dead and I don't care —he will be.

I give his limp body a shove and when his eyes remain open and I don't see any movement in his chest, I'm convinced he is, in fact, dead. Nothing can begin to explain what I feel in this moment.

I'm free.

That sums it all up. I'm free, and he can't hurt me anymore.

The smell of gasoline sweeps through the air as the wind blows. Taking the can from Tommy, I douse the interior and pour it all over Mike Porter's dead body. "Fry mother fucker," I whisper into the small space of the car before I draw back. I don't even look around to see if there are people nearby. I wave for Tommy to get back, and once he does and is at the truck with it running, I pull out a box of matches.

My hands shake as I look down at the matches, but I savor every moment. Feeling as if this brief moment in time is the sole reason that I exist. Everything I've been through and the constant up-hill battle has brought me to this point. It's my destiny to rid this man's death grip on society.

This is for Blakely.

This is for Mom.

This is for every soul this man has burned.

I pull a matchstick from the box. Swiping it across the striker, it ignites and offers me a sense of warmth. The fire inside me burns. I stare at the stranger through the flame then give it a toss. When it's in mid-air, I whisper, "This is for me."

Strike a match. Watch em' burn.

Then I run like hell.

I'm hauling ass through the parking lot when Tommy pulls up beside me with the window down. "Get in now!" he shouts.

He's leaning over the seat, trying to open the door for me, while the truck is still creeping through the parking lot. I pull it open and jump inside. Burning rubber, he rips out, but I watch in the side mirror as the flames engulf the vehicle. Crimson and burnt orange flickers of light fade into the distance, and I exhale a drawn-out breath.

"He's really gone," I say. At least, I think I said it out loud. Adrenaline is still rushing through me, and I've never felt this alive in my life.

"Regrets?" Tommy asks, as he leans forward and checks for traffic, before turning onto the main road.

"Not a damn one." I look at his phone sitting between us. "Did you get ahold of Lars or Marni yet?"

"No, man. No one is answering. I'm sure they're at the hotel."

Ten minutes later, we're pulling into the hotel that I booked for us over three weeks ago. My blood has settled and my heart rate is back to normal. I glance around the parking lot that is packed with cars and don't see Tommy's car anywhere.

The stench of chlorine hits me as soon as we walk into the lobby. I head straight to the front desk to get a room number since Lars already checked us in. Dropping my bag to the floor, I reach in my bag pocket and pull out my wallet.

"Good evening. Do you have a reservation?" the young blonde from behind the counter asks.

I slide my ID to her. "Room's under my name. We've already checked in, but I need the room number, and I'd like to add another suite if you have any vacancies." When I booked the room, I was planning for us to all share one room. At the time, Marni was merely another body taking up space. Now, I plan to devour that body tonight and I don't need Tommy and Lars as an audience.

Tommy's standing next to me typing into his phone. "Reach him yet?" I ask.

He shakes his head no.

"Thank you, Mr. Porter." She hands me back my ID. "I've added a suite to your reservation. That will be on the fourth floor as well." She begins going over check-out, breakfast, blah blah blah, but I cut her off.

"Lars Tyson has already checked in for the original room. Is he here now?"

"No. No one has checked in under this reservation. You're the first to arrive."

I look at Tommy, who lifts his head from his phone. "Alright, thank you." I take the keys.

"That's not right. Maybe someone else was working when Lars got here earlier," I say, as I push the elevator button. "Something feels off. Do you feel it?"

With hooded brows, Tommy side-eyes me. "Yeah. Something is definitely off. Marni isn't answering your phone and Lars' is going straight to voicemail."

We step into the elevator, and I press the button for the fourth floor. When the doors slide back open, hurried steps take me to the original suite. The room that they should be in.

The key clicks the door unlocked and I shove it open. "What the hell? Where are they?" My bag slides off my shoulder and hits the floor with a thud. "Gimme that." I grab Tommy's phone from his hand.

I tap Lars' name and then info to go to the map of his location.

Location Unavailable.

I tap my name and a darkness consumes me as it's loading. Like my mind is preparing for the same result.

But it's not. The location pings.

"Dalton? What the actual fuck is my phone doing in Dalton?"

Tommy grabs it back out of my hand. "That's over an hour away from here and in the direction of Redwood. That can't be right."

I grab my bag off the floor. "We've gotta go. Wherever she's headed, I'm ninety-nine percent sure that Lars is with her."

24

MARNI

The Welcome to Redwood sign has come and gone. We drove through the town, and we're headed down the outskirts of a familiar location.

"Why are you doing this?" I ask for the hundredth time. And the response is always the same.

"Just shut up." Though his response is calloused, his tone is warm.

Lars held me at gunpoint while he made me climb over the seat and switch him spots so that he could drive. The entire ride, I've had the pistol pointed at my stomach. I've thought of countless ways that I could try and overturn this hostage situation, but in my mind, each one ended with a gunshot to the gut. Needless to say, I'm at his mercy until I'm handed over to the devil himself.

"You don't have to do this. Tommy and Talon will protect you—I'll protect you. Zed doesn't—"

"Shut up." He repeats again.

"I'm just saying that if you're scared—"

"God damnit, Marni. Will you just shut the fuck up!" He shouts for the first time during this three-hour drive. Straightening my back, my body tenses up again when we make a turn down the long gravel drive.

"What are we doing at Briarwood?"

Zed's car is parked out front and he's leaning against it in a pair of black jeans and a dark gray hoodie that's pulled over his head. But, what makes my skin crawl is the sinister smirk on his face. It's unearthly and loaded with intentions that I can't even fathom.

"Lars, please." I try one more time. "Just turn around. There's still time."

He looks over at me, offering me a brief moment of comfort with his eyes. "Whatever you do, don't try and fight him. It sends him to a dark place and nothing good ever comes out of it." He stops the car and hits the unlock button.

When Zed begins strutting over and Lars stays put, my heart jumps, and I struggle to speak. "Aren't you getting out?" He looks straight ahead. He can't even look at me now. "You're a fucking coward!" I shriek when the door opens and Zed grabs hold of me. I wail and my legs kick, trying to hit him, but my eyes are still glued to a mute Lars. "Do you hear me? A coward!"

As soon as I'm out of the vehicle, Zed slams the door shut, without even a word to his friend who drove me here. Lars speeds off, kicking gravel up behind him.

At the top of my lungs I scream, "Come back!" A lump lodges in my throat, and I choke out, "Please come back." Tears begin falling carelessly down my face as Zed drags me up the driveway to Briarwood.

"Scream as loud as you want. No one can hear you."

"Why are you doing this? What have I ever done to you?"

"This isn't about you. This is about him." His grip tightens as we walk up the concrete steps to the dilapidated building. Kicking the door open, he pulls me inside.

It's just as I remember it; only, this time, a sliver of light from the setting sun shines through the old windows. The smell of burning leaves still lingers throughout the main entrance, and I'm immediately taken back to that night. The night that it all began.

Talon led me here. He sought me out, tricked me, gave me no choice but to fall for him, and because of that, I'm caged in this house with a psychopathic lion. "Who? Talon?" I have to dig. I need to know what Zed's endgame here is. He says it's not about me, but who is trying to hurt through me?

Leading me down the steps to the basement, memories of that night come flooding back. It's all too familiar. It was only a month ago that I was in the same position with Talon, but it didn't feel like this. With Talon, it was about the thrill of walking into the unknown. With Zed, it's a fear of walking into a death trap.

No one knows I'm here. No one can save me—except for Lars. It's apparent he's not on my side in this. For whatever reason, Zed forced him to deliver me. Even if he didn't want to, he did it, and he's just earned a name on my shit list if I make it out of here alive.

If.

Hope is slowly slipping away as Zed shoves me into a chair and begins strapping my hands to the side of it. Giving up my fight, I surrender. At this point, I wish he'd just knock me out so that I don't feel what's coming.

Zed begins pacing in front of me, brushing his chin with his thumb. "Oh, Little Thorn. What am I going to do with you?"

"Zed," I say pleadingly, "you can just let me go now. We can forget this ever happened."

Stopping in front of me, he stoops forward and places both hands over mine as they remain still on the arm of the chair. "You know what I like about this place? No cameras. Everyone has those damn things these days, and it feels like someone is always watching. Lurking, spying, getting off on watching someone when they don't even know they're being watched."

Dipping my head down, I avoid eye contact. "He'll find me," I say in a hushed voice.

"Oh, he *will* find you." He perks up. "That's a fact. But not until I'm ready for him to find you." Pacing in front of me again, he continues, "You see, Talon is probably racking his brain right now trying to figure out where you are. He might even be losing his mind, unable to come up with a logical explanation about how his girl and one of his best friends just disappeared. Talon might be a loose cannon, but he's smart." Leaning forward again, he gets right in my face and taps the side of his head with one finger. "But I'm smarter."

"And what? You plan to kill him when he gets here?" I chuckle, but I don't find it funny in the least bit.

"Ding Ding Ding." He chimes. "She's beginning to catch on."

My stomach twists and sweat dampens my palms as they grip the arm of the chair. "Talon is one of your best friends. You have that little pact thing with the tattoos. Why would you wanna kill him?" I'm not even sure why I'm asking him any questions at all, something tells me that he is going to give me all the answers, whether I ask for them or not.

Zed grabs an old rusted chair and pulls it over. The sound of the metal scraping across the concrete echoes in my ears. Lifting and twisting the chair around, he sits down on it with his legs straddling the back as he faces me. My legs dangle free, and if I could kick high enough, I could get him right in the face.

"You ever hear of a lady named Rose Monte?" he asks. When I don't answer, he continues, "Of course you haven't. No one has, except for Talon. You see, Rose was an agoraphobic. Her body hadn't seen sunlight in seven years before it was taken out of the house on a sunny Tuesday afternoon. Only, she couldn't feel the warmth of the sun or the cool of the breeze because she was dead as a door knob. Wanna know how she died?"

This time I nod. I don't wanna know. I *have* to know. Did Talon kill her? How many people has he killed? First Josh, then his dad. Is Zed about to tell me that he killed this Rose lady, too?"

His eyes widen. Dark, empty, and unapologetic. "Your druggie boyfriend fed her a handful of Methadone then left her to die."

Oh no. Talon, what have you done?

"Rose Monte was my mom. That is until Talon assisted her in a planned suicide."

"I'm sure there is more to the story. Talon wouldn't—"

"There isn't! And he did!" he shouts, jolting my body upward.

Zed walks away in a fury and I fear that his entire body is filling with a rage that he plans to unleash on me. I wiggle my hands to try and free them, but nothing budges. These damn straps are so tight. There is no way I'm getting them free any time soon. I kick up my legs that are still loose, and it grabs Zed's attention. He turns around, shooting daggers at me, then eats up the space between us.

"No!" I shout, as he grabs my left leg and holds it against the chair then straps it in. I kick my other leg out and nail him in the crotch, but it has no effect on him as he straps the other one in as well. "Just let me out of here," I cry out. "Please."

"Talon says that he had no idea that Rose was planning to take all the pills at once. Even if he didn't know, he still supplied them to her. It could have been any Tom, Dick, or Harry. But no, it was my best fucking friend. He got caught up in the wrong shit and ran around town, feeding everyone pills because it made him feel less alone." His voice raises, "in the end, it left me alone and without a mother."

I try to reason with him. He's hurting. I get it. "I'm sorry you lost your mom, Zed. I really am."

He doesn't even look at me. He just turns around and walks into the darkest area of the room, and I lose sight of him. The next thing I know, I hear a loud thud and the repeated sound of metal on cement.

He's chipping away at the cement floor.

He's digging.

Holy shit. Is he digging up Josh?

Resting my chin on my chest with my eyes closed, the sounds begin to fade. Like a storm passing, but still striking in the distance.

I'm not sure how much time has passed when I feel him at my side again. My eyes pop open, and I lift my head. "What did you do?" He's waving something in front of me, but I can't make out what it is. I lean closer and catch a glimpse: the SD card.

"Remember when you went to hell and back for this card. You even let me dip my fingers inside of you just for answers. What are you willing to do for it now?" He smirks.

I don't need that card anymore. Little does he know, I had the phone, and I already have my answers.

"Nothing. I don't want it."

He perks up. "Oh? You don't wanna know what your boyfriend has been keeping from you?"

"I already know everything." I smirk right back at him.

He laughs. "You *think* you know everything."

"I do. I already know that Talon killed Josh. So you can shove that card right up your ass." I snuff my nose in the air and turn my head.

Stepping closer, then even closer—until his legs are level with mine—he climbs on top of me. His knees hit my sides, and we're face to face. "Naive little Marni." He tsks. "You don't know a damn thing." Leaning over, his mouth hits the lobe of my ear. "Talon didn't kill Josh. Your daddy did."

Everything stills. My heart, my breath. Zed's body and his words. He's frozen on top of me, waiting for a reaction.

He's lying.

Laughter erupts from inside me. "Shut the hell up. There is no way that my dad killed Josh, and don't even try and pin this shit on him."

"You think I'm joking? That's cute. But it's true." He leans back and his eyes bore into mine. "Sure, Talon wanted to kill him. Josh was peeping through your windows and Talon had a fetish for you. Talon was at Tommy's that night. Josh parked his car nearby, and they knew exactly where he was. So they walked over there to confront him. They planned on recording Josh as he stood at the end of your driveway with a pair of binoculars. They were gonna tell him that they'd show the entire school if he didn't stay away from you."

"Why should I believe anything you say to me?"

"Because I have no reason to lie."

He's right. He has nothing to gain from this. Aside from turning me against Talon—again. "Alright, humor me. What happened next?"

"So the guys were getting a good laugh and just as they switched on the camera and hit record, your dad came flying down the road at full speed and took the fucker out. Hit him and killed him. Instantly."

Gasping, I begin to squirm again. "Let me up. Please, Zed. I need to get up." The walls feel like they are closing in around me. Sucking all the air out and smothering me.

He continues to talk, as I buck my knees up. "Tommy and Talon hid behind a bush but kept recording. Your dad got out of the car, took one look at Josh, panicked and got back in and drove off. Never called an ambulance. He never even went home."

Words that don't feel like mine escape me. "He was supposed to come home that night. He called and told me that he had a last-minute meeting in Phoenix and he'd be home a couple days later."

"Later that night, we all got together and came up with the elaborate scheme to get you right where we wanted you. We went to your dad with the video and threatened to hand it over to the police if he didn't do exactly what we wanted."

"What did you want?"

"You." Zed hops off of me and grabs a shovel that's leaning against the wall. He goes back over to the corner where he was and it sounds like he's digging up dirt now. There's the scrape of the shovel and then the drop of dirt onto the cement. He continues talking as he digs. "Your dad handed over his little girl just to keep his reputation and freedom."

This whole time, it was my dad. I have so many questions that I need answered. Only, I don't want answers from Zed. I want them from Talon.

There's a brief pause in digging and the light on Zed's phone shines from the other end of the eerie basement. "They're almost here." He whistles, way too chipper for someone in his position. He's digging a manmade grave and, deep down, I know that he plans on filling it with another body —Talon's.

25

TALON

The rain is hammering on the windshield. "Could ya press the gas a little harder. Come on, man." I lean forward in the passenger seat. To say that I'm tense is an understatement of epic proportion. I've chewed half of my thumbnail off and the fucking thing won't stop bleeding. Add that to the scratches on my neck, and the diced skin under my shirt and I look like I just stepped out of some fucked-up horror film.

"I'm already going seventy in a fifty-five and I can't see shit." Tommy presses down on the peddle with a little more tenacity, and I finally sit back in the seat.

We're only five minutes away from Briarwood, but five minutes feels like a lifetime. "I can't believe fucking Lars. How the hell could he do this shit?" I slap my hand on the dashboard. "When this is all over with, I've got a few choice words for that backstabbing son of a bitch."

"Yeah, what he did was pretty messed up. But at least he's trying to atone for his fuck-up."

"Well, he's atoning a little too late. Zed could have done just about anything to her at this point." I can't let my mind go there. I swear to God if he laid one harmful finger on her, I'll break 'em all. I resume chewing on my nail and suck the drop of blood into my mouth.

Tommy snarls in disgust as he side-eyes me. "Would you quit that shit."

I slap both hands on my legs, rubbing my sweaty palms onto my jeans. This is a disaster. If anything happens to Marni, I'll never forgive myself. Should have just found another way once I felt that first twinge in my chest. That new feeling that told me she was more than just another girl—that she was special. Instead, I got her tangled up in this mess and now she's under the hands of a guy who has not a single ounce of empathy in his heartless body. "Bout damn time." I huff, as we pull down the driveway of Briarwood.

Zed's car is parked right out front and I'm well aware that he's expecting us. Lars filled me in on that much. What Zed doesn't know is that Tommy and I have brought backup. Didn't wanna do it. Really didn't want to. I hate Axel Thorn with a passion, but we have the same agenda here. Get Marni out alive, while keeping our asses alive as well.

I shoot Lars a text from Tommy's phone to let him know we're here. "They'll be coming through the back. My guess is that he has Marni in the basement, so I'll head straight there. You search the upstairs while Lars and Axel hide out until it's time."

"Not gonna lie, bro. I'm really fucking nervous about this," Tommy says, killing the engine and tugging his hood up.

"We all are." I lift my hood up as well, but waste no time jumping out and booking it to the front door. Thunder ripples all around me, followed by a strike of lightning that shoots across the sky. Looking behind me, before I open the door, I see Tommy trailing me, none too eagerly. "C'mon."

When he's finally at the top of the stairs, I slowly open the door. Not that it matters much, the old wooden structure scrapes so loudly against the floor that I've just announced our presence to everyone inside, dead and alive.

"Ah, there's the man of the hour," Zed says, as he stands in the middle of the narrow hallway with his hands in the air. "We've been expecting you."

My first instinct is to charge at him and rip his fucking head off for touching Marni. Then every other limb on his body for this mess he's stirred. Everything I've replayed in my head the entire drive is a scrambled mess. "Cut the shit. Where is she?"

"She's around. And trust me, she's not going anywhere this time. You see, I know how to keep the ladies right where I want them. You, on the other hand, let them run amuck and fuck shit up." He holds up the SD card. "You're lucky I got my hands on her...I mean this, when I did." He corrects himself, although it's crystal clear that it was intentional.

"Give that to me." I hold my hand out, knowing full on that he won't just hand it over. I'm just buying time for Lars and Axel to get in the house.

"Could you imagine if she would have stuck this baby into her computer? Your entire secret would have crashed down on you before she even knew she had feelings for you. She would have run right to Daddy."

"Doesn't matter. None of that shit matters anymore."

"Oh," he perks up. "You won't care if she knows that her dad killed the boy in the basement?"

I take a step closer to him and he doesn't budge. "Just give me the card and tell me where she is." My hands pat my puffed-out chest. "It's me you want. I'm right here."

"You're right. It is you. But it's also her. You don't deserve a girl like that." His voice raises a few octaves. "Because of you, my mom is dead and she's never coming back."

"My mom's gone too, Zed. You think that I don't mourn

her, even though she's living. At least you had a mom for most of your life. Mine never even deserved that title."

"And that makes it ok? Your mom was a fuck-up, so it doesn't matter that you killed mine?"

"Zed," I take another step, "your mom committed suicide. It doesn't matter who gave her the pills, one way or another, she would have gotten her hands on them. I had no idea that was her plan when I gave them to her. I know I screwed up."

I'd been doing pill drops for Zed's mom for weeks. Didn't think that day was any different. She was an addict, like me. I didn't have two cents to rub together since I blew through my savings and Dad cut me off. At that time, I thought my trust fund was years away, so I started selling for a high-end dealer. I was making damn good money and I was getting my fix. It was a win-win.

I had no idea that Rose was planning to overdose that day. I ended up going to the football game, living my life like nothing had happened. We played hard, won the game, and that's when Axel threw his two cents in about my fucked-up family life. Everything became too much that night. Rose died, Zed would soon know that I brought her the pills, and I was ready to end it all. Only, fate had other plans for me. I went to rehab and got clean. It was the best thing to come from that whole messed-up situation. Zed eventually forgave me. At least, I thought he did.

"You screw up when you take a left instead of a right. Not when you hand a manic depressive a loaded gun."

"I'm sorry, man." I really am. I'm so damn sorry for the way that all unfolded. I was at a really bad place and made a lotta bad choices.

Zed takes a step forward and reaches out his hand with the SD card. "She already knows." He slaps it into my open palm.

"Knows what?" I ask, but just as the words leave my lips,

Zed grabs my arm. He gives it a twist behind my back, then spins me around to face Tommy. The card digs into the skin of my palm as I grip it tightly. Zed's other arm crosses over my throat while my back is pressed firmly to his chest. I'm pretty much fucked as far as getting out of this hold.

"She knows everything." His voice is unfamiliar. I've always known that Zed's heart is as black as coal, but he's shown us streaks of color over the years. Only us. Only his boys.

When we were eleven years old, I was staying over at his house. He had stretched up to do something, I can't even remember what he was doing. Pulling off his sweatshirt, maybe. I noticed a mark on his back. It was the perfect shape of a handprint with little bruises on the rest of his back, and with my history, I knew exactly what it was. It was a secret.

Something he didn't wanna talk about and something I didn't dare ask about. Only, I had no idea who'd done it. Was his dad giving him beatings, too? It didn't seem likely. While his dad wasn't the friendliest man in existence, he didn't come off as angry or bitter. No. It was someone else.

From that day on, I was hell-bent on finding out what happened to Zed. I couldn't figure out if I was worried for him or if it was because I needed to know that I wasn't the only one who was living a life under the clutches of Satan himself.

I followed him everywhere. My eyes were always on him. Weeks went by, and eventually, it began to slip my mind until it was just a distant memory.

Three months later, it was Christmas break and we were all hanging out at Tommy's house and Zed had to get ready to leave for some Christmas play at his family's church. Yeah, Zed went to church. Religiously. His mom made him attend every single Sunday, and they were at every gathering the church held. This night was no different. Zed made a comment about hating the pastor and how one day he'd pay for his sins.

Everyone brushed it off as Zed being Zed. At this point, his darkness was starting to creep out like black tar. So, I became suspicious again. There was something about the look in his eyes that told me this was more than Zed just hating church.

Making jokes about seeing Zed dressed up as a shepherd, I talked Tommy and Lars into going. Zed put up a fight and wasn't happy in the least. But we went anyway. The three of us were lined up in a row, waiting for the play to start, when I saw Pastor Jeffries pull Zed aside. Zed's eyes danced around the room in fear, as if he was searching for someone to stop him. Though no one did. I excused myself and told the guys that I had to use the bathroom.

That's when I saw it. After months of wondering what was turning Zed ice cold and leaving those marks on his body, I had my answer. Staring at a plain white wall, Zed looked numb. But it wasn't the black of darkness in him I saw that night. It was shades of blue sadness, red angered, and crimson fire. I saw his true colors. Pastor Jeffries was the one hurting Zed. Not just physically, but sexually.

I never told a single soul. I didn't know how. I was just a kid. As years went by, I always regretted it, and eventually it felt too late. I knew what these secrets felt like, and I knew what would happen if they got out. To this day, Zed isn't even aware that I know.

Until now.

We all have our inner demons that we battle day in and day out. Just because the world doesn't see them, doesn't mean they don't exist. My father created a monster inside of me. Pastor Jeffries unleashed the monster in Zed.

"We aren't your enemy, Zed." I speak calmly in an attempt to alleviate his rage.

His jaw clenches. "The world is my enemy."

"Talon!" I hear Marni shout in the distance. My body jolts

up and I wanna scream back. Tell her I'm here, but I don't. Instead, I motion Tommy to the staircase with my eyes.

Just as his feet slowly slide in the direction of the basement, I hear the thud of footsteps come from the kitchen. Many footsteps. Sloshing and squeaking from the rain across the hardwood floor. Zed spins my body around, and I catch Tommy ducking out to go to Marni.

"Where the fuck is my sister, King?" Axel growls as he repeatedly taps the tip of a baseball bat to the palm of his hand. The shadow of the others casts off the wall, and I immediately know he brought back up.

Just like us, where there is one, there are four. With Axel's boys, where there is one, there are three. Kip and Knox come into view, sporting the same displeasure in their expressions.

Axel takes a step closer while Zed's grip on me strengthens. "I'm gonna ask you one more time where the hell my sister is, and if you don't tell me, this bat will meet your skull." His voice grows louder with each word and even on his side in this, I feel the wrath of his fury.

Zed chuckles. "Should'a known these guys would call big brother for help."

"I don't give a shit what you do to these guys you call your friends. I'm here for Marni and I will be leaving with her." Knox and Kip close in as Axel steps even closer to us.

Lars has yet to show his face, but I know he's around.

The flapping of feet on the steps draws closer and closer until Marni is fleeing into the room and throwing herself in Axel's arms. He takes a step back, examining her and running his fingers through her hair. "Are you ok? Did he hurt you?"

"I'm fine." She turns around and looks at me. Our eyes catch and a sadness lingers behind them. Zed said he told her everything. What she doesn't know is that I didn't divulge that information to protect her. Also, because there is so much more that even Zed doesn't know. The fleeting moment of our locked gazes passes, then her eyes drop and she turns back to Axel. "Let's get the hell outta here."

Axel looks from Marni to me. "What about them?"

"They can take care of themselves. It's what they do best." She grabs his arm and pulls him toward the direction of the kitchen, while Knox and Kip follow behind.

Axel points his finger at Zed before leaving. "This isn't over, King. There will come a time when you're alone with no witnesses around. When that time comes, you better run, mother fucker."

I wanna scream at Marni to stop and to let me explain, but I have to handle Zed first. Once I do, I'll make her understand. She'll come back to me. She has to.

"Well, you lost the girl. Ready to give up the fight?" Zed grumbles in my ear as he continues to brace me.

Tommy stands by idly with apprehension in his eyes. Unsure what he should do to help, but there isn't anything he can do. I have to do this one on my own. "Go find Lars and wait for me at the truck. I'll be out soon," I tell him.

Tommy's eyes question my sanity, but I nod. "Just go."

Once he's gone, Zed continues with his threats and insults. "That was fucking stupid. And here I thought you were the smart one of this bunch."

"I'm not your enemy, Zed." I repeat the words again.

His hold on my shoulder tightens, causing his forearm to press aggressively against my throat. "You are the enemy."

With my voice box constricted, I sputter, "He did this to you. Not me. Pastor Jeffries is the enemy." It's the first time I've ever mentioned the old man to Zed. As far as he's been concerned, no one knows what happened. But I know. I know every dirty detail.

"What the hell did you just say?" He squeezes with so much force that I can feel my air supply diminish with each passing second.

"I know." I manage to choke out.

"Know what?" Zed releases his grip on me and I buckle over, drawing in long breaths.

My back is to him while I'm gripping my knees, bent over coughing and sucking in air. "I've known for a long time. Seen it with my own eyes at the Christmas party in sixth grade."

"Fucking liar." He spits.

"Why would I lie about this? How else could I possibly know?"

"Who else knows?" He stomps his foot to the floor. "Who else?"

Straightening my back, I turn around to face him. "No one else. I've never told anyone what I saw."

He sweeps his hand through the air. "You didn't see anything. You're making shit up."

"Am I?" He knows damn well that I'm telling the truth. Making this up would be too much of a crazy coincidence. "We can make him pay, Zed. You deserve your peace, just as much as the rest of us."

Something ticks inside of him, and he's at my front, gripping the collar of my shirt. "You paying is all that will bring me peace."

"I think you're just searching so deep that you're looking for any answers, even if they're the wrong ones. It's not me you want. Deep down you know that your mom's death was on her own hands." When there's a flicker in his eyes and he releases my shirt, I know that I'm breaking through his walls.

"Get the hell out of here." He points to the door and screams, "Go!"

"From start to finish, Zed. You've done some fucked-up shit, but I know what it feels like to have your insides twisted and drained because someone stole your dignity. You fight like hell to hide the pain, but eventually, you have no fight left inside, because the only person you're battling is yourself."

With that, I walk out and leave him standing there. Alone in his own misery. I'm not sure if he's gonna be ok. But that's not my problem anymore. If he needs a hand getting his salvation, I'll be there. Because we made this pact in blood and I stand by my word. I'll never forgive him for what he did to Marni, though. There's no going back after that.

26

"Again?" Shay asks from the doorway of her bedroom.

I nod. "Yep." Tucking my phone under the pillow, I roll over and face the wall.

"Just shut it off. Maybe he'll take a hint."

That would be the logical thing to do. But I don't. Talon hasn't taken a break from calling me since last night. His finger must be hovering over the redial button, because every time I hit end, it starts again. The crazy thing is, he hasn't sent any text messages or left any voicemails. It's probably for the best. If he did, I'd feel tempted to read them and it would defeat the purpose of taking this time for myself. I just need to process everything. I haven't totally given up on Talon. He's still in my heart and my head. But so much has happened and I'm unsure where I go from here.

I can't go home. Apparently, my own father was in on this and sold me to the wolves, just so he wasn't implicated in Josh's murder. It's a sad truth when you're smacked in the face with the reality that, in the end, you only have yourself.

"Shane's having a kickoff to Thanksgiving break party tonight. What'd ya say? Should we make an appearance?"

What I want to do is shout to Shay that I was held at gunpoint for three hours, strapped to an electric chair in an old asylum, and found out that my dad killed Josh. *No, I don't wanna go to a party.* But, I can't say any of that. "I'm just really tired. You go ahead and I'll stay here."

I mean, where else would I go? Not home. Not Talon's. Axel is back in LA. I don't even know where home exists anymore.

"Ya know," she walks over and sits on the edge of the bed, "they say that vodka is the best medicine for heartbreak. Seals that sucker right up."

I laugh. "Vodka is the last thing I need. Besides, if he knows I'm there, he'll probably seek me out."

Who am I kidding? Talon doesn't go to other parties; he only attends his own. Maybe that's why I'm not thrilled to go. Maybe part of me wants to see him.

"Is that such a bad thing? I mean, you do like him, don't you? Unless you tell me what happened, that's all I have to go on." Her shoulders shrug. "You like him. He likes you."

If only it were that simple. "Yeah, I do like him. More than I should. But he's been lying to me. I feel like everything that happened between us was all just a lie."

"Is it possible that he lied to protect you?" When I shoot her the evil eye, she holds her hands up in defeat. "Just throwing it out there as a possibility."

With my left leg, I kick one of her hands down and chuckle. "No, you're right. In fact, I'm pretty sure that's exactly why he lied. I just need more time is all."

My phone vibrates for the umpteenth time beneath my pillow. Only, this time, it's not the steady vibration of a ring. It's just one buzz. Ten seconds later, it buzzes again. Digging my hand under the pillow, I pull it out. My eyes dart from the phone to Shay. "He texted me."

She raises a brow. "Well, I'm gonna leave you to that while

I get ready. When you're done, join me. Because you're going to this party, Ms. Debbie Downer."

I return to the phone and let my finger linger over his name. Temptation getting the best of me, I tap it.

Talon: Please, Marni. I need to talk to you. I really don't want this conversation to happen over a text message. There's so much you don't know. I'll tell you everything. I'll do whatever it takes. Hell, I'll run away with you and leave all this behind if I have to. Just give me five minutes.

I could really use some clarity right now. At this point, I have nothing left to lose.

Me: Meet me at Shane's party at eight o'clock.

His response comes instantly.

Talon: I'll be there.

∞

"Are you sure I don't look too sleazy?" I ask Shay, as I tug the skintight dress down a tad while we walk up the lawn of Shane's house.

Her eyes skim the length of my body. "You look hot."

Music blasts through the speakers and people are already staggering around in the grass with beverages in their hands. It's officially Thanksgiving break, and when schools out, the students of Redwood High celebrate the only way we know how—music and booze.

It feels surreal to be surrounded by all these people after everything that happened in the last month. Granted, I haven't exactly been in isolation, but my mind has been there for a while. Alone and full of irrational thoughts that provoke irrational behavior. My eyes immediately search the party for Talon. I've been a ball of nerves and I'm so anxious to see him. To get answers and to try and move on from this. If that's even possible. Josh is still dead. The cops are still investigating. And now, I have to worry about Dad going to prison.

I'm pushing my way through the crowd, trying to keep up with Shay, when I spot Tommy. Then…"Talon," I say, when his eyes catch mine.

A smile tugs at the corners of his mouth and mine threaten to do the same, but I bite back and pull my lips between my teeth.

"Hey," he says, while he's still at least six feet away from me. Slow steps lead him closer and when we're face to face, I see who's behind him.

"Lars!" I spit. "Are you seriously hanging out with this guy right now? Do you have any idea what he did to me?" I shake my head and go to walk away, but Talon grabs ahold of my arm.

"Wait. Please. Let me explain."

Jerking my arm back, I huff, "There's nothing to explain." I begin dodging people and heading out the house the same way I came in.

"Marni," Talon shouts, "Would you just wait a damn minute?"

I look over my shoulder and see him coming closer. Along with Lars, and then Tommy.

I pick up my pace and walk faster, but as soon as my feet hit the steps outside, I stumble forward. "Easy there," Jordan says, when he catches me mid-fall. I brace myself by gripping the shoulders of his purple and black Ravens jersey. He smiles big and wide, like seeing me is the highlight of his night. "I was hoping you'd be here."

"Jordan," Talon grumbles from behind me as he comes closer, "Get your dirty fucking hands off her now!"

"I need to get out of here." I push myself off from Jordan. *Damnit, my car isn't even here.*

Regardless, I keep trudging back down the lawn. I'll walk home if I have to, err back to Shay's. My arms cross over my chest, and I heave a drawn-out breath with each step because I know they're right behind me. So close that I can smell Talon's cologne.

"Haven't you realized by now that you can't escape me?" He speaks casually, like his words have little to no effect.

"Watch me." We're walking side by side now. I don't slow down, and I don't speed up. I just keep walking, unsure of where I'm even going. "Where'd your posse go?"

"Left them behind. We were planning to talk to you together, but apparently, that didn't work out like we planned."

"How can you even talk to Lars after what he did to me? Are you buddy-buddy with Zed again, too?" I chuckle, and it's loaded with sarcasm. "Oh, right. The pact. Your loyalty lies with them."

"It's not like that. Lars was being blackmailed. He's just as much of a victim as you were. Zed threatened to expose him for some serious shit if he didn't do what he was told. But he tried to amend the situation. He called and told me everything and offered to help once the guilt ate away at him."

I smirk, with even more sarcasm this time. "Oh, good. All is forgiven."

He grabs my hand, stopping my movements, but I jerk it away again. "Would you stop walking and listen to me for a damn minute."

Crossing arms over my chest, I grumble, "I'm listening."

"Lars would have never hurt you. He knew we'd come find you, and you're safe. Isn't that enough?"

"Alright. Let's forget Lars for a minute. I don't even care about fucking Lars. I wanna know about my dad and his place in all this."

His fingers weave through his hair and he lets out a sigh. "It's messy, Marni. And really fucked up."

I speak each word slowly. "Did my dad really hand me over to you guys just to keep his secret?"

"Yes." *That's all I need to know.* "But there's more."

27

TALON

O ne month earlier

"His car is right fucking there." I point out the window. "I know he's watching her. Probably jerking off in her front yard as we speak."

Josh Moran is going to pay for not listening to me. He will pay.

"What do you wanna do about it?" Tommy asks, as he lingers beside me from his bedroom window.

"He needs to be stopped," I tell him, while he pulls a black hoodie over his head and slides on his tennis shoes. "What are you doing?"

"Let's go stop him." He opens his drawer and pulls out a taser.

"Where the hell did you get that?" I laugh, as I grab it from him and inspect the little device.

"Stole it from the cop that tried arresting me for spray-painting under the bridge."

I stuff the taser in my pocket. "Alright. Let's just give him a little scare. We only use this if we have to. We're not hurting the boy. Not yet."

We walk outside and the night is completely still. Not even a cricket chirps. "So what's with this guy? Why's he honing in on your girl?"

"She's not my girl. She's my pawn. I just need to find a way to get her on my side, so I can lure that bastard Mike Porter in. She's got the body and she's got the guts. Shouldn't be too hard."

As soon as we round the corner, I notice a flicker of light coming from the road. "What the hell is that?" I jog closer. "Holy shit." My hand claps over my mouth.

"Is that—"

"Yeah. Dude. I think he's fucking dead." I lean closer to get a better look. The flashlight of his phone is on about five inches from his body. "It's definitely Josh."

"Fuck, man. We need to call the cops—an ambulance—someone."

Giving Tommy a shove, I push him out of the way. "Get back, there's a car coming." We run and hide behind a bush. "Get out your phone," I urge him. When he does, I grab it from his hand and press record on the camera app. Holding the phone up, I record the car coming down the road. "He might have just got hit. They might be coming back."

"Fuck!" Tommy shrieks at the same time I do.

"Oh my god." My hand covers my mouth once more as I continue to hold the phone up.

The car rolled right over Josh's body like he wasn't even there. Then backed up.

"The driver's getting out," I say in a hushed tone. "Wait a minute. That's Anderson Thorn, Marni's dad."

Anderson takes in his surroundings, checking for witnesses. Takes one look at Josh, mumbles something with wide eyes, then gets back in his car and keeps heading straight. This time, driving around his body. Driving right past us while we hide behind the bush. I stop recording. "Do you think he's the one who killed him?" I ask Tommy.

"Nah. He looked scared shitless. No way. Someone else did this. Someone hit him and left his body out here."

"Who would fucking do that?"

We sit quietly for a good ten minutes then a devious plan creeps into my mind. I try and shove it back down, but it keeps crawling back in and filling every crack and crevice of my head. "Anderson did look scared. Like he thought he hit and killed him. Then he drove off out of fear." I look at

233

Tommy, who isn't following one bit. "We have a video of him running over Josh. What if we crop it and make him think he did kill him? We could get whatever we want."

I can immediately tell that Tommy doesn't like this idea. "What could he possibly have that we want?"

A smile spreads across my face. Sinister and full of mischief. "His daughter."

"What a damn minute," Marni cuts me off, "You mean to tell me that my dad *didn't* kill Josh?" Her face drops into her hands. "Then who the hell did?"

"I'm not finished. We then decided to call the guys and fill them in on the plan. We scooped up Josh's body, tossed it in the trunk of Zed's grandma's car, and took him to Briarwood."

"You're telling me that her dad just hit him and drove off and you guys actually caught the entire thing on video. This is fucking epic." Zed beams all too eagerly. *"We've got that fucker in the palm of our hands and we're gonna squeeze the life out of him. I've never liked that bastard."* He begins pacing the basement floor while Josh's body lies next to him wrapped in an old afghan.

"We can't push him too far. We tell him that we want Marni for a while and we make a deal. No one touches her. She will not be harmed. Got it?" I say, making myself perfectly clear.

"Works for me," Lars says. Tommy follows in agreement.

"What the hell is in it for us?" Zed huffs. *"Doesn't seem fair that we do all the dirty work and you get to carry out your plan with no gain for us."*

"How about this," I tap my fingers together. *"We all have people who have done us wrong. We all get our shot at revenge. When I'm done, someone else gets their chance. One shot. Four acts. We stick together no matter what."*

"That sounds a little bit better. I can handle that. I've already got a poor soul in mind who needs to atone for his sins."

I put my hand out, and the guys pile theirs on top. "One shot. Four acts. We're in this together from start to finish."

Tommy chimes in, "And anything that happens in between."

We break.

"We need to get rid of this fucking body before he starts stinking up the place." Zed pinches his nose.

"We could just bury him down here. No one comes to this place, except for the occasional scarefest. Chip up the cement, dig a hole, and drop him in, and we'll cement the surface again," Lars says.

Tommy gags as he walks toward the stairs. "I can't stomach this shit. You guys have to do that part without me."

"I'll take care of Josh and grab a few bags of cement tomorrow. You all go home. I'll text you when it's done. Then we need to talk about what we're doing with his car that's parked in front of Tommy's house." Zed surprises us all by taking some initiative.

"Thanks, man. When you're done, meet us over at Tommy's house. We'll come up with a game plan."

"Wait. Zed buried Josh in the basement. So why was he digging up a spot down there last night?"

"He was?"

"Yeah. I assumed he was planning to toss one of you guys in there with Josh, but you all seem fine to me."

"I guess that could have been his plan. But, I got through to him and left. Haven't heard a word from him since and don't plan to."

Marni nods in agreement. "Yeah, let's hope that none of us do. Is that all to the story?"

"Pretty much sums it up. You know what happened next."

I pull out my phone and hold a finger up to Marni. "Hey, Lars. We need to go check on things at Briarwood. It seems Zed was stirring shit up in the basement. Pick us up at the end of the driveway."

I end the call.

"We?" Marni questions.

"We're in this together. Remember? You're one of us now."

I hook an arm around her, and this time she doesn't toss it off like it's infected.

"Alright. So, Josh is dead. We have no idea who did it. Lars and Zed still think that it was my dad and could use that against him at any given moment. Should we tell them the truth?"

"I've filled Lars in. He knows now."

"And, Zed? Do you plan to tell him so he doesn't do something stupid that could send my dad to prison?"

I shake my head. "No. Not until we find out who really killed Josh. He could turn it around on us. Someone out there knows something and eventually, we'll find out who that someone is. When we do, let's hope for their sake they don't have something we want."

"You don't think it could have been Zed who hit him, do you?"

I shrug a shoulder. "At this point, everyone is a suspect."

"We'll meet you guys inside," I tell Tommy and Lars when they get out of the car.

Marni tucks a leg under the other and turns toward me in the back seat. The back of my hand grazes over her cheek. "I've missed you."

She chuckles and turns her head to look out the window. "It's only been a day."

"It felt longer."

Turning back to me, her expression is solemn. "Talon, I just don't know how this could ever work between us. Everything is so messed up."

"That's because we're messed up. You and I both. Nothing has ever been easy for us, so why would it be now?"

"I'm just not sure that a relationship is the best thing for me right now."

"I agree. Besides, I don't do relationships. Never wanna get married. Definitely not having kids."

She smiles. "Same." Then she takes my hand from her cheek and holds it in hers, tracing the lines of my palm. "What if we just take things slow?"

My eyes dart to hers. "As long as it's fast in the bed."

"Such a man." She snickers.

I lean forward and press my lips to hers. "Your man."

"I thought we just agreed to take it slow."

"This is slow. But I don't want anyone else and you better not be with anyone else."

"Or what?"

"You've seen what I'm capable of my little rebel." I kiss her lips again, and again, and again. Then I pull back.

"Are you happy now that you carried out your revenge? Do you feel fulfilled?"

"Honestly, I've got everything I've ever wanted. Money, power, my revenge on the man I hate. But, it means nothing without you. I didn't know it at the time, but my plans changed the first time I saw you cry. I'd give it all back if it meant I could keep you forever."

"Ok then."

"Ok?"

"Keep me."

Our lips collide with so much intensity that even the strongest force of nature couldn't pry them apart.

The strongest force of nature couldn't stop it, but the loud thudding on the window could. "Unlock the fucking door." Lars growls from the other side. I didn't even know it was locked. I pull the handle, and the door flies open.

"He's fucking gone."

"What do you mean *he's gone?*"

"Josh. He isn't down there. The hole is dug but nothing's in it. Fuck man, I don't think he ever was."

"No. That can't be." I slide out of the car, and Marni follows.

Tommy comes hurling down the driveway. "Nothing." He throws his arms in the air.

"So Zed never buried him here like he said?" Marni asks.

I pinch the bridge of my nose and exhale a drawn-out breath. "That mother fucker." I pull out my phone and hit his name.

"What are you doing?" Lars steps forward. "Don't call him."

"We need answers and he's the only one who has them."

Zed picks up on the second ring, "Miss me already?"

"Where is he?" I huff.

"Oh, Josh. He's safe. Don't you worry about that."

"Did you ever even bury him like you were supposed to?"

"Oh, he's buried. But not where you wanted. Never was."

"Where the fuck is he?"

"I told you I'd take care of him and I did. Now, I have you all right where I want you and you'll do exactly what I say. If you don't, everyone goes down."

I look around at the concerned faces staring back at me.

We're all screwed.

EPILOGUE

I f someone would have told me a month ago, or even two weeks ago, that I'd be spending Thanksgiving with these guys, and actually enjoying it, I would have rolled over dead. Yet, here I am. Squeezing my eyes shut because I was told to—not much has changed.

"Can I open them now?" I ask Talon, as he leads me down the sidewalk to who knows where. I'm pretty sure we're in Las Verdes, but I have no idea where we're going.

He turns my body and positions me to his liking. "Ok, open them."

"Inked in Attitude? What is this? A tattoo shop?" I laugh. "It's Thanksgiving. I highly doubt they're open."

"Have you forgotten who you're dating." Talon smirks.

I can feel the heat rise in my cheeks. "Oh," I tease, "Is that what we're doing? I thought we both agreed that we were not doing that."

"Well, you *are* living with me." He wraps his arms around my waist, locking his hands behind my back. "And sleeping in my bed, pretty much every night. So, maybe you should stop biting my tongue and let me call you my girlfriend."

"For the record, my living with you is pure convenience on my behalf. Since my dad sold me to the highest bidder to keep his ass out of prison, I have no desire to go home."

"Just fucking say it. Don't make me beg."

"I feel like such a teenager right now." I tilt my head down to hide the blush color on my face. "Ok," I look back up, "you can have your title."

His hands drop down to my ass and give it a squeeze. "Good. Because I don't like to share. And you," his lips press to mine, "are all mine."

I look up at the sign on the shop. "So, what the hell are we doing here, anyways?"

"Waiting on Lars and Tommy. They should be here any minute."

"And can you tell me why?"

"Because you're getting some ink, baby."

I chuckle. "Ahh, no I'm not."

Tommy's car pulls up beside us and he and Lars jump out. Lars throws his arms across the hood. "You ready to do this?"

I'm pretty sure he's talking to me but not completely. "Me?"

"Yeah you. You're one of us now. You need to get branded for life."

Ah, the infinity symbol. I'm not sure if I should be honored or scared for my life. They say I'm one of them. That comes with more baggage then I'm ready to carry. I'll admit, I've grown pretty fond of these guys. Especially the one who won't take his hands off my ass and claims I'm his girlfriend. "Alright." I shrug my shoulders. "Let's do this damn thing."

I'm sitting in the chair, getting prepped, when Tommy whispers in my ear, "Do you trust me?"

My eyes widen, and my heart rate excels. Every time someone asks me that something insane happens. "Should I?"

"You definitely should."

Honestly, Tommy might be the one that I trust the most. Talon has it on some levels, but we're still working on the communication aspect of things. He agreed not to leave me in the dark anymore, and I'm trying to believe him.

"Alright. I'll give you my trust this one time. Don't disappoint me."

He pulls out his phone and shows something to the tattoo artist then looks at me. "Where do ya want it?" The big burly guy asks.

"Depends on what it is. But, I've always wanted one on my wrist."

"Wrist it is."

After an hour and a half of being told that I couldn't look to my right, the guy finally steps back. "All done."

The guys come over to my side, all too eager to see what I think of it. I look down at my wrist and there it is.

"You got your wings. What do you plan to do with them?" Tommy asks, with a huge grin on his face.

I smile back. A real, genuine smile. "Eeeek. I love it!"

I can't stop staring at it. It's the angel wings that Tommy painted underneath the bleachers and, right in the middle, is the snake infinity symbol.

"I'll be up front. Come out when you're ready to pay," the artist tells us.

Once he's gone, Talon sits on the edge of the bed. "It's official. You're a Rebel. Now you get to choose what you wanna do with that honor."

My brows raise. "What do you mean?"

"You get your one shot of revenge. Have anyone in mind?"

I think about it for a minute while the guys linger over me —watching and waiting.

"As a matter of fact, I do. But my act isn't quite as deadly as yours. I love my dad and I don't want him hurt. But he betrayed me. Now it's my turn to get what I deserve. I don't want him to know the truth. Let him think he killed Josh for awhile. In return, I want my trust fund that he plans to withhold until I'm married."

"You got it," Talon quips.

Tommy holds out his hand in front of me. "From start to finish."

Lars tops it with his. Followed by Talon. Then I place mine on top. "And everything in between."

TALON

She's lying in bed tapping on her phone when I push her bedroom door open. Seeing her smile immediately draws a smile to my face. Ironic how just a month ago, she cringed every time that door opened.

"How you doing?" I ask as I join her at the bed. She slides up into a sitting position and lets her phone fall to the side.

Her shoulders shrug. "As good as can be expected."

"Maybe this will help." I slope my body over hers and kiss her lips gently. I can feel her smile against my mouth and my heart pitter patters at her touch. "Is it working?"

Her body slides down the bed until she's on her back. "Almost, but I'm still pretty tense."

When I climb on top of her, her legs bend and invite me between them. Grinding against her through the fabric of our clothes, I feel my dick throb in agony. I need to feel her from the inside and make her come. Erase her worries, even if it's just temporary.

Skating my fingers up her shirt, she lets out a subtle moan when I pinch the bud of her nipple. "I need you, Talon."

With that, I sit up and take the hem of her pants in my hands and slide them down. She's not wearing any panties so the bare skin of her pussy looks back at me.

Pushing her thighs apart, I can see her desire for me already moistening her folds.

When I look up at her, lust-filled eyes gaze into mine. She leans forward and begins fussing with my pants, but I push her hand away. "Not yet."

On my knees in front of her, I press the tip of my finger to her swollen nub and begin rubbing in a clocklike motion.

She begins moving subtly at first, then forces her hips up to try and gain momentum. She wants these fingers inside of her so damn bad, but I need to tease her clit a little bit longer. "Take your shirt off."

She leans forward and pulls it over her head. Her tits pop out and greet me with hard nipples.

Still rubbing her sex, I lean over top of her and take her right nipple into my mouth, grazing my teeth over it and giving it a gentle tug.

Fuck, she's so damn sexy and if I keep this shit up, I'll be exploding before I even get my dick out of my pants. I slide two fingers inside of her but hold them in place with no movement. "Relaxed yet?"

She chuckles. "Just fuck me, then I'll answer your question."

I tsk. "You're too tense, you need to relax." My smirk sets her cheeks on fire and I know she's getting pissed. She's so wet that her arousal slides down my fingers. I begin gliding them in and out and she breathes out a sigh of relief.

Pressing my lips to hers, I suck her bottom lip between my

teeth and pump my fingers faster. Sticking my tongue inside her mouth, she tangles it with her own. Twisting and tasting, while forcing her mouth harder against mine.

She lets out another moan with my two fingers inside of her. "I love the way you taste," I mutter into her mouth. "Can I taste more of you?"

When she nods, I kiss my way down her body. Her breasts, her nipples, the smooth skin of her stomach.

I tug her belly ring between my teeth and give it a gentle pull, before making my way between her legs.

Darting my tongue at her clit, I continue to slide my fingers in and out of her dripping wet pussy.

Her fingers tangle in my hair, and she guides my movement. I pick up my pace and she rocks her hips as she begins riding my face. "Oh God," she cries out in pleasure. "I'm gonna come."

"That's right, baby." I look up at her as I shove my fingers deeper inside of her.

Her eyes close and she lets out a strangled moan, before pooling her arousal in the palm of my hand.

I pull out my fingers and rub aggressively over her throbbing clit causing her to shudder. Her hand slaps over mine and she thanks me with a smile.

It's only seconds before my sweatpants are flying over the other side of the bed. I lean forward and press my lips to hers. Just as I'm about to slide inside of her, she tugs at the bottom of my shirt. I lift my head and look into her eyes that are questioning me. I shake my head, no.

"Do you trust me?" she asks in a muffled voice.

"Trust has nothing to do with this."

"It has everything to do with it."

She's already saw the scars that night in the bathroom. Not that I wanted her to. She just barged in and took matters into her own hands. This is different. To willingly take off my shirt and bare my ugly skin to another person is unnerving. It's something I've never done. Ever since I was a kid, I've swam in a t-shirt. When the guys tore off their shirts because they were sweating, I kept mine on. Hiding the horrid marks and swearing no one would ever see them.

But she's seen them. And she didn't turn up her nose or act like I was infected.

"Just this one time," I tell her as I slowly pull my shirt up over my head. I watch her expression the entire time. Unfazed, she pulls my face back to hers. Her fingers trail up my side and graze over the rigid bumps of my scars. Then to my back where they continue to spread like wildfire. The intensity in this moment is unfathomable. A feeling I've never felt before. Trusting someone with my scars—my heart. It's frightening, but it's also beautiful.

I slide my dick inside of her and feel her walls collapse around me. Taking things slow, I savor every moment. When I lift my head, our eyes catch and I stare back into her baby blues while feeding her every inch of my cock.

"Mine," I breathe out, "all mine." My head drops and her arms wrap around me. This is so much more than just sex with a girl. It's passionate, intense, and completely mind-blowing. A feeling I've never experienced. She keeps taking me to this new high that I can't get enough of. Dare I say, love?

No, that's not possible. Is it?

With one final thrust, I lift myself up and pull out. My cock pulsates as my cum shoots all over her bare stomach.

"And you're all mine." She pulls my face to hers, and our mouths collide with so much intensity that I feel like I could do this all over again, every minute, for the rest of my life.

We get cleaned up and lie down for a minute, still completely naked, before she breaks the silence. "Any word on Zed?"

I begin trailing my fingers up and down her stomach, watching as goosebumps cascade. "We'll talk about that later."

"Please just tell me what you think about all of this."

"Nothing from Zed. But I'm not surprised. He'll be in touch when he's ready."

"I don't like the waiting. I wish he'd just voice what he wants and get it over with so we can all move on."

Pushing myself up, my elbow presses into the mattress on her side. "I didn't say anything before, but Zed took something from your dad's office when we were at your house. I think it has something to do with Josh."

Her eyes open wider. "What kind of *something*?"

"I don't know. A piece of paper, maybe. Does your dad have any property or any place that Zed would take Josh's body?"

"He has property all over. And there's the warehouse where Axel used to have his fight club. But Dad shut that place down and it's secured with a passcode and an alarm now."

"That could be what he took. A paper with the passcode. It's worth a shot to find out. We need to find his body, bury him someplace that no one knows about and destroy all evidence that connects us to Josh before Zed turns this whole thing around and buries us all."

"Do you think Zed did it? Killed Josh, I mean?"

No, I don't think Zed killed him. If he did, he wouldn't be tampering with his body. He'd stay as far as hell away from it as he could to protect himself. No, he's doing this because he wants power and he knows that he's safe from incrimination.

Someone else killed Josh. We just have to figure out who it was before Zed goes too far.

"Anything's possible. Right now, we can't trust anyone but each other."

. . .

The End.

Book Two of the Redwood Rebels
series is available! Read Heathen now!

Message From the Author

First of all, I want to send a big thank you to readers who gave Striker a chance. I hope you enjoyed these twisted boys and Talon's story.

Thank you so much to Amanda, and Aurora for beta reading. And, Sara for putting up with my constant back and forth, mental breakdowns, and for talking me through it all!

Thank you to Britt and Red Hatter for all that you do for me. You all rock!

Greys Promo, thank you for helping get the word out about my books and for being so easy to work with.

Thank you to all the bloggers who like, love, share, and review. I appreciate you all so much.

My amazing street team, thank you for your daily support and shares!

I'd love to hear what you thought of Striker by leaving a review. It would be greatly appreciated. I'd also like to invite you to join my readers group Rachel's Ramblers.

xoxo-Rachel

ABOUT THE AUTHOR

Rachel Leigh resides in West Michigan with her husband, three kids, and a couple fur babies.

Rachel overuses emojis and lol. Coffee is her guilty pleasure. Writing is her passion. Her goal is to brighten at least one person's day with the worlds she creates between the pages of her books.

Printed in Great Britain
by Amazon